HORSE

HORSE

Talley English

ALFRED A. KNOPF New York

2018

THIS IS A BORZOI BOOK
PUBLISHED BY ALFRED A. KNOPF

Copyright © 2018 by Catherine Talley English Tillack

Knopf, Borzoi Books, and the colophon are registered trademarks
of Penguin Random House LLC.

Library of Congress Cataloging-in-Publication Data
Names: English, Talley, author.
Title: Horse : a novel / by Talley English.
Description: First edition. | New York : Alfred A. Knopf, 2018.
Identifiers: LCCN 2017039634 (print) | LCCN 2017051407 (ebook) |
ISBN 9781101874332 (hardcover : acid-free paper) |
ISBN 9781101874349 (ebook)
Subjects: LCSH: Families—Fiction. | Horses—Fiction. | Girls—Fiction. |
Domestic fiction. | GSAFD: Bildungsromans.
Classification: LCC PS3605.N53 (ebook) | LCC PS3605.N53 H67 2018 (print) |
DDC 813/.6—dc23
LC record available at https://lccn.loc.gov/2017039634

Jacket photograph by Thomas Kelley / iStock / Getty Images
Jacket design by Jenny Carrow

Manufactured in the United States of America
First Edition

For Isabel, always

And for Margaret, Catherine, Susan, and Anna

Oh I miss you so
and I long to know . . .

—*Lucinda Williams, "Death Came"*
  The Ghosts of Highway 20

Contents

HORSE

Sonnet I

Now in the father's place a horse is placed,
accounted here is why the horse will stand.
Love for the father's love is all disgrace,
a horse is waiting here, and not a man.
And what was left behind compares to what
now is, the first, the last, between undreamed.
See there, the horse across a field, it trots,
a memory may not be what it seemed.

    He was my father's horse who is now mine,
this love constrains what is and what is not.
And though I see this time, it bends toward time,
nothing is solved by what I have forgotten—

        not horse, not him, not me, or all our love.

Prologue

Ian was broken English. The language he spoke was horse, a form of sign language: it involved eye contact; it was mostly touch. The English saddle was plain, sloped up in front and back; the bridle had a noseband and a throat lash; the bit was a snaffle. Watch how the horse stood, and see how the rider swung onto his back. (I am reminded that a horse is not born able to carry a rider; the muscles of his back must strengthen over time. If the horse is well trained, then the rider can think a word, *walk,* rather than say it, and the horse will respond to a nuanced shift in the rider's body, and follow the command.) See the rider, who feels a pull in her arms as the horse's head moves with his stride; watch the swing of his rib cage from side to side. The horse; the rider. The image was not new, but there was something to it: when horse and rider are one body within a web of language.

ONE

Found

From a way off she saw the movement of the dog and knew it was after something. The dog leaped in and out of the weeds, huffing and panting, running along the bank. When she was closer she saw the gosling. She yelled at the dog. The gosling drifted to a submerged branch. She waded into the creek and the dog followed. She yelled and the dog turned and ran back up the bank. She captured the gosling and tucked it against her chest. The little bird gave a few hard nips on the soft fat of her arm, but she ignored it and climbed the bank, turning her back to the dog, who jumped up to get the bird. The gosling struggled, but she tightened her hold. The dog followed her at a distance before it turned and ran off. She opened the narrow gate and closed it behind her. The bird was warm and limp. Its head jostled as she walked over the uneven ground of the field. She wondered why it was alone. If the adult geese had been able, they would have fought off the dog, batting the air with strong wings, sticking out their narrow pink tongues and hissing and honking. She'd seen Canada geese at the creek before, and occasionally blue heron, with long legs, narrow head, and crest of feathers. With a free hand, she climbed where the fence was sturdiest, near a post, and swung her leg over, the wood sun-warmed and splintery on her bare skin. The pasture was for horses, and the grass was short. She could see Zephyr's light shape under the lip of the barn's green tin roof. She cut through the middle of the field. The horse lifted his head and flicked his ears forward. He dipped his head to the ground and grazed, then lifted it again. He turned and traced a thin ribbon of dusty ground through the grass, his habitual path. His head bobbed as he walked. She usually had a carrot for him. When they met, he sniffed her hand, then his ears flicked forward. His big nostrils flared. The down on the head of the gosling moved in his hot breath. The horse was white with brown spots, an Appaloosa, and he had one brown eye and one blue.

She said, "No, Zep, not for you," and walked on. Zephyr followed her. Duchess, the gray dapple mare, was coming up the hill. At the fence she let the two horses sniff the gosling and then let herself out of the field and walked between the wheel ruts of a dirt track, past the paddock connected to the newer barn. Beyond the barn was the yard of the house. Her mother was weeding in the garden. She recognized the familiar motions of her mother's hands. The dog was on his side under the apple tree, as if dead in the heat. Her father had bought the dog. Barker. There was a trend in her family when it came to naming house pets. Her parents' first dog was a black Labrador named Blackie, and there had been a cat with four white paws called Boots. A white rabbit had been Snow, and three chickens had been Cluck, Spots, and Mrs. Brown. Her own first pet was a guinea pig she called Piggy. And then Barker. The day her father brought him home, the puppy made a high-pitched yapping and didn't stop. She called him Barker and that was his name. Her own family name was straightforward. French. She was Teagan French. Whenever she had to give her name she preemptively offered, *French, like the language,* to avoid having to say *Yes, like french fries.* There was also French's yellow mustard, but nobody said *Like the mustard.* Teagan asked her father where their name came from, but he didn't have an answer, except that he said he was pretty sure his ancestors had been English.

Robert French came out of the garage, his white crew-neck undershirt smeared with grease. He wore worn blue jeans and a tatty leather belt. His weekend-project clothes. During the week his shirt would be clean and have a collar, his khakis would be creased, and his brown penny loafers would be spotless. His face was molded into a frown. He had obviously been trying to fix something. He seemed to like to try to fix things, even though it always made him angry in the end, or at the beginning, depending on how complicated the thing was. She guessed it was the lawn mower. She had heard him telling her mother that there was no point in buying a new one if the old one worked perfectly fine. It didn't work; he meant that he was going to make it work. If Teagan had not been holding her own small project in her hands, she would have avoided the garage altogether and joined her mother in the garden, or slipped upstairs to her bedroom. Her father's face lifted to look at what she held.

"What's that?"

"I found a gosling."

"Gosling? A goose?"

"A baby. A baby Canada goose."

"It could be a duck," he said.

"We never have ducks. Those Canada geese are usually at the creek."

"Is it hurt?" He peered closer.

"I don't know. It was by itself and there was a dog after it."

"Barker?"

"No, I don't know what dog," she said.

"Where was it?"

"In the creek."

"You should have left it alone."

"The parents were gone. There was just this one and the dog was after it."

"Now Barker's going to go after it," he said.

"Not if we don't let him."

"How are you going to do that?" It was always like this. The obstacles set before her.

"I don't know."

"Are you going to try to feed it?" he asked.

"What should I feed it?" Now he would help her, when he could tell her what to do.

"When your mother and I raised some baby chipmunks," Robert began.

She knew this story. The chipmunks had been found after a storm. Her mother and father had raised them and then released them into a tree in the yard, but they kept coming back, even jumping onto their shoulders. They had to drive off in their car and stay away for a weekend before the chipmunks would stop coming back to them. Robert, all in all, liked animals. He got along especially well with dogs. He had a special tone of voice for dogs. She had seen dogs strain against their leashes to thrust their heads under his hands.

"We fed them dog food and bread soaked in milk. Try that. Put it in your bathroom. I've got to see if I can get this damn piece of junk lawn mower to start," he said but walked through the kitchen door. Now that she had permission from her father, she hoped the gosling would live. Robert washed his hands.

They were large and powerful, the knuckles thick. She had her father's hands, wide palms, thick fingers. She looked under the sink for a dish towel.

"Not those," he said. "Don't let it out of your bathroom or you'll be cleaning up after it, or I'll be cleaning up after it. And wash your hands."

From the narrow upstairs closet she pulled out a frayed bath towel. Her bathroom was a pastel yellow that she hated. She set the gosling on the towel. It walked off, but she caught it and put it back on, bunching the sides around it. It stayed and seemed to settle. The knobby black beak sunk down and touched the towel. It startled, then closed its eyes. Teagan left the light on in the bathroom and pulled the door tight. In the kitchen she looked for an opened can of dog food in the refrigerator. There wasn't one. She took out bread and the milk. When she looked into the bathroom the bird didn't stir. She tipped the milk down her own throat and ate the bread. In her bedroom she stripped out of her damp and sweaty clothes. Her shoes were smelly. She rubbed down her arms and legs with her T-shirt because they itched from the grass and her own salt. She pulled on fresh shorts and a T-shirt and lay on her bed, and thought about finding the gosling. She fell asleep and when she woke up the sky was indigo. She stretched and was thirsty. In the kitchen Barker wagged his tail and pressed his wide head against the inside of her knee. She patted him. Her mother stood at the double sink. Susanna French was picking out stems and cutting them. Two paper grocery bags full of flowers stood on the counter. This was Susanna's method. When her garden was in bloom, she filled paper bags with her cuttings, then selected, cut, and arranged them in vases. Teagan often walked into a kitchen full of blossoms.

"Did Dad tell you what I found?" Teagan asked, a glass in her hand.

Susanna poked a stem into her arrangement. "What?"

"A gosling. It's in my bathroom. Will you check on her with me?"

"Where did you find it? By the creek?" Susanna asked, rinsing her hands. Teagan told the story and filled her glass with water and drank it down.

"Did you put down some newspaper?" Susanna asked.

"I forgot," Teagan said. "Stay, Barker," she said, shutting him in the kitchen.

"I don't know anything about a goose. We'll have to look up how to feed it," Susanna said.

"Dad said dog food, or bread soaked in milk."

"That might work," Susanna said.

The bathroom door creaked, and they heard chirping.

"Goodness, that is a baby goose," Susanna said, squeezing past her daughter into the bathroom. The gosling was standing on the towel, chirping and flapping its tiny points of wings. Then it waddled off on black webbed feet.

"Should we feed her?" Teagan asked.

"You have the bread?" Susanna said.

Teagan went to get some. When she walked in her mother was sitting on the pastel yellow toilet and the gosling was exploring behind it.

"I forgot milk."

"Soak it in some water. She might not even eat it," Susanna said.

Teagan dripped water from the tap on the bread, ripped it, and held a piece in front of the bird's small beak. It ignored her and waddled away. She sat down and captured the bird in her lap, and wiggled the bread against the beak. The gosling ate a piece, and then another.

"Well," Susanna said, sounding satisfied.

"Barker will want to eat her," Teagan said.

"Keep her in here for now, and put down some newspaper," Susanna said.

Robert was freshly showered, wearing a green short-sleeved polo shirt. "Are we having goose for supper?" he asked.

"No," said Teagan. Across from her, her brother, Charlie, was drinking a Fresca. Robert had picked him up from playing paintball with friends. He was wearing camouflage pants and a green T-shirt.

"It wouldn't be enough for one bite," Charlie said.

"She's not for eating," Teagan said.

"How do you know it's a she?" Charlie asked.

"Goose is supposed to be delicious," Robert said.

Susanna smiled and spooned boiled potatoes. "Somebody see if the chicken is burning?"

Robert cracked open the door of the oven. "Roast gosling!" he said.

"No it isn't," Teagan said.

"Have you seen the goose lately?" Charlie said.

"It's in my bathroom."

"It was in your bathroom," Charlie said.

"Can we keep her?" Teagan directed the question at her mother.

"Oh . . ." Susanna began, spooning peas into bowl.

"You want to keep it?" Robert stood behind his daughter and put his hand on her head.

Teagan tilted her head against his chest. "Yes," she said.

"Fatten it for Thanksgiving?" he said.

"No." Teagan dropped her chin.

Charlie laughed.

"You know, it could be a Newfoundland goose," Robert said.

"What's that?" Teagan said.

"A goose from Newfoundland."

Charlie caught Teagan's eye.

"You found it, right? That makes it a *Newfound goose,*" Robert said.

Susanna held up the big spoon and laughed.

End

An end marks a beginning; memory needs sorting, but my heart keeps love, beat after beat, like a tail wagging, like a mat to wipe your boots on. What it would say, I think I know.

Saddle

The garage is so full no car can park in it. In front is the holly tree, grown to the top of the shingled roof since I last saw it. I sift my keys, looking for the one that fits the dead bolt. The smell of the house is familiar. The dog comes, hair raised, but when she knows it's me she whines and waits for me to stroke her head. She looks into my face with round yellow-brown eyes. I say, "Good Kitten." Mom went to the ASPCA to adopt a cat and came home with a puppy named Kitten.

My mother's house seems to me like rereading a book. I seem to visit myself here. I have changed; I don't eat breakfast in this kitchen anymore, or sleep in the bed upstairs, or walk down the wooden steps on my way to the barn, and today I am here to remove something, to take it with me.

After my dad left, my mother filled empty spaces with new furniture; now there are lots of places to sit down, and more thriving green things and flowering plants that make the place feel like it's living.

She changed the color on the living room walls, the pattern on the couch, and added my and Charlie's faces in frames everywhere. Some things are the same. The kitchen closet spills out bags of birdseed, dog food, and worn pairs of boots. A wasp buzzes on the window glass, making an angry sound against the solid sky. The wasps come through gaps in the stones that make the outer kitchen wall.

I see my mother's ubiquitous coffee mug next to a notebook, and several pens scattered nearby that will never again have caps. The sun comes in the same way, though a different dog lies down in its light. Outside, a pileated woodpecker, with his currant cap, taps up and down a dogwood tree.

From the house I remove the boxes my mother set aside for me, and when that's done, Kitten and I go to the barn. On the way, I don't look carefully through the fields. They are empty of horses now.

The big wood doors slide; dust swirls in the sunlight. The stalls are dry. Cobwebs trace the ropes. There is a white coat of bird droppings on the cement floor. Pigeons. The barn cats did their job while they lived. I open the heavy door of the tack room and kick a block of wood in place to hold it. Each saddle is on its rack, and each is shrouded in a towel. Each bridle hangs on a half-moon of wood.

I expose my saddle and use the dusty towel to wipe the leather. There's no horse for this saddle now, but I still want to take it. Lifting it by the pommel, I fit the smooth underside against my thigh, and call the dog, and slide the heavy doors shut behind me.

Trail Ride

More than once Teagan had returned to the barn while the sky faded. More than once she'd sponged sweat from her horse, smoothed his sleek hair with a stiff brush, before leading him to the field, slipping off halter and rope, and watching him disappear into a darkness he knew well. More than once she'd lingered at the fence to watch a mottled moon rise and stretch weird shadows from the trees.

She walked through the kitchen wearing riding britches, a pair of thin kneesocks pulled over them. From the jumble of things in the closet, hammers and pruning clippers, clay pots and winter coats, dog food and birdseed, she pulled her short leather paddock boots. She laced them, then clapped her hand against her thigh, a signal for Barker to get up from where he lay directly on the air-conditioning vent. He heaved himself from the floor and stood with his nose at the door, his thick tail waving lazily. She plucked a few long carrots from a plastic bag. Susanna had once kept a vegetable garden but grew tired of competing with the groundhogs and deer that came to eat. She allowed Charlie and his friends to roll cherry bombs down the groundhog holes, but despite the bombs and the presence of Barker, the groundhogs dug new holes. One day, when Susanna discovered that her fat, sun-ripened tomatoes had exactly one bite taken out of each, she resigned from vegetables. Teagan missed her mother's zucchini bread, sweet and flecked with green. Next, Susanna planted sunflowers, but the deer nibbled the shoots, and when the giants bloomed they were barely two feet tall, their heavy yellow heads bent to the ground. Now Susanna grew what the deer and groundhogs would leave mostly alone: tall lavender, quick-lived irises, hydrangea, and peony.

Outside, the humidity covered Teagan like a blanket. Her armpits went swampy. In the yard her toe caught in a divot and she stumbled. Barker had been digging for moles. He smelled them under the dirt, and dug trenches to unearth them. Susanna put the order to her family to stop him from digging big pits in the yard. He never caught a mole, but he left bare patches of dirt where he had tried. With Teagan near him, the dog trotted through the yard as if a mole had never concerned him. At the edge of the yard was a more interesting animal anyway. A groundhog, the summer resident, made a quiet escape to the field, shuffling its low body. The dog flattened himself under the bottom board of the fence and gave chase. More than once the dog had made a killing bite to rodent flesh. Teagan didn't mind whistle-pigs, but the deep holes they dug in the fields were a danger to a horse's slender leg.

She slid the barn doors open and clicked on the fan to move the warm, stale air. In the tack room, bridles hung in a row on the wall. Two-by-fours made saddle racks. The last saddle in the row was a child's western saddle. It had a stitched, cushioned seat and a small horn. She had seen black and white photographs of Charlie sitting in this saddle. When she looked at the saddle she could imagine her parents as a young couple, lifting their firstborn onto a horse, telling him to hold tight to the horn.

Teagan was thirsty. She stuck her head under the tap of the large sink. Maybe it was because she was hot, but she thought the water at the barn was colder than at the house. She hung a bridle on her shoulder and carried her saddle against her leg. Dropping them off where she would tie her horse, she picked up ropes and halters and walked to the field. She stepped up on the fence and cupped her hands at her mouth, calling out "Horses," in the voice her mother used, stretching the *o*. They were in sight, but she wanted them to come to her. Zephyr raised his head, then flipped his tail and cantered toward her. The gray mare wasn't going to be left behind. They galloped. They didn't always run, but she loved it when they did. They halted suddenly, swinging their heavy heads and stirring up dust from the beaten-down dirt beside the gate. And then the wild moment was over, and they were tame animals looking for a handout. Zephyr nosed her hip. She snapped the carrot in two and handed over the pieces.

She cross-tied the horses, clipping ropes to either side of the halter. From a bucket she grabbed two brushes and a hoof pick. She ran her hand down the tendon of the leg and said, "Foot please, sir." Zephyr had been taught, so the horse lifted his hoof. She held the hoof in her palm and scraped the flat underside with the pick, and dug into the V-shaped groove called the frog. (A horse has a frog under each foot; four frogs squashed silent in the press of hooves.) With the stiff brush she followed the grain of his hair, pulling clouds of dust onto herself. She knocked the brush against the wall to clean it. With a soft-bristled brush she went over his face. He liked this and tried to rub his head against her. She spent a little more time around his ears and eyes, getting the places he couldn't scratch himself.

Susanna walked in followed by Barker. The dog went to the water bucket under the pump and lapped through a skin of drowned bugs.

"Thanks for getting my horse," Susanna said.

"Sure."

"She's a good girl," Susanna cooed to the mare and picked up brushes.

Teagan took down her helmet and half chaps. She slipped the elastic band under her boot and zipped the side. The chaps gave her a little more sticking power and protected her leg from the saddle's stirrup straps. When she unclipped her horse he took a step forward. With a hand against his nose she said, "Stand."

Pinching the cheek pieces of the bridle she slid the bit down his nose and pressed it against his lips, and he accepted the bit, which settled over his tongue in the back of his mouth, where he had no teeth. She slipped the crown piece over his ears and pulled them through. She buckled the throat latch and noseband and checked that all of it fit right and nothing pinched.

"Stand," she said, pressing her hand against his nose briefly, and she left him there to pick up her riding crop.

"Your horse is leaving," Susanna said.

Teagan turned to see Zephyr walking into the barnyard.

"You can't leave him untied," Susanna said.

"He usually stands," Teagan said, quickly retrieving the reins, which had slid down his neck, so he wouldn't step on them. She stood on his left side, lifted the saddle flap, and cinched the girth. She stood in front of the horse, her hands around one of his front legs, at the knee. She tugged the leg toward her and said, "Give." The horse allowed her to raise his leg and stretch it forward. He leaned back into the stretch until she let go of the leg. She figured, if people stretched before exercise, then a horse who would carry a person should, too. They repeated with the other leg. Then she moved to his belly, reached under to the far hind leg, and when he gave it, she moved it toward her, stretching the large muscles of his flank. It was not something she would have attempted with a horse who might kick. She was confident with Zephyr, and he was familiar with the routine. Then she patted his neck, gathered the reins, stuck her toe in the stirrup, planted her hands on the pommel, and swung up, settling softly on the saddle out of respect for his back. Her arms and the reins, from her elbows to his mouth, made a line. When her horse moved, she received his motion in her hands. In a few minutes Susanna was ready to go on Duchess.

———

They called Blue View a farm, but the biggest parcel was tree-covered. Robert was a high school principal, and Susanna taught preschool. They were not farmers. The barns were always going to be for horses, and the two best fields were for horses. Robert had tried maintaining a cow-calf operation himself, enlisting Susanna's help, even though she didn't like cows. He kept Angus, because he liked Angus beef. The cows developed a knack for trampling the fence or escaping underneath it. Charlie drove his four-wheeler illegally on the highway to herd them toward home. Robert eventually gave in to his lack of ability to work cattle and sold and slaughtered the herd. For a while after that the freezer was packed with beef wrapped in white butcher paper, and Robert was happier with a freezer full of beef than he had ever been with a field full of cattle. He rented the lower field to a neighbor who built up a small herd of mixed cattle, and calves were born from them each year.

Teagan walked her horse beside her mother's on the wide track in the woods. She reached a hand to her mother, who squeezed it. Zephyr dropped back and followed Duchess, his nose in line with her lightly swishing black tail, as if a herd of two. The clop of hooves was like a metronome.

Teagan knew the story. When Susanna was pregnant with Charlie, she asked her doctor how long she could continue to ride. He told her, *Absolutely no riding*. She went for a second opinion and was told, *No riding while pregnant*. She went to a third doctor, who said, *You can ride until you can't get up on the horse by your-self.* That was the advice Susanna followed.

There was no breeze. The horses walked. Teagan took up a handful of Zephyr's brown-white mane. She let the side-to-side motion of the stepping horse, left hind, right front, right hind, left front, exaggerate her shoulders, swaying left, right, left, right. She imagined a baby in its mother's womb, rocking.

"Teagan, what are you doing?" Susanna called, looking back at her daughter.

Teagan straightened up. "Napping?" she said with a guilty smile.

"I don't think so. If your horse shied, you'd be on the ground in a minute."

"Sorry," Teagan said, but knew that Zephyr wouldn't surprise her. He never had.

They turned onto a trail that snaked up the hill. Teagan stood in her stirrups to take weight off her horse's back and felt a spiderweb break across her face. She wiped it off and inspected her arms for the spider. The grass on the trail was tall.

"I have to ask Jason to bush-hog this," Susanna said.

"We have a bush hog."

"Your dad sold it," Susanna said.

"To who?"

"Jason."

"So Jason clears the trails with our bush hog Dad sold him?"

"Right," Susanna said.

"I guess that makes sense," Teagan said.

"Should we trot?" Susanna suggested.

They trotted their horses until Susanna lifted her hand in the air and Teagan slowed her horse. The signal was borrowed from foxhunting. They left the woods and walked the cleared hilltop. Teagan reached down to pat her horse's neck, and he bucked, kicking out with both back legs. She sat, confused, and he did it again.

"Mom, hold up," Teagan called.

Susanna glanced over her shoulder and saw the horse kicking out. "He's got a fly."

Teagan twisted in her saddle and peered down his flanks. A thick horsefly, its plated abdomen visible, buzzed past Teagan's head. She ducked.

"Swat it," Susanna said.

"It's huge," Teagan said.

The big fly landed on the horse's neck. She slapped with a stiff hand and the thing dropped to the ground. A little blood spotted the horse's white hair. "Got it," she said, wiping the blood from his neck and cleaning her hand on her shirt.

By the time they made a loop and were back on the wide track, the air was cooler. Teagan felt more awake, her muscles warmed from riding. "Let's race," she said.

Susanna halted her horse near the blue gate. "We just did a big loop."

"It's not so hot and we mostly walked. Just up the straight-away. We stop at the bend."

"Duchess, what do you have to say about this?" Susanna said, but she turned her horse. "I don't want to go flat-out."

"If you want to lose," Teagan said, scrubbing Zephyr's neck

with her knuckles. "That's the start line." She pointed to an oak tree with a curving branch. "Ready?"

The Appaloosa was the faster horse. She held fistfuls of his mane and her arms jerked forward each time he stretched his neck.

Beyond the bend, she couldn't see three does emerge to cross to the woods on the other side. When her horse saw them, he halted. One moment he was at a full gallop, and the next he stood still. Teagan did not transition so well. The sudden stop unseated her, and she flew into the air, turning over. She had not even let go of the reins and gripped them in her hand. And then she landed, hard, on the soles of both boots, and stepped forward to catch her balance. For a moment the deer stood, their long ears upright, and she stood, the reins in her hand, and the horse stood. Then the deer leapt away, the white undersides of their tails flipped up like signal flags. She turned to her horse and the horse swung his head around at the sound of hooves coming closer. When the mare rounded the bend Susanna slowed her, and she saw Teagan standing beside her horse. Teagan looked up at her mother's shocked face.

Song

That night, I wanted to sleep, but close to the house a bird was singing. Its single clear voice trailed through its repertoire. But it was still dark, still night, no matter how close the horizon might be to turning toward the sun, it wasn't daybreak. I lay in bed and listened, and thought that either the bird or I might be disturbed. I got out of bed. In the backyard I followed the sound. It came from the fir tree, a perfect bird tree, feathery leaves layered in a dense cover. A bird-full tree, I knew, because constantly they flew in and out, chickadee, cardinal, titmouse, nuthatch, and finch. There the hidden bird belted, as if it thought everyone else must be too sleepy to care. A dog across the field barked, *Shut up, shut up.* The singer tried some scales and fit them into phrases. Was it confused? Had the world run a fever, and all things were hallucinating, the night and the dog, the bird and myself? I knew that a flashlight might end it, and went to find the flashlight. The eye of light hit repeating green points on the tree. The song stopped. I walked around the tree anyway, seeing only leaves and dried droppings like fake snow on the red-brown branches. The dog gone quiet. The singer done. Only a pinch of guilt in my gut for cutting off the notes, but it was night, and it was strange, and I couldn't sleep for all that purposeful singing.

Susanna's Game

Charlie positioned the foot of the tube so that the opening faced away from the house.

"You made that?" Teagan said, weighting down a pile of napkins on the outdoor table with a fork.

"Of course."

"How did you know how to make it?"

"I kind of made it up," Charlie said.

"So, it might set the house on fire?" Teagan crossed her arms.

"That's why I point it this way."

"So, it will just set the yard on fire. What is this for, again?" Teagan asked.

"It's how we signal the start and end of our games," Charlie said.

"And why do you need a bottle rocket to start your game?"

"It's cool."

"Dangerous," Teagan said.

"Horses are dangerous," Charlie said, scooting the launcher a little farther forward.

"You fire rockets into trees and shoot your friends with guns," Teagan said.

"We don't fire them into trees. We fire into fields of dry grass. And we shoot with paint."

"It's aiming and firing at people," Teagan said.

"As long as it's not at close range, it doesn't hurt, much."

Robert walked out onto the deck.

"I don't believe that," Teagan said.

"Don't believe what? You don't believe this will fire?" Robert said.

"That's not what I'm worried about," Teagan said.

Robert held the back of Teagan's neck in his large hand. "Worried that we'll blow up?"

"Yes."

"Boom!" Robert shook her a little.

"Dad."

Susanna walked out. She tucked her dark hair behind her ears and crossed her arms. "Okay. Let me see it once and never again."

"Mom, I'm careful," Charlie said.

"You better be," Susanna said.

Charlie selected a long-stemmed bottle rocket from a plastic sleeve and inspected it as if looking for flaws. He fit the stem into the tube of the launcher. "Ready?"

"Fire away," Robert said.

Charlie struck a match and the fuse smoked. He backed away. The rocket began a piercing whistle. Teagan covered her ears and backed into her father. There was a crackling, and then it went out.

"What happened?" Susanna said.

"Dud," Charlie said, looking at the tube.

"Don't go near it," Susanna yelled, balling her hands into fists.

"It's done," Robert said.

"You don't know that. It could blow up in your face," Susanna said to him.

Charlie quickly pulled the rocket out of the tube and tossed it aside.

"Oh my god. Why do I let you do this?" Susanna said.

"Why do you?" Teagan said.

"Try again," Robert said. "Second time's a charm."

Charlie loaded another rocket. This time the whistling and crackling ended in a sound like a gunshot and a trail of smoke that made an arc over the yard.

There was a hint of gunpowder in the air as they sat down outside to eat.

"Looks good," Robert said, cutting into his steak.

The table was set with blue place mats and yellow plastic drinking glasses.

"Thanks, Mom," Charlie said.

"Teagan helped," Susanna said.

"I set the table."

"Thanks for setting the table, Teagan," Charlie said.

"You are welcome," Teagan said.

"I'm just glad we all survived," Susanna said, passing the basket of rolls.

"There was no danger," Robert said, spreading butter on his steak.

"Horses aren't exactly safe either, Mom," Charlie said.

"Are too," Teagan lied, starting to work on an ear of corn.

Robert took a swig from his beer. "Did I tell you about Try Again? My father had a horse that was really difficult to ride. It threw everyone, that's why its name was Try Again."

"That's funny," Charlie said.

"Your mother has even better stories," Robert said.

"Better?" Charlie asked.

———

Susanna wiped her mouth and lined up her fork and knife beside her plate. "When I was a little girl, I would stay with my two cousins for part of the summer. They had a mean pony. It was tied to a stake in a field, because no one could catch it if it was loose."

"That sounds unhappy," Teagan said.

"It was unhappy, and it hated to be ridden, but, of course, we rode it anyway. It would try to bite us when we saddled it. It would try to stomp on our feet. To get onto the saddle, we'd have to distract it so one of us could climb up. It would try its best to bite us and kick some of us, and then someone would run in and climb on. Once you succeeded in getting on, the pony would run along the fence line and try to scrape you off, or it would run under a tree, and if you didn't duck, then you risked getting knocked in the head by a branch. Every summer we would ride that pony. It was the best entertainment we had."

Teagan smiled into her plate. She had never imagined her mother being so determined and unafraid of getting hurt. "What's another story?" Teagan asked.

"Another story?" Susanna said.

"Tell them about Chase," Robert said.

"Oh, yes. Chase. When I was older, my father took in a crazy ex-racehorse. He was a little bit dangerous, but I loved him, and, if he didn't love me, at least he thought I was interesting, because we used to play a game. We played it day after day. It was such a dumb game. I would perch on the top rail of the fence and pretend I just wanted to feed him a carrot, and he would come over, pretending he was just going to eat a carrot, and when he was close enough, I'd leap onto his back, and he'd go galloping and bucking into the field, and I'd hold on as long as I could."

"What happened then?" Teagan asked.

"I always fell off, in the end."

Teagan sat on the top railing of the fence and held out the carrot. Just a little closer and she could make it onto Zephyr's back. She wondered, as the horse seemed to hesitate, then stepped forward, did he already guess the game?

Barn Cats

Charlie suggested shooting them, but there was a problem about the legality of it. Poison was difficult, because something else might be killed by mistake. Trapping meant purchasing a trap, setting it, and checking it. A predator was needed. Something that would go after them. Everyone was sick of them. Sick of hearing them scratching in the rafters, sick of the poop on everything in the barn. And they were breeding. Barker was no help. As much as he liked moles and groundhogs, he was not interested in pigeons.

"Cats," Susanna said.

"Cats kill rats," Robert said.

"We have pigeons, Dad," Teagan said.

"You mean get cats? And keep them?" Charlie asked, helping himself to another slice of pizza. Robert steadied the flat cardboard box on the table and took a swig of beer. Teagan excused herself to fill her water glass.

"Teagan, grab me another beer," Robert said.

"This green bottle?" Teagan called back.

"Yes," Robert said.

"Mom, you want one?" Teagan called.

"No, thank you," Susanna said.

"Charlie?" Teagan said.

"No, thanks," Charlie said.

"You can have a beer if you want," Robert said.

"He can have a taste," Susanna said.

"That's okay," Charlie said.

"You can have one. Want one?" Robert said.

"No."

"I do," Teagan said, giving over the bottle.

"You won't like it," Robert said.

"I might," Teagan said, sitting down. Robert held the cold bottle to her. She took it and glanced at her mother. Susanna picked up her pizza and bit into it. Teagan took a sip and handed the bottle back.

"What do you think?" Robert asked.

"I don't like it," Teagan said.

Robert laughed.

"Are we really getting cats?" Charlie asked.

"Sure," Robert said.

"They would have to be barn cats," Susanna said.

"Why wouldn't we keep them in the house?" Teagan said.

"Teagan, you already have a goose," Charlie said.

"I don't want cats to eat Newfound Goose," Teagan said.

"You just said you wanted them in the house."

"They can live in the barn," Teagan said.

Robert set down his beer. "Newfound Goose is going to a new home," he said, looking at his daughter.

Teagan sipped her water. She didn't agree with him.

"Where?" Charlie looked at his sister.

"I haven't heard this," Susanna said.

"Teagan and I have come to a decision. Teagan?"

"Newfound Goose is going to the wildlife center," she said and sipped her water.

Susanna slid a hand on the table toward Teagan but didn't touch her. "Is that okay?"

Teagan wanted to think that her mother could change things. "It's better," she said and shook her head unconsciously, brushing her hair from her face.

"Good girl," Robert said.

Teagan gave a quick smile and then her eyes clouded up.

"Honey," Susanna said.

Charlie laid a hand on her back.

Teagan smeared a palm across her eye. "It's just a stupid bird!" she said, pushing back her chair and walking into the kitchen. She hadn't picked up her glass or paper plate, and stood in front of the sink with nothing in her hands. She poured a glass of milk and walked back to the table.

"I'll have a glass of milk," Charlie said.

She went back for another. "We should get cats," she said, sitting down.

Susanna backed the car away, waving a hand out of the window. Charlie had already gone in. Teagan pulled the door open and walked into the white room with a linoleum floor. It smelled strongly of disinfectant. On the wall hung colorful dog leashes and pet collars. Under them were cardboard cat carriers, the handles peaked like a row of tiny houses. Displayed on a table was a cage holding skinny orange and white kittens. They were curled on a fluffy blanket. Teagan peered down at them.

"May I help you?" the woman at the desk asked. She was an obese woman with short oily dark hair. Patches of skin on her neck flushed red and she wore a purple T-shirt with a cartoon image of a dog, cat, bird, and rabbit standing on the large block letters of ASPCA. Teagan liked the T-shirt and wondered how she could get one.

"I'm here to look at the cats."

"You want to hold a kitten?"

"No, thanks. I'm looking for the grown ones."

"Through there are the dogs. Next door is cats."

"Thank you," Teagan said. She walked through the door. The smell in the room was densely of dog and disinfectant. The kennels were cement and each had a black rubber flap that led outside. Two or three dogs were in each narrow kennel. A dog started barking and then they all did. The sound was deafening. She opened the door to the cat room and found Charlie.

"Look," he said, standing in front of a barred cage. "Look at its ear."

Teagan saw a small tabby cat. One ear was cleanly in half, as if it had been cut with scissors. They wandered down the rows, looking at cats who mostly blinked at them from the backs of cages. Charlie pointed out some choices. She vetoed one that was extremely friendly.

"We want something that doesn't care about people."

A girl a little older than Teagan walked in, wearing an aqua blue ASPCA T-shirt. "Y'all have any questions?"

"We're looking for barn cats," Charlie said.

"What do you have on death row?" Teagan said.

The girl looked at her. "Take a look in here." She led them into a closet-size room. On one wall was a double row of cages. "These are the ones less likely to be adopted."

It was quiet in the room. Some dull faces looked through the white bars.

"Are these sick?" Charlie asked.

"No, they're either old or look kind of rough."

"Teagan," Charlie said.

Teagan looked in at a brown-and-white cat. His ears were withered and folded down. He was wheezing and making a wet rattling sound as he breathed. His eyes were squinted almost closed. His head rested on his paws and he was huge, filling up the small cage.

"Why is he making that noise?" Charlie asked.

"URI. Upper respiratory infection. They get colds. It goes away," she said.

Teagan couldn't wait to hold the giant cat in her arms.

"Did you get some good ones?" Susanna asked.

They stood by the counter with two cardboard cat carriers. From one came a muted scraping sound and from the other a soft wheezing.

"We got real winners," Charlie said.

Susanna looked at him.

"They're perfect barn cats," Teagan said.

Susanna clicked a pen to fill out the adoption forms.

"All righty," the purple-T-shirted, obese woman said, tapping buttons on a calculator. "That's fifteen times two cat carriers, and total is one hundred and eighty."

Susanna put down her pen. "How much are the cats?"

"Seventy-five," the woman said.

"Per cat?"

"Seventy-five per cat. That covers the cost of vaccinations and other care," the woman said, her chin wobbling.

"These are lucky cats," Susanna said, writing the check.

"Do you want to make a donation along with your adoption?" the woman added, her chubby finger poised above the calculator.

Susanna stared at her, then said, "Five dollars," and flipped to a blank check.

Cat and Cat

Susanna was appalled at what came out of the cat carriers. The big brown-and-white cat wheezed and snuffled. The shy tabby with half an ear stared untrustingly from a corner of the tack room. Teagan defended them, repeating that they were perfect barn cats. Susanna said she was taking both cats to the vet. When the big cat sneezed, he sprayed droplets. His long back dipped down so he carried his hind end close to the ground. Susanna thought it could be an old injury. The tabby had a stunted look. She was unusually short from head to tail. Both cats were shut in the tack room for a week. The idea was that when they were let out, they would stick around. Teagan set down new blue food and water bowls. The big cat had a tiny meow that did not match his size. He ate immediately. Susanna tried to pet the tabby, but each time she approached, the little cat slunk away to a corner.

"She slinks away from me," Susanna complained.

"Slinky," Charlie suggested.

"Slinky," Teagan agreed.

"That's a terrible name," Susanna said, "but it suits her."

In the morning, Teagan went down to feed the animals and found Slinky by herself. She looked around, but there wasn't anywhere a large cat could hide. From the saddles to the ceiling was blank wall. Slinky cautiously approached her food bowl. "Slinky, where's your friend?" Teagan said. She looked up the wall. Along the ceiling was a gap. Shutting Slinky in the room, Teagan climbed to the hayloft and pulled the string attached to a bulb. The warm air was stifling. She didn't think the cat could be up there, but she heard a high-pitched mew behind her. She turned around. The big cat was on a hay bale, his squinted eyes and withered ears. He let her carry him down the ladder one-handed, the cat's long body slung against her leg. She shut him in the tack room.

Teagan told her family about the escaped cat. Robert suggested he had slipped out the night before. Charlie had fed them and said that he'd shut the door on both cats. There was no explanation except that the cat had climbed the wall. Robert said it was possible, a cat that size. The next morning Slinky was alone again. Teagan climbed to the hayloft and collected the big cat, again. As soon as she dropped him on the tack room floor, he sprang up onto a saddle, then leapt up the wall and caught the lip of the gap into the hayloft. He slipped through it. Teagan put his food bowl in the hayloft.

Susanna said the only thing to do was to let the other one out, too, and maybe they would decide to stay. Neither cat was seen for two days. Susanna said that it was money down the drain, but Robert said that they would be back. One evening both cats were eating from their bowls. After that, Susanna said she thought the pigeons were gone.

Teeth

Teagan and Charlie were making sandwiches. Jars, a pack of cheese, a bag of cold cuts, lettuce, and tomatoes sat out. Susanna dropped her purse on the counter and tightened the lid on the mayonnaise and stuck it in the fridge.

"I need that," Charlie said, taking it out again.

Susanna sealed up the pack of cheese.

"Can I have that?" Teagan took it from her hand.

"Two hundred dollars, medicines for two weeks, and the big cat has to have teeth pulled."

Charlie laughed, pressing his sandwich together with his hand.

"These are the most expensive cats I've ever heard of," Susanna said, sweeping crumbs off the counter and into her hand. She shook them into the sink.

"Well, at least they get to live, and I haven't seen any pigeons," Teagan said.

"A cat with no teeth is supposed to catch pigeons," Susanna said, running the tap.

"He'll have to gum them to death," Charlie said.

"Gums!" Teagan said, raising a knife like she was making a toast.

"That's it. Gums. That's perfect," Charlie said.

"*Purr*-fect," Teagan said, licking the knife.

"A geriatric, toothless cat. This is what I pay money for?" Susanna said.

"Mom, can I make you a sandwich?" Charlie offered.

Roof

I know the sky above the mountain. Sometimes clouds seem to catch on the hills. I know the rain sky, soft gray. I know the morning and night sky. The sky is constantly shifting, but the mountain is regular, like a clock: winding through seasons. Fall reds and yellows start at the top. Spring greens and purples start at the bottom. Fall down. Spring up.

The barn is often the same. It smells of hay, grain, dust. The hayloft fills and empties. In winter, even with bales stacked to the ceiling, the air in there is cold. In summer, even empty, the loft feels hot and dense. Anytime, I can move through it without thinking. My hands and feet climb the wood ladder rungs. My fingers untie the baling twine that winds around a metal latch that the wind would otherwise unlock. The door opens to the roof.

Truck

"What time can your mom drop you off?" Teagan said, holding the phone against her shoulder with her cheek and spreading peanut butter on bread. "Okay. I'm sure that's fine. My mom's not in the house right now. I don't know where she is. But she said it was okay. Are you spending the night? We could camp if you want. Just in the woods. I have an extra sleeping bag, but we probably would be fine with blankets. Yeah, they might get damp. Okay, bring yours. Okay, see you soon. Bye." She hung up the phone and wiped the knife with her finger and licked off the extra peanut butter. From a plastic honey bear she streamed honey onto the sandwich and pressed the top piece of bread down. She looked in the fridge and found a big bowl of fruit salad, mostly cantaloupe and green grapes. She filled a smaller bowl with some and finished it quickly. She poured a tall glass of milk and drank it down. She hunted in the cabinets for some kind of dessert but came up empty. Her parents must be dieting again. She thought longingly of a big bowl of vanilla ice cream with chocolate sauce. Maybe she could convince her dad to go to the store for her, since Grace was coming over. He understood her love of dessert.

They usually stayed up late and would need something to keep them going. Ice cream was the best, but cookies or even cheese and crackers would do. She wondered where her mother was. Maybe in the garden, maybe at the barn, maybe in her parents' room? Then Teagan remembered that she'd said she had errands to run. She glanced out the window and didn't see any cars. Charlie must be off somewhere, too. He wouldn't buy ice cream for her unless Susanna okayed it. What good was a brother with a car if she couldn't get him to do things for her? In the fall they would be at the same school again, and he'd promised to drive her so she wouldn't have to catch the bus by herself. Her mother and father drove the same car in different colors, Ford sedans. Teagan wondered what, in two years, she would drive. Then there'd be four cars in the driveway, plus the truck.

The old blue Chevrolet was always parked down by the barn but rarely in the same place, as if it went off on its own and parked itself each day. It was driven by whoever needed it and for whatever purpose. Jason Brill sometimes took it out for hauling hay. Charlie sometimes took it for his weekend paintball wars (the trees showed the aftermath of the games, splotched blue and yellow). Susanna used it for barn chores. Robert drove them through the woods to the upper field for sunsets and picnics. Teagan drove it just to drive it, because she was allowed. It was registered as a farm vehicle. She wouldn't get pulled over driving from the barn to the woods and up to the upper field. Robert had given her lessons, and eventually she'd graduated to driving it on her own. She never asked permission to take it, unless she was going to keep it up in the woods for a campout. The woods were easy enough to walk to, but that wasn't the point. The point was bouncing over the fields, lining up the truck to fit exactly through gates, and then winding up the uneven path, branches scraping the roof and sides, bumping over rocks, trying to keep the wheels going straight. The alignment on the truck was never adjusted. Neither were the brakes serviced nor the air pressure in the wheels checked. The truck seemed to be an organic thing. (Maybe it grazed in the fields at night with the horses.) No one ever spoke about repairs or maintenance. The truck was as it was. A few more bounces, and dings, grinding of the gears, and riding the clutch weren't going to make a difference to anybody.

At about two o'clock, Leta Penn pulled up in her familiar blue Volvo station wagon. Grace got out carrying a backpack, a loose sleeping bag spilling from her arm. She was a little taller than Teagan, with dark brown hair. Teagan's was a lighter brown, and straight. Her hair didn't have the natural curl at the ends that Grace's had. They both had athletic builds, and the same pale skin, but Grace's tanned where Teagan's burned. Teagan saw that, once again, they'd cut their hair the same way without having talked about it. Grace's new short bob matched Teagan's. They seemed to be parallels of each other and sometimes bought the same T-shirts just to emphasize their similarity.

"Thanks for bringing Grace over. I think my mom can take her home," Teagan said, hugging Leta, who had gotten out of the car.

"Yes, we already figured that out. Grace, I'll see you tomorrow around three. Are you two going camping?"

"We might spend the night in the woods. It's not going to rain," Teagan said.

"Okay. I know you'll be careful," Leta said.

"Do you want to come in?" Teagan said to Leta. She didn't know what Leta would do if she came in, because Grace and Teagan didn't want to stay around, but it was something Susanna would have asked, so Teagan extended the invitation.

"Is your mom here?"

"No. I don't know where she is," said Teagan. But as she said it, Susanna pulled into the driveway. "There she is."

"I'll go and say hi. You girls be good," Leta said. She walked over to Susanna's car and Teagan scooped up the sleeping bag from Grace, and they went inside to make plans.

"We don't have anything good in the house, so we might have to convince one of my parents to go to the store with us. We'll need supplies if we're camping. We could even build a fire and cook, or heat up soup or something. Charlie and I built a fire ring and we've already tried it out," Teagan said.

"Do you have soup?" Grace asked.

Teagan opened some deep drawers. Grace checked the cabinets.

"I don't see any."

"Me either."

"Okay, let's make a list. What kind of soup do you like?" Teagan said, flipping through some bills Susanna had stacked next to her checkbook and finding a scrap of paper and a pen.

"Tomato is good. We could make grilled cheese."

"Tomato, grilled cheese. And maybe some s'mores stuff?" said Teagan.

"I don't really like s'mores," said Grace.

"You don't like s'mores? What's wrong with you?" Teagan said.

"I like the chocolate. I just don't like the marshmallow and the graham crackers."

"Okay, then just hot chocolate?" said Teagan.

"What about tea?" said Grace.

"What are you, British? Okay, tea. Boring."

"Are we making breakfast?" said Grace.

"How about some granola bars or something? We can always come back to the house for breakfast stuff," Teagan suggested.

Susanna came in the door backward, a paper grocery bag in each arm.

"Hello, Grace," she said.

"Hi, Mrs. French," said Grace.

"You can call her Susanna, you know," Teagan said.

Susanna set down the bags and pulled Grace into a hug. "I don't mind politeness. But you can call me Susanna." She released Grace and craned over the list Teagan was writing. "What's that?"

"We're camping and we need supplies. Can you take us to the store?" Teagan said.

"Honey, I just came from the store."

"Okay," Teagan said, not keeping disappointment from her voice.

"Let's see if I have anything you want, before you get upset," Susanna said.

"We're not upset," Grace said.

"Help me unload these and you might be surprised," said Susanna. She'd bought canned chicken noodle soup, granola bars, apples, chocolate bars, marshmallows, and graham crackers, which Teagan added to the paper bag designated for camping food, despite Grace pretending to not like them.

"This is perfect. Thanks, Mom."

"See. I know you two better than you think," Susanna said. She began unloading the other groceries and Teagan directed Grace where to put things.

"So, what do you girls think about high school in the fall?"

Teagan said she didn't know, and Grace gave a noncommittal shrug. The truth was that they had no idea what to expect, and so couldn't talk about it.

"It'll be bigger," Teagan said.

"I'm going to take Latin," Grace said.

"Really, Latin," said Susanna.

"Why? It's a dead language," said Teagan.

"Exactly. I don't have to learn how to speak it," said Grace.

"You'll be with Charlie," Susanna said.

"Yeah. We'll probably never see him," Teagan said. Charlie was three years ahead of her.

"It'll still be nice to be at the same school, won't it?" Susanna said.

"Sure," said Teagan. "Grace, come see the new barn cats."

The girls carried their backpacks, sleeping bags, and the paper bag of groceries down to the barn and piled everything in the back of the blue truck. Gums came up to them to have his withered ears rubbed. Slinky lay in the sun and flipped her tail occasionally. Grace told Teagan that they were nice cats, and they moved on with their plans. They climbed into the cab of the truck. The cracked bench smelled strongly of vinyl warmed in the sun. A crushed Diet Coke can sat in the well of the passenger's side.

"Key is in the glove compartment," Teagan said to Grace. Grace handed it over.

"Your parents let you drive?"

"Yeah, didn't you know? I've been driving the truck for a while now," Teagan said. She pushed the clutch to the floor, turned the key, and rested her hand on the stick shift. "Hold on to something, because I don't drive it that often," Teagan said.

"We could just walk," Grace said.

"That's not as much fun. Hold on," Teagan said.

"What about seat belts?" Grace asked.

"There aren't any. Sorry. But we won't go very fast at all," Teagan said. She shifted into first and slowly let up the clutch, trying to feel when it caught. The truck lurched forward, bucked, and stalled.

"Shit!" said Grace, pushing against the dashboard with both hands.

"Sorry. Sometimes it takes a few tries," said Teagan. She was already restarting the engine. On the second try the truck rolled forward, but not because the gear had engaged, and when Teagan let up the clutch the truck ran for a few seconds and then stalled and shuddered again. Grace looked at Teagan and said that she would rather walk.

"One more time. This is it," Teagan said and turned the key. The truck rolled forward and Teagan eased it into first gear, and when the engine began to roar she eased it into second gear, and they bumped down the hill through the field, the horses lifting their heads from grazing to stare. As they neared the gate, Teagan told Grace to get out and open it, and she would drive slowly toward it. Grace looked doubtful at this suggestion.

"The brakes don't hold very well on the downhill anyway, so it's better just to keep it moving," Teagan explained. She slowed the truck to a crawl, and Grace got out, slammed the truck door, and ran ahead and opened the gate. Teagan leaned over the steering wheel to try to see how much clearance she had on both sides, which was about an inch. She eased the truck through but turned too soon and the side of the bed scraped against the fence post, the metal protesting as it was scratched by the wood. Grace closed the gate, then ran to catch up. She opened the door and ran a little more to get momentum into the cab while the truck meandered forward. She pulled the door shut.

"Good work," Teagan said and shifted into second.

"Next time, you get the gate," Grace said.

"You don't know how to drive it," Teagan said.

"I don't think it's that hard," Grace said.

"I'll teach you. After we put our stuff down I'll give you a lesson," Teagan said. She steered the truck up the trail toward the top field, and they were thrown side to side as the wheels bounced over rocks. Teagan tried to keep the tires in the tracks and wasn't entirely successful. Before the woods opened to the field, there was a small clearing that Charlie and Teagan used as a camping spot. There they'd built the fire ring, digging down to the dirt and fitting rocks close together. The girls spread out their plastic tarp and tossed their sleeping bags on it. They'd decided against the trouble of putting up a tent. The weather was warm. They scavenged for sticks for their small fire. They argued over how to build the fire, A-frame or log cabin, and Grace won with log cabin. A pile of extra wood next to the unlit fire and they were moved in. They sat on their sleeping bags and ate some chocolate.

"Ready for your lesson?" Teagan said.

"Tell me how it works first, before I try it," Grace said.

Teagan described the clutch, and how to press it down to shift gears, and let it up to engage the engine. She mimicked the movement of the clutch with one hand, and shifting the gears with the other, and told Grace how to feel when the clutch caught. Teagan asked if the explanation made sense, and Grace said forget it, she would just figure it out. Teagan drove into the field, where there was less chance of hitting a tree, and killed the engine. They traded places, and Grace stepped on the clutch and the brake and started the engine. She tried shifting into second gear, and the truck groaned.

"You have to use the gas. Forget the brake. If it rolls a little, that's fine," said Teagan.

Grace stepped on the clutch, shifted from neutral into first, and then gunned the gas and let up the clutch. The truck sped forward toward the woods.

"Use the brake," Teagan yelled.

Grace slammed on the brake, throwing them both forward, and the truck shuddered and died.

"A little bit of gas, Grace. You're going to kill us," Teagan said.

"I've never done this before," Grace said back.

"Okay. It's fine. Just use a little less gas this time, and steer toward the trail," Teagan said.

Grace stepped on the clutch, and this time she eased down the gas pedal and shifted smoothly. The truck moved forward with no lurching at all.

"That was great," Teagan said.

"It's not that hard," Grace said.

"Once you get the hang of it. It could be beginner's luck," said Teagan.

"Should I go down the hill?"

"Sure. Go down to the dirt road. It'll be easier to drive there," said Teagan.

Grace drove slowly down the trail, pulling hard on the wheel when the truck didn't respond right away. She went more slowly than Teagan had, and Teagan gave her encouragement. Grace turned onto the road and then shifted into second, only gunning it a little bit.

"You're doing really well," Teagan said.

Grace shifted into third and gave it more gas.

"I don't usually use third here. You don't really need to," Teagan said.

Grace said nothing and kept driving, and then shifted into fourth.

"Grace, I think it's too fast," Teagan said. She looked over at the speedometer. The needle crept past forty, to forty-five.

"You're going too fast, okay? Slow down some, okay?" Teagan said.

"This isn't that fast," Grace said.

The dirt road was not long. Soon they would reach the gate between the dirt road and the paved two-lane road.

"Okay, you should slow it down now," Teagan said, after they'd traveled a little ways more at speed. "Slow down."

"Stop telling me what to do," Grace said.

"It's my truck and I want you to slow it," Teagan said.

"Fine. I won't drive at all," Grace said. She took her hands off the wheel and folded them across her chest.

"Grace, hold the wheel. You can't do that," Teagan yelled, bracing herself on the seat. The truck veered off the road and two wheels fell into the ditch. It drove forward, tilted precariously, two wheels on the road and two in the ditch. And then it bounced as if it had hit something and ricocheted off, and then stopped. Grace had hit the brake.

"Oh my god. Don't do that ever again," said Teagan, quietly.

"I can't drive with you telling me what to do the whole time," Grace said.

"I won't tell you what to do. I just thought it was a little fast. Please, don't ever take your hands off the wheel again, please."

"I won't," Grace said. She started up the engine and pulled forward, out of the ditch, and drove them back to the campsite.

They lay on their sleeping bags, talking about whatever came to mind. Songs they liked, books they'd read, their lack of boy-friends, and who they knew had dated in the past year. They lit some newspaper and stuffed it between the twigs of their fire, and when the twigs lit, they fed it larger sticks. When the woodsmoke began to rise, the woods became a place far away from the lives they lived in houses, with parents and broth-ers. Even though the truck was parked nearby, and they were making canned soup, they seemed a little bit distant. The soup bubbled, and they didn't say much to each other. They ate from bowls that they stacked, unwashed, in the paper bag, and Tea-gan ripped open the bag of marshmallows. They stabbed the marshmallows through with thin sticks, and dunked them in the fire, and watched the sugar skin turn brown and then black in the orange flames, and then pulled them off the sticks with their mouths and ate the hot sweetness, along with the bits of bark that stuck to the soft melt. Teagan did not even point out to Grace that she was enjoying the marshmallows.

Car

In the morning they packed up everything into the bed of the truck. Grace drove down the hill, and at the gate they switched and Teagan drove back to the barn. At the house they found Susanna and Charlie fixing lunches. The girls had bowls of cereal and went up to Teagan's room and fell asleep, because they'd stayed up most of the night talking. It was late afternoon when they woke up. Grace remembered that she was supposed to be home at three o'clock, and they went outside to look for Susanna, who was coming up from the barn.

"Did you ride?" Teagan asked.

"No, I fed. Your dad and I are going out to dinner. I wanted to get the feeding out of the way."

"Susanna, I'm supposed to go home now, I think," Grace said.

"I talked to your mother and let her know that you all were asleep. How late did you stay up?"

Neither of them could say for sure. The sky had been a weak blue when they finally slept.

"I'm going to take both of you to Leta, and Teagan, you can stay there tonight. Sound good?"

On Susanna's insistence, the girls took showers and Grace borrowed some clean clothes of Teagan's. Susanna didn't want to drop them off smelling like a campfire. It was six o'clock when Susanna came out of her bedroom, smelling sweet with perfume and her hair pulled back in a clip. She wore black leather heels.

Grace and Teagan had their backpacks by the kitchen door like Susanna had asked and were sitting at the kitchen table.

"You smell nice," Teagan said.

"Thank you, baby," Susanna said. She took a compact from her purse and held it up high while she applied lipstick. The cap made a little click when she closed it. She popped it into the purse. "Your father should be here any minute." Susanna looked at her delicate watch and then opened up the dishwasher and began putting clean dishes away.

"Mom, don't do that. You're all dressed up." Teagan took a dish from her mother and slid it onto a cabinet shelf. Grace got up to help.

"Thank you," Susanna said.

The sound of car wheels was audible in the driveway.

"Here he is. Get your things," Susanna said and walked out the door.

"Let's just finish this," Teagan said, grabbing a fistful of spoons and forks that clinked together.

Charlie walked in carrying a duffel. "Doing chores? Is this punishment for something?" he said.

"No," Teagan said. She wasn't going to argue in front of Grace. "Where are you going?"

"Mike's."

"Dad's here. Are you coming with us?" Teagan said.

"No. I'm driving myself. Is Mom waiting for you?" he said.

"We're going. Mom's outside," Teagan said.

"What is that?" Charlie was looking through the window. He went out the kitchen door.

Teagan paused with a bread knife in her hand. She heard Charlie talking with her father but couldn't figure out what the excitement was about. She thrust a whisk and spatula at Grace. "These go there," she said and put the knife away and closed the dishwasher, lifting the door with her foot. "C'mon," she said, preventing Grace from picking up her backpack.

Robert was standing with his hand on the silver hood of a sleek, expensive-looking car. Charlie was in the driver's seat, and they were pointing to different things inside. Teagan looked at the shiny, silver, brand-new hubcaps. She'd never seen a car so clean. Barker tried to stick his nose in the open car door, and Robert pushed his head away.

"Barker, come," Susanna said.

"What is it?" Teagan said.

"It's a car," Susanna said.

Teagan smiled at her mother, but Susanna wasn't looking at her. She was looking at the car. Robert straightened up.

"What do you think?" he said, looking at Teagan. Grace hung back. Teagan said it was pretty. She wasn't sure what else to say. She would have never guessed that her parents would buy a car like this one. It was fancy. She didn't want to get too close to it.

"Teagan, come sit in the driver's seat," Charlie said.

She walked forward and sat down. The seat was black leather. It was soft and hugged her. It smelled like new carpet and new leather. The steering wheel was also leather. The panel was full of discreet black buttons. Where there wasn't leather there was what looked like polished wood.

"Nice, isn't it?" Robert said to her.

"Yeah," Teagan said.

"This is a German BMW."

"Was it made in Germany?" Teagan said.

"Yes. It was made there and shipped over here," Robert said.

"Wow," Teagan said. "What happened to your car?" she said.

"I traded it in for this one."

"You traded it?" she said.

"Well. The car dealership buys it and takes the amount off the price of the new car. I still had to pay the difference. But this is a much better car," Robert said.

"I didn't know you could do that," Teagan said.

"Okay, hop out," Robert said.

"Nice wheels, Dad," Charlie said and waved goodbye and got in his own car.

Robert looked at Susanna, who stood with her arms by her sides.

"We should get going," he said.

"Girls, get your stuff," she said.

They ran.

When they came back out Robert was still standing near the car and Susanna was standing away from it.

"Let's take my car," Susanna said.

Teagan headed for the green car.

"No. We'll take this one. Girls, get in," Robert said.

Teagan looked at her mother, who stood and didn't speak.

"Come on. Hurry," Robert said.

Teagan and Grace crawled carefully into the smooth seats, their backpacks on their laps and both looking at the rich interior of the car. Robert shut the door on them. Grace looked at Teagan, but she just shrugged. Susanna sat in the passenger's seat.

"Do you like it?" Teagan asked her, quietly.

Susanna reached back and squeezed Teagan's knee but didn't say anything. Robert started up the car, and it hummed.

"You hear how quiet that is?" he said.

"I can hardly hear it," Teagan said.

Down the driveway, down the road, no one said anything. Teagan looked through the impeccably clear windows, and tried the automatic button, which seemed to operate smoothly and instantly.

"Can we listen to the radio?" Grace whispered to Teagan.

"Can we listen to the radio?" Teagan asked her parents.

Neither of them said anything.

Teagan asked about the radio again.

"What station do you want?" Susanna said, searching the dashboard for the right button.

Cake

In my apartment, I pour a cup of coffee and push one of the cardboard boxes I picked up from my mother's house into the middle of the floor. My saddle lies upside-down in the corner, like a giant flayed bug. I sip my coffee and stare at a box. I'd rather do anything than sort through its contents, but I pull the box to me. I consider just taking all of the boxes to the dump, except I don't actually know where the dump is, and I know that the boxes contain a lot of paper, which I will recycle, especially because I picture my old journals lying open on a pile of tires and toilet seats, my adolescent misgivings exposed.

I pop open a box and pull out papers. On top is a school essay on the greenhouse effect. This is worse than I'd guessed. I am going to have to sort through the detritus of my childhood. The essay is an appropriate start to the recycling pile. There are poems written on yellowed wide-lined paper and drawings done in crayon. There is a letter to my grandmother, written on a card decorated with a bird, which I never sent to her. There are several journals, full of angst and teenage self-discovery: three pages dedicated to the merits of a boy I liked. I hold my mug of coffee close for support.

My mother saved this stuff and somehow decided I would want it all back. Maybe there is one thing I might want in all this, but I feel there isn't enough time to go back in time. I commit to sorting quickly and making a no pile and a yes pile. The no pile will be decidedly the larger.

What I want is to move on, to move forward, and also to take a shower. I don't want this reek of nostalgia. I will julienne the past and it will not be profound; it is a simple chore. I give myself this pep talk, pour more coffee, and dig out the contents of another box.

Three slow hours later, the no pile is tall and the yes pile is tiny. I chose to keep a note from my grandmother, a card from my mother, and another card from my father, because in each handwritten message I can hear a voice stored in letters. There is one final box, and from it I pull a fabric-covered photo album that my mother put together for me. I have been missing it for a couple of years, not wanting to admit that it might be lost. I can't believe it is in my lap.

The photos were taken on film. The colors are faded and muted and the photos are pasted behind clear, flimsy plastic. Like frames from a film they show a progression of moments.

My grandmother, younger than I ever remember, holds me as an infant in a blanket. My mother stands with my father, looking at me. Charlie stands beside them, but his gaze to the ground and he turns slightly away. He looks disappointed. He is no longer his parents' only darling. Another picture of Charlie shows him on the couch. His feet don't yet reach the end of the cushion, and there I am, his monkey-faced infant sister, draped across his legs. He is smiling but looks unsure as to what he's holding on to.

Another series of photos is arranged vertically on an album page. They show a one-year-old me and my dad. I am sitting in his lap. His thick forearm hugs me. Smiling, he holds his baby daughter as she focuses on a piece of cake on the table. My fingers curl on my father's arm. In the next picture, he lifts a spoon with yellow cake and fluffy icing. The snapshot catches the spoon almost to my opened mouth. My father leans to the side to catch the expression on my face. In the last picture, my cheeks are smeared with frosting, and my dad looks down at the top of my head. We wear the same squinted smile.

Obsidian

"Your mother and I found a horse," Robert said.

"Really? What is it?" Teagan said.

"A Thoroughbred."

"Mare or gelding?"

"Gelding."

"What color?"

"He's a dark bay. He looks black, with a white mark on his face."

"A star?"

"No, a blaze. And one white sock on a hind leg."

"A foxhunter?"

"A seasoned foxhunter."

"He sounds good."

"We're bringing him here."

"When?"

"Tomorrow afternoon."

"Can I ride him?"

"Probably not."

"Why not?"

"He's a strong horse."

"I'm strong."

"He won't be a horse for a girl."

Foxhunt

Robert was told a story about Obsidian. At the time the gelding belonged to a man whose fields happened to lie along a route the River County Hunt often rode. The horse was in his usual field. When the riders passed by, Obsidian jumped the fence and took his place. He halted with the hunt, galloped when they galloped. At the end of the day the riders passed by the field, and he jumped back in.

Susanna Told Teagan a Story

Susanna told Teagan a story about the first time she and Robert tried to load the horse, Obsidian, onto the trailer to go fox-hunting. It was early in the morning. Susanna said they were all beautiful and clean (the horses, the tack, and they in their riding clothes). The horse wouldn't walk onto the trailer.

"He acted like he'd never seen a trailer," Susanna said.

Robert tried to lead him up the ramp, but Ian stepped off to the side. Susanna couldn't believe it. They were ready to go, and the new horse, an experienced hunter, wouldn't load. Desperate to get the horse on the trailer, Susanna called Hope Graves, her friend who was a horse trainer.

Hope drove up in her truck, a long whip and a sturdy rope on the passenger seat. She stepped out of her car and looked at the horse. Ian walked onto the trailer.

Hope said, "That's a smart horse."

Curriculum Vitae (Abstract)

Obsidian. Nicknamed Ian. Color: bay. Sex: gelding. Height: 16.2 hands (one hand equaling four inches). Excellent conformation (that is the symmetry of his bones). Service: River County Hunt; Fox Grove Hunt. Miscellaneous: Called handsome by strangers who follow the compliment with an offer. (He's not for sale.) Ian is called a made horse. Has exceptional knowledge, has exceptional talent, is an exceptional athlete, is seemingly vain and lazy. When jumping a coop (a triangular obstacle with closed sides, which is slat of wood touching slat of wood, built in a fence line to allow jumping from one field to another) three or four feet in height, he gathers himself early and leaves the ground from a distance away, sails above the obstacle, and touches down lightly on the other side.

First Ride and Foxes

Susanna explained to Teagan that she wanted Teagan to ride Obsidian, who was called Ian. Teagan wondered if her mother was nervous about him or if she simply guessed that, if anything happened, her daughter's bones would knit faster than her own. When Teagan saw the horse in the field, he was holding his head high and he flared his nostrils, sniffing the air. If she had been braver, she would have refused to ride him. Hope pulled up in her truck. Susanna wanted Hope to evaluate Ian.

Teagan was impressed by Hope, who could tack a horse in ten minutes, whose arms were ropes of muscle. Hope handled horses with authority and efficiency, and she could command her Jack Russell dog with a glance. Teagan tried to approximate Hope's approach, but she always felt she was too slow.

Teagan had heard her mother say that a horse could read a rider's mind. She tried to feel calm when she went to mount up, but her heart pounded. She didn't speak reassuringly to Ian or pat his neck. It seemed that would patronize him. She stepped in the stirrup and pulled up on the pommel of the saddle, but she didn't sit down right away. She slipped gently onto the smooth seat on her inner thighs and settled on the small bones of her pelvis. She'd never sat in the saddle quite that way before. Teagan let the reins loop a little. The horse's stride, even at the walk, was enormous. She sat easy in the saddle, trying to figure him out. To match his rhythm she had to let her body shift with the movement of his shoulders. In a matter of seconds she had adjusted. He was eager to go forward, and she felt he carried her.

Hope rode in front and Susanna rode behind. The strategy of this order wasn't lost on her. They'd put Teagan in the safest place. If Ian tried to run forward, Hope could use her horse to block him, and if he backed up, Susanna could use her horse to push him forward. Ian walked comfortably, and he seemed calm, interested in his new surroundings. Teagan couldn't shake the impression that he wasn't paying much attention to her. She seemed insignificant, even though she was supposed to be important, in control, his rider, after all. He should pay attention to her. She wasn't sure he cared.

Ian seemed to be speeding up, his long strides getting longer as they started downhill. She prepared to slow him, and as soon as she lifted the reins he slouched back onto his hind end and slowed. It was clear to her that he was well trained and responsive, obviously athletic, but also unafraid and powerful. He was a little bit frightening. If Ian decided to get rid of her, he would have no trouble doing it. But his big rib cage swung side to side in an easy rhythm as he stretched out his neck and walked with a ground-covering stride, as if moving was what he was made to do.

Ian was going to be her father's horse. Susanna and Robert hunted, and if Ian passed his trial, they would have a pair of hunters again. Teagan didn't mind that her parents hunted. She was aware that their version of foxhunting had very little to do with killing foxes, and more to do with riding across fields and through woods. It also involved a certain amount of ceremony and pomp, the way the horses and riders arrived clean and shiny; the way riders bid good morning to the field master; the way a (sometimes silver) tray of doughnut holes was offered, lifted up to the riders in their saddles; the way the (sometimes silver) stirrup cup was passed, a deep blood-color port drunk from a communal cup; the idiomatic *cup of courage;* the way the huntsman called the hounds together, the way he blew his horn, the way the hounds began to run, the way horses followed on, the way the fox outwitted even thirty hounds, the way the fox crossed a stream to break the trail of his own scent, the way the fox crossed the stream again to leave his scent in two directions, the way the fox walked the top of the fence, up where hounds couldn't smell him, and when the fox was treed or went underground, the hunt gave him up. No wiry terriers were sent down a fox hole, and, as far as she knew, no one carried a gun. Her parents' hunt club went so far as to monitor the fox population year-round. It made sense to her. If they wanted foxes, then they should care about the health and habitat of foxes.

She has seen the flash of rust color disappearing up a grassy bank when she looked at the right moment from the car window. The red coat and white-tipped tail she has seen from a distance across some fields. She has come face-to-face with the red-and-white face, the black paws, the black-tipped ears, when she was in the woods. It was evening, the daylight was fading, and the fox came trotting, always as if he had a purpose, a place he was heading to. The fox stopped and she stopped. The fox left first, turning to go back into the woods, and she walked on.

Once, at Blue View Farm, she was having a riding lesson from Hope. They were in the riding ring, a grassy oval marked by a wooden fence. Hope told her to stop, so Teagan halted. A silver fox, the body supple like a cat's, but on tall legs, and the head like a dog's pointed muzzle, was carrying something in her jaws. She trotted quickly across the grass arena and loped up and over the hill. Hope said it was unusual. They kept going with the lesson, but soon Hope told her to stop again. The fox was back. From atop her horse Teagan could see the gray body disappear into the woods. She on her horse, and Hope standing nearby, waited for something to happen. The fox crossed again, another small thing in her mouth, and again up and over the hill. Hope guessed that she was moving her family. The things she carried in her mouth, one by one, were her pups. Each time the momma fox came with her pup in her mouth, they held still. Teagan silently wished her well.

She sometimes saw the evidence of a fox killed by a car, the tail blowing in a breeze, the body eternally still on the roadside. Once she begged her mother to stop the car. She had seen two foxes, a few yards apart. She pleaded with her mother, her need unexplainable, and Susanna, against her better judgment, pulled over. Teagan ran down the road shoulder to the first body and searched in the ditch for some sticks. The first fox was whole. The undersides of the dark paws had leathery pads. She worked the sticks under the body and carried it, bier-like, to the stiff grass beyond the ditch. The second fox had an eye popped almost out of the socket, like a cartoon illustration of surprise. The eye was round and almost all white, except for the deep brown iris. She pried the red body off the road. She couldn't think what had caused them both to die so close together, and she couldn't explain why she wanted to move them.

They walked the horses on the dirt track. Alongside it a finger of a creek trickled, hidden below a treed bank. They turned in to the woods and after a while came to the clearing on the hill. They walked their horses down the hill a different way, and at the bottom was the creek again. There were two skinny logs along the track next to the cow field. Hope wanted all of them to jump. They first jumped away from home, meaning they jumped so the horses weren't running in the direction of the barn. It didn't matter that the barn was across a field, through the woods, and up another hill. Horses know where the barn is. *Don't stop riding until you are off your horse* was a saying of Hope's.

They jumped as they might in the hunt field, one after the other, with Hope leading. Ian passed that test. When he led off he did fine, too. Then Hope wanted them to jump separately. She explained to Teagan that it takes discipline for a horse to stand while another horse moves away from it. Horses tend to want to stay together, like in a herd. To begin, Teagan jumped Ian first and halted him, waiting for the others to come over the jump. He kept his head turned toward them but otherwise stood quietly. Then it was time to take the jump toward home, which was always harder. Hope jumped first and Susanna waited with Teagan. Ian seemed happy to wait with the mare.

Susanna started to move her horse toward the jump. Ian stepped forward to follow, but Teagan held him back. He didn't like that. He didn't want to be left. He tossed his head and shifted sideways. She held him. Duchess was just over the jump when Ian threw his head high in the air. Teagan had no leverage on the bit with his head so high, and Ian charged forward. When his head dropped she pulled him back, but only for a moment. As if it was her idea to go, she raised out of the saddle to let him move forward. He went from standing still into a canter, took a few enormous strides, and jumped, galloping even faster on the other side to catch up with the other horses. As soon as he did, he halted himself. Ian seemed happy. Teagan was shaken. The horse was too difficult for her to handle. She took a deep breath and quickly assessed herself. She was fine, really, and the horse was suddenly calm. A stronger rider could have held Ian. Her father would be able to handle him.

Hope and Susanna had been talking when Teagan jumped, and they turned around as she reached them. They were surprised to see her right behind them. When Hope asked what had happened, Teagan had to tell them that Ian had fought her and she'd decided to let him go rather than hold him. Susanna wasn't happy to hear that. Teagan, lying before she could stop herself, said it wasn't a big deal.

"He just pulled a little," Teagan said, playing it down, although she wasn't sure why. Ian's bony skull had come within an inch of her face when he had tossed his head. The ratio of the horse's power to her ability to handle him definitely favored the horse. But he would be ridden by her father. She wasn't worried. As they walked up the hill to the barn on their horses, Susanna told them the story of when she and Robert went to look at Ian for the first time.

Robert had been standing next to Ian, and the horse had reached over and bit him on the arm. Robert had laughed and made an offer on the horse right there. When they loaded him on the trailer to bring him to Blue View Farm, the wife had said, "I hope you're good riders. I'm afraid of that horse."

Susanna had pretended she hadn't heard.

Dobb

On a Saturday, when Robert had to go into the office for a few hours, Susanna got an interesting piece of mail. It was a hand-addressed envelope, and she said it was from her old college roommate. She opened it at the table and took out a newspaper clipping. As she read it, her hand went to her mouth and she sighed deeply. Charlie looked up from his magazine. Teagan walked through the kitchen. Something about her mother and brother caused her to stop.

"An old friend died," Susanna said. She folded up the newspaper and read the letter that came with it. "The funeral is next week."

"Who was it, Mom?" Charlie asked.

"His name is Dobb. He was my high school boyfriend. He was married and he had at least one child. A son," she said.

"How did he die?" Teagan asked.

"He's had health problems," Susanna said.

"What was wrong with him?" Teagan asked.

Charlie gave her a look, but Teagan wanted to know.

"He had stomach problems, or intestinal problems. He got injured, and he was sick a lot after that." Susanna stuffed the letter and clipping back into the envelope.

"Was it a car accident?" Charlie asked.

"No. But it was really tragic. He was hunting with his brother, Mick, and they were climbing over a fence, and Mick's gun went off accidentally, and the bullet lodged in Dobb's stomach. It was awful. I remember he was in the hospital a long time. It really changed him. His system was just so damaged. Anyway. I'm

sure it had something to do with that. His poor wife. I met her.
She's very nice. He was my year in school. You just don't expect
it." She made a noise, a little hum, and dropped the envelope
on the table and got up and walked out of the kitchen. Teagan
picked up the envelope.

"That's Mom's personal stuff," Charlie said, reaching out and
taking hold of it.

"I want to read the obituary. It's from the newspaper," she said.

Charlie let go and went back to his magazine, sipping a
Fresca. Teagan fished out the thin, gray newspaper clipping and
looked it over, but it wasn't that interesting to her. There was no
photograph. She slid the clipping back inside the card.

"I guess she'll go to the funeral. Do you think we'll go, too?"
Teagan said.

"Probably not. We didn't know him," Charlie said.

"I'd go though, if Mom wanted us to. Did you know about
her boyfriend?" Teagan said.

Charlie gave a one-shouldered shrug and shook his head, still
reading. Teagan picked up a pencil and balanced it between her
pointer fingers, the dull tip pressing into the pad of her fingertip.
Then she held it vertical, aimed, and flipped it at the back of
Charlie's magazine. It hit. He frowned.

"Teagan," he said, and he moved the pencil to the side. "Go
do something."

Later in the week, Teagan sought out her mother in her bedroom. It seemed that she hadn't seen much of her mother in the
past few days. She was folding sheets on the big double bed.

"Hi," Teagan said.

"Hi," Susanna said, continuing to fold.

Teagan sat down on the opposite edge of the bed.

"Teagan, don't get in my way. If you're going to do that, take this," Susanna said, tossing the end of a sheet to her. Teagan picked it up and they folded it in half, to the side, and Teagan reached across to hand her corners to her mother. Susanna picked up a new sheet.

"When are you going to the funeral?" Teagan asked.

"What funeral?" Susanna said.

Teagan was suddenly embarrassed. "Your high school boyfriend."

"Oh. It's already happened. It was Monday," Susanna said, waiting for Teagan to line up corners.

"Why didn't you go? Was it far away?" Teagan asked.

"It wasn't that. It was just we couldn't get a babysitter for you and Charlie, and anyway, it was too expensive," Susanna said. She wasn't looking up.

"Charlie and I could have stayed by ourselves," Teagan said, a little confused.

"No. You're too young for me to leave you without an adult in the house. I wouldn't be comfortable with that."

"I don't think we're too young," Teagan said.

Susanna took the sheet from her. "I'll finish these. You go find something to do," she said.

"Why was it too expensive?" Teagan said.

Susanna bent down and fluffed out a fitted sheet. "We've made a big purchase recently."

"The BMW?" Teagan asked.

Her mother lined up the unruly edges of the elastic. "I need you to go somewhere else now, so I can finish this. You're getting in my way," Susanna said.

Teagan walked into the hallway. The house was quiet. She decided to go to the barn.

After she'd cleaned her saddle and bridle and girth, and her mother's, too, she pulled Zephyr out of his field and groomed him thoroughly, just for something to do. When she turned him out again, she followed him, just to see where he would go. He stopped to sniff her, looking for food, then walked away. She sat in the field, looking out at the mountains. She wondered if it would be possible to walk in a straight line from where she was to the top of the mountain directly in front of her. She sat until the insects began to whine. When she got to the house, Charlie was watching TV on the couch.

"Where's Mom?"

"In her room," Charlie said.

"What are you watching?" Teagan said.

"Cop show," Charlie said. "It's not that good."

"Why are you watching it?"

"Why don't you go bother someone else?" he said.

"Like who?" she asked and sat down to watch the show.

Charlie flipped through the channels during the commercials, and Teagan couldn't stand it. She asked him to stop.

"This is my show. You don't have to watch it," he said.

"There's no point in flipping channels if you're not going to watch any of them."

Susanna emerged. "I'm going to start dinner," she said and was gone.

"Go help Mom," Charlie said.

Teagan ran up the stairs to her bedroom and lay on her bed.

———————

It was late when they sat down to eat dinner. Four places were set. Susanna told Teagan to eat her salad.

"When's Dad getting home?" Charlie asked.

"Later," Susanna said, picking up a forkful of lettuce.

"I want dessert," Teagan said.

"I don't think we have anything for dessert," Susanna said. "We have fruit."

"Fruit isn't dessert. Ice cream is dessert," Teagan said.

The kitchen door opened, and Robert walked in wearing his work clothes, khaki pants and a button-down shirt and a tie.

Teagan leaned back in her chair. "Hi, Dad," she said.

"Hi, girl," he said. He stopped at the fridge and popped open a beer and sat down. "Sorry I'm late. What are we eating?"

"Salad on the counter. Pasta is on the stove," Susanna said.

Robert got up to fill his plate.

Teagan woke to the sound of voices. She got out of bed and listened in the hallway. It was like hearing a storm coming over the mountain, the thunder rumbling and getting louder. A door slammed. Then she heard her mother yelling. Her father's deep voice was yelling, too. Teagan walked to Charlie's door and knocked softly. He didn't answer, but she opened the door a crack and looked in. He was sitting at his desk, the lamp on, a magazine open. She walked over to him. He didn't look up. Something else made a loud noise below their feet, and the voices rose and fell again.

"Charlie," she said. Her voice shook. "Charlie?"

"Go back to bed," he said.

"What's going on?" she said.

"Go to bed," he said, still not looking at her. She stared at him, then walked back to her bedroom and pulled a pillow over her head.

Phone

Teagan couldn't sleep. She looked at the shadows in her room. The house was quiet. She got up and looked out the window. One floodlight was on at the barn. She couldn't see any animals. She wondered if the cats were asleep or hunting. She decided she wanted something to drink. In the hallway she heard a voice speaking softly. She walked into the kitchen and saw her dad, in jeans and polo shirt, wearing his shoes. She stood and listened to him whisper something into the telephone. He turned and saw her, and slammed the phone down.

"I couldn't sleep," she said.

"Me either," he said.

"I'm going to get a glass of milk," she said.

"That'll help you sleep," he said and left the room.

Mornings Are Repetitive

Barbecue sauce, chicken juices dried with oil circles at the bottom of the Dutch oven, peas shriveled in a pot on the stove, a yellow bowl crusted with salt where the potatoes had been, and plates stacked like the leaning tower stuck to a pan stuck with sauce. The forks and knives lay in a swampy grave at the bottom of the sink. I filled the carafe under the tap and then poured water into the coffeemaker. With dull fingers I fit a paper filter in the plastic cone. The coffeemaker gurgled and steamed. The coffee made, I poured it black and took greedy sips. The corners of my eyes leaked tears, because of the canyon of dishes, I thought. On the table was a notepad. Near it was a pen. I wrote, "Barbecue sauce, chicken juices dried with oil circles at the bottom of the Dutch oven, peas shriveled in a pot on the stove."

Bedroom

Teagan couldn't sleep, again. She seemed to have trouble getting to sleep, or staying asleep, and both were new to her. She wondered who her father had been talking to on the phone the other night. She was wide awake. Maybe her father was awake, too. Maybe she could talk to him. She got up. She looked out at the barn. A floodlight was on. There weren't any animals. She walked downstairs. A light was on at the end of the hallway. She walked toward it. Her parents' door was open. She walked in. Her father was talking on the phone.

"Just a minute," he said and put the receiver on the side table. "Teagan, go to bed," he said.

"Who are you talking to? Where's Mom?" she said.

"What did I just say to you?" He was angry.

"I can't sleep," she said.

"You can't sleep because you're not in bed," he said and grabbed her shoulder and pushed her out the door and closed it. She stared at the closed door, then knocked softly.

"Dad?" she said. She could hear his voice talking again. "Dad," she said. "Will you open the door? Please?" She knocked again and tried the doorknob, her heart beating fast. It was locked. "Dad," she yelled. "Dad, open the door. Open the door, Dad, please." She yelled and pounded on the door with the side of her fist until it rattled in its frame. She shook the doorknob. On the other side of the door was silence. She thought that Charlie would hear and come tell her to be quiet. No one told her to be quiet. She went back to her bedroom and lay in bed.

Ball

Occasionally, Teagan went to Charlie's games. She would sit next to her father while he threw his fist in the air and clapped and yelled. She would wait for him to calm down and then lean lazily against him and watch her brother run back and forth on the court.

Somehow Teagan's job was to practice basketball with Charlie whenever he told her it was time to practice. She never questioned it. He would track her down in the house, basketball in hand, and tell her to put her shoes on. Not questioning it was easiest. She thought that maybe if she said no, her parents would yell at her. Later, she realized that that didn't make sense. No one made her practice with her brother. It was his air of authority that made her tie the laces on her sneakers, as if she'd been given a decree: one shall put on one's shoes when one's sibling says to put on one's shoes.

It was as if her compliance was a thing inherited, like a recessive gene or a tendency toward risk taking. They would go to the school gym, which was kept open after school and some on weekends. She didn't really like basketball, but she didn't dislike it, either. Maybe it was that she was never allowed to do what she wanted with the ball. If she dribbled the ball, Charlie would tell her to stop, and if she went for a layup, he would tell her not to waste time. She caught his rebounds and passed him the ball again.

"Pass me the ball," Charlie would yell.

Teagan wondered why he almost always said this, as though it was a different command.

Teagan shoved the ball back to him in a two-handed throw, then she would stroll backward from the net to see if his shot would go in. Wherever it went, she sprang forward to grab it, even though there was no one to compete with.

Charlie usually stayed where he was and waited, and said, "Pass me the ball," but one day he asked Teagan to play defense.

"Man to man," Charlie said.

"That won't work," Teagan said.

"Yes, it will. I'll teach you," Charlie said.

He didn't get the joke.

"Woman to man," Teagan said.

Charlie just launched into telling her what he wanted her to do. "Don't let me get to the net," he said.

"Okay," Teagan said, and she didn't. She defended so well that she ended up stealing the ball from Charlie while he was dribbling.

"If you don't let me get to the net at all, I can't practice," he said.

"I take my instructions seriously," Teagan said.

After that, Charlie didn't ask her to play defense again.

Railing

Gums balanced on a fence post. She went up to him and he rubbed against her. She climbed up and sat on the next post. He trotted along the top rail on wide paws. He walked over her lap, then back again, and resumed his spot. After a while he seemed to get annoyed with her sitting there, watching him, and he walked away across another railing to another fence post. Shakily, Teagan stood up with her arms out and walked the railing to him. Seeing her coming, he walked to the next post. She followed him and figured out that going quickly from post to post was easier. If she could maintain her balance across the railing, then she could steady herself for a moment on the wide fence post. Gums jumped down. Teagan kept going along the fence line, to see how far she could get before she fell.

Robert

He was away. His clothes were in the closet. His tools were in the garage. Susanna said that he would be home that weekend, but a couple of weekends passed and Robert wasn't back. Charlie shut himself in his room. Her mother was quiet, and she was gone from the house more. Instead of doing her homework after school, Teagan went to the barn. She wasn't supposed to ride by herself, but she did.

The dark bay horse, Ian, was in the field. Didn't Robert need his horse? It was his horse. Charlie and Teagan had been born into a family with horses. She'd never known life without them. It was Ian who made Teagan think her father would be back. It didn't make sense to her that he would leave a horse.

Teagan walked out of the bathroom at the same moment Charlie walked out of his bedroom. She felt she hadn't seen him in days. No one in the house seemed to be talking, as if silence had infected all of their voices. She put her arms around her brother. He let her and patted her on the back, then broke away.

Away

Charlie said that their parents' problems were none of their business. He wouldn't talk about it.

Teagan had thought of going to a school somewhere else. "I just want to," she said.

A few days later Susanna told Teagan to get on the phone. Hope was on the line. She had gone to high school at a girls' boarding school with a riding program. The school was in the state and a few hours away. Teagan wouldn't have to leave Virginia.

"Can I really go?" Teagan asked her mother.

"Are you sure about this?" Susanna frowned at her daughter.

"Yes," Teagan said. "Can we afford it?" she asked.

"Do you want to go or not?" Susanna said.

"I want to go," Teagan said.

Susanna and Charlie drove Teagan up to Hunting Hill School for a tour. The main building of classrooms was large and looked like a house, with a peaked roof, rows and rows of windows, and a double front door. The "school yard" was long and green with giant old oak and elm trees. The tour guide from the admissions department showed the group of girls Miss Guinevere's Garden, a sunken lawn lined with flowers and flowering bushes, where graduation took place every year. Teagan couldn't believe how beautiful everything was. She even agreed to the dress code without arguing with her mother about it. Charlie was quiet on the trip. He didn't seem to have anything to say about the school, but he was one year away from graduating. She doubted he was interested in high schools. Teagan was just starting. And she'd have her horse, too. She couldn't believe her luck that such a place existed. She didn't like leaving Grace, but they would see each other on holidays. Teagan would write to her.

Drink

Grace didn't ask where Teagan's father was, and if she had, Teagan couldn't have told her. She knew he wouldn't come home again, although this thought was vague. Grace was spending the night. They talked about school and how Teagan was going away. Grace sat on the floor of Teagan's room, sorting through a pile of T-shirts. Teagan explained that she had to wear collared shirts to class and "no denim" (Susanna had to explain that meant no jeans), but on the weekends she could wear what she wanted. Grace was helping her go through her clothes. Their priority was which real clothes to take, ones she could wear on weekends.

"I might come home a lot of weekends anyway," Teagan said.

"You still need to wear something, don't you?" Grace said, holding up a soft, faded blue T-shirt with a starburst across the chest. "Can I borrow this?"

"I guess so," Teagan said.

Grace put it in a pile of things for herself. "We can trade on weekends," she said. "Do you think you'll have parties there?" she said.

"I don't know," Teagan said. Then, feeling like she should make the school sound better, she said, "I know you can sign out to go to things. Plays, and stuff like that, I think. And, I think there are things with other schools. Dances with boys' schools," Teagan said.

"Dances?" Grace paused, a yellow shirt in her hand to go into her "borrow" pile.

"I know," Teagan said. "Are you going to parties next year?"

"It depends, I guess," Grace said.

"Druggie parties," Teagan said.

"That was so weird when Scott and those guys did that at the end-of-year party," Grace said.

"They're stupid. Getting a head start on high school, I guess," Teagan said. She grabbed a red T-shirt that had THE PHILIP-PINES written across it in yellow and was printed with a volcano and palm trees, which Grace was holding up. "I want that one. I don't think I'd want to be drunk. At a party, I mean. Especially if you don't know people there. You'd just end up acting stupid," Teagan said.

"Have you been drunk?" Grace said.

"No. I've never really had anything. I mean, I've had sips at supper. Charlie will have a beer sometimes. But I haven't, like, really had a drink," Teagan said.

"Me either. But I was thinking that I probably should try it out beforehand," Grace said.

"Try out getting drunk?" Teagan said.

"Well, I'd rather do it at home instead of in front of a bunch of strangers."

"That kind of makes sense," Teagan said. "What do I wear to class if I can't wear jeans?"

"Khakis," Grace said.

"Gross," Teagan said. "So are you going to do it? Get drunk?"

"I don't see why not. My parents have a liquor cabinet. I looked in there. It's mostly sherry."

"What's sherry?" Teagan said.

"Tastes like vinegar," Grace said.

"I can't believe you've already been in your parents' liquor cabinet. You're a budding alcoholic. Hey, we could drink here. My parents have a cabinet, or my mom does, and there's beer in the pantry, but it's warm. I think you drink beer cold, but whatever. Do you want to try?" Teagan said.

They went to sleep, but Teagan set an alarm. At two in the morning, they went shopping in the kitchen. Grace suggested a snack so they wouldn't get sick. Then they took turns taking little sips of everything in the cabinet. They found some bourbon and gin, and bright green crème de menthe. They split one of the warm, foamy beers. Grace liked the crème de menthe the best and continued drinking it. Teagan took sips of the bourbon. Her eyes watered while it burned her throat, then it tasted sweet like honey. They wondered how they would know when they were drunk. Grace suggested trying to write something, and when they couldn't write anymore, they would probably be drunk. Before Teagan could find paper, Grace said she had to pee, right away. Teagan said she had to pee right away, too. They couldn't decide who should go first. Grace said that they had the whole yard. Teagan said she was so right, and they went outside to pee in the yard. Teagan had trouble squatting and sat in her pee. Grace had taken her shorts and underwear completely off and then couldn't find them. Teagan laughed and couldn't get up. Grace finally found her clothes but said she couldn't remember how to put them back on. They had a fit of laughing until Teagan said they'd wake up her mother. Grace got dressed and they lay down in the grass, even though it was wet and the night was cold. Grace said she was sure they were drunk. Teagan said that the stars looked really, really bright. Grace vomited.

Injured

Zephyr didn't come when she called him. Teagan walked his field and found him.

"What is this, Zep? Are you hiding from me?" She held the carrot out, and he crunched it. She put on the halter and pulled on the rope, but he wouldn't step forward. She turned her back on him and gave small tugs on the rope, but he wouldn't budge. Finally, she reached back and hauled him forward by the halter. He took a few steps and then stopped again. "What's going on, boy? Something bothering you?" she said. She looked him over but couldn't see anything wrong. She pulled on the rope again and he walked forward, and she walked faster, trying to keep his momentum up, and then she noticed that he was limping. She stopped and stared at the leg. It looked fine, but she knew something was wrong and didn't want to believe it. She walked him forward, and he limped behind her. She led him up to the gate, stopping every few yards to let him rest. By the time she got him to the barn, she was fighting back tears. She wanted to blame someone. She put him in a stall and jogged to the house.

"Mom," she yelled as soon as she was in the door. Susanna didn't answer. Teagan banged on her mother's bedroom door before pushing the door open. Susanna was on the phone. She put a hand over the mouthpiece. "Teagan, I'm on the phone with your new school."

Teagan sat in the kitchen, staring ahead of her, as if in a waiting room.

Susanna came in. "What's going on?" she said.

"Come look. Zep is limping," Teagan said.

Susanna seemed to loosen. She said, "Show me."

Teagan led the horse into the barnyard.

"Walk him in a circle," Susanna said.

Teagan led him in a circle in both directions.

"He's favoring that back leg," Susanna said. "I'll call Hope. I'd say we should wrap the leg, but I don't know. I don't want to make it worse."

"It's bad, right?" Teagan said.

"It's not good. But this is lucky. The vet is coming tomorrow."

"Why tomorrow?" Teagan said.

"We need a certificate for a negative Coggins test before I can send him with you. Put him in a stall and give him some hay."

The official letter of acceptance from Hunting Hill School came in the mail the next day, and the vet came in a white pickup truck. In the truck bed a white metal box folded out into trays full of instruments, medicines, and bandages. Susanna walked the horse in a circle, both directions, like Teagan had done, and the vet watched. He picked up each leg in turn. Both back legs were having trouble holding weight, he said. "In here," he said, running his hand over the front of the leg, just below the belly, "is the stifle joint. It connects the femur with the lower bones, fibula and tibia. That could be the problem." He ran his hand lower, to the next joint, where the leg narrowed. "Or here, the tarsus. You probably call it the hock, between the tibia and cannon bones. An X-ray could confirm it, or both."

"Both?" Susanna said.

"Some horses are prone to joint problems, especially in the back legs. Do you jump him? Go up or down steep hills?" the vet asked.

"Both," Teagan said.

"That may have caused this to present itself, but it was probably just a matter of time."

Teagan felt guilty. All the hills she'd been taking Zephyr up and down, and not at the walk. She loved to let him canter up hills.

"Can he recover?" Susanna said.

"He can, but probably not all the way. He shouldn't jump anymore."

Teagan froze. "He can't ever jump?"

"Jumping him would probably take things beyond repair," the vet said. "He'll need stall rest, and then if he improves, he can start out on the flat, walking, and then if that goes well, he can move on to gradual hills, about five minutes, no more, at the walk, increasing the length of time over a period of days. Then we can assess him and see if he can do more," he said.

"And how long does he need to do that?" Susanna said.

"Maybe four months, maybe six, maybe more. It depends on him, really," he said.

"Do you need me here?" Teagan said quietly to Susanna.

"No, you can go," Susanna said.

"Do you want to bring him to the clinic for more tests?" the vet asked.

Teagan couldn't listen to any more bad news.

In the afternoon Susanna forced Teagan into shopping for khakis and collared shirts. Then she tried to discourage Teagan from packing any of her old T-shirts and offered to buy her new ones in plain colors. Teagan said there was nothing wrong with her clothes, and Susanna went on to list everything that was, in fact, wrong with them. They were both in horrible moods. Teagan couldn't wait to get out of the car and get away from her mother, and she was irritated when Susanna pulled into a parking lot.

"What now?" she said.

"Stay in the car. I'll be right back," Susanna said.

"I'm not staying in the car," Teagan said and got out.

"I'll only be a minute. I'm dropping something off for your dad."

"I want to see Dad," Teagan said.

"He's not here. He just has a mailbox here."

This was fascinating information to Teagan. The idea that her mother had to send mail to her father, that he didn't get mail at the house anymore, was strange.

"When is he coming back?" Teagan asked and immediately regretted it.

Susanna started walking toward the dull, brown building. Teagan caught up with her and didn't say anything more. They walked into the empty hallway, lined with blue metal lockers. Susanna didn't have to read the board listing names and offices. She pulled open a door, and Teagan followed her up a flight of metal steps and into another hallway. This one had fewer lockers, and more posters and projects on the walls, made by students. Susanna opened another door, and Teagan followed her into a strange, short hallway that had a door on either side. Next to one of the doors was a plaque that said ROBERT FRENCH, and under it was a narrow metal mailbox. Susanna fed the long envelope into it, then she stood in front of the door, as if waiting. Teagan looked at her mother, who didn't speak.

"Is this Dad's?" Teagan asked. She had never been to her father's office.

Susanna reached out and turned the knob, then let it go

and knocked, many rapping knocks. She turned the knob and opened the door. The room was small and had one narrow window across from the desk. Robert was in a swivel chair in front of his computer. He stood up and looked at Susanna.

"Dad." Teagan hugged him.

"Teagan," Robert said. His hug was weak.

"I didn't know you were here," Susanna said.

"I didn't know you were coming. What do you need?" he said.

"I dropped the papers in your box," she said. They stood looking at each other. Susanna walked to the narrow coat closet and opened it. A woman was standing there. She was skinny and wore a purple jacket and matching skirt. Her hair was brown, not as dark as Susanna's, and cut short.

"You are pitiful," Susanna said to the woman and shut the closet door again. She yanked Teagan's arm and dragged her to the stairwell, and they ran down the stairs.

Teagan stared at her mother in the car. She was afraid that her mother would explode at any minute and have a wreck. "It's okay, Mom, it's okay," she said and couldn't stop herself.

When they reached the house Susanna went directly to her own bedroom, and Teagan went to hers. She fell asleep and woke up in the night, still in her clothes, on top of the bedcover.

Wait

By the time she was where she wanted to be, it was a letdown that it had taken all that effort to stand in front of a door in a quiet parking lot. Teagan found herself feeling guilty at how easy it was to get the people who trusted her to believe her. She'd told her mother that she wanted to meet Grace at the library, which was a lie, because Teagan hadn't told Grace anything about meeting at the library.

Susanna didn't seem to think it was odd, so she dropped Teagan off without asking when she wanted to be picked up. Teagan said that she would probably spend the night at Grace's house since it was a Friday.

"Do you want me to wait here until you find her?" Susanna asked.

"No, I'm sure she's inside," Teagan said. She walked into the building, waited a few minutes, and walked out again. Her mother's car was gone.

It took longer to walk to his building than she'd planned. She worried that someone might recognize her, so she kept her head down and let her hair fall over her ears, and at intersections she pretended to be interested in the contents of her bag. She had wanted to go to the place her father worked and look for something. She wasn't sure what. She felt she was doing that, lately, looking for something and not finding it. She would walk to the barn, stand in the field, stare at the mountains, none of which felt different from lying on her bed, starring at the brass handles of the drawers in her dresser.

She stood near a door that she guessed was on the same side as her father's office. It had one window above the handle, with thick glass etched with a crisscross pattern. Teagan's feet felt hot from walking and she was thirsty. There wasn't anyone around, and people walking on the sidewalk did not look at her, so she crossed her arms and stood. She wasn't sure why. Maybe she was waiting for her father, but she wasn't sure he was even in the building. A man in khakis and a blue button-down shirt smiled at her. The only person who paused was a short, fat woman who reminded Teagan of her middle school social studies teacher, who held the door open for her, but Teagan shook her head. "I'm just waiting," she said. After the woman walked away, Teagan tried the door. It was locked. She looked at the sky and decided she'd been there too long.

Another woman came around the corner of the building on a different sidewalk. Although she'd only seen her once, and briefly, and in a closet, Teagan knew it was her. She wanted to walk away, or pretend to have lost something, but she simply stood. The woman stopped in front of her.

"Are you waiting for someone?" she asked. Her voice was low and toneless.

Teagan stared at her. The woman wore the same purple clothes. Her hair was short and brown. She was thin in the way Teagan thought people who tried hard to be thin were thin. Teagan wanted to maybe punch her, but she didn't know how to punch. She wanted to dirty that light purple suit, but she didn't want to touch it. She wanted to make the woman afraid of her, but she didn't know how.

"Do you know someone who works here?" she asked Teagan.

Teagan realized that the woman knew who she was. She knew Teagan, but Teagan wasn't supposed to know about her.

Teagan walked past the woman toward the street. Her legs felt restrained. She felt like she was walking through deep grass, having to push her way through. She didn't look back. At the library she called Grace's house collect. She asked Grace to ask her mom if she could spend the night. Leta didn't notice anything out of place. Grace and Teagan made up the foldout couch in the family room and watched a movie. Teagan kept going to the kitchen to drink glasses of milk. Grace didn't even ask her why. Finally, Teagan admitted to Grace what had happened.

"What was the point of that?" Grace asked.

"I don't know," Teagan said.

"Did you see your dad?" Grace asked.

"No," Teagan said.

"So you just stood on a sidewalk?" Grace asked.

"Pretty much," Teagan said. She got up from the creaky foldout couch bed.

"For how long?" Grace said, fast-forwarding through the credits of the next movie.

"More milk," Teagan said.

"You're going to get sick," Grace said.

Sometime after they had finally fallen asleep, Teagan woke up with stomach cramps. She crawled over Grace's legs to get to the edge of the bed and walked bent over to the bathroom. The milk came out of her mouth and her nose. She washed her face and then brushed her teeth with a trembling hand. She crawled back into bed, kneeing Grace in the leg by accident.

"What's going on?" Grace sat up.

"I'm sick," Teagan said.

"Are you okay?" Grace found Teagan's arm in the dark.

"I puked."

"You did?"

"Yes."

Grace sat there, her hand on Teagan's arm. She yawned. "Do you need anything?"

"No," Teagan said.

"Do you want some more milk?" Grace asked, smiling.

"I'm going to throw up on your pillow next," Teagan said.

"I told you," Grace said, scrunching her pillow more comfortably under her head.

Blind

Zep recovered enough to be let out into his field, which was relatively flat. Teagan was surprised to find him standing alone near the barn, his cheeks swollen and his jaw lumpy, like it was broken. She heard the wheels of a car crunch the gravel on the other side of the barn and heard Charlie yell for her.

"What?" she yelled back.

"C'mere," he yelled.

She rounded the side of the barn.

Charlie leaned over to the passenger-side window. "Tell Mom I'm going to Chris's, okay?"

"Charlie, come help me with Zep," Teagan said.

"You take care of your own horse," he said.

"I need your help. Come help me."

He looked at her and grudgingly threw the car into park. "I can give you one minute."

He helped her urge the horse into the barn. They had to stand on either side of him and push.

"What do you think happened?" Charlie said.

"I don't know. You go. I'm going to tell Mom."

"You sure?" Charlie said.

Teagan was already turning and running to the house. When Charlie walked in the door, she was screaming at her mother, accusing her of not taking care of Zephyr. Teagan picked up a coffee mug and threw it at the wall. It broke. Charlie grabbed Teagan's arm and yelled at her. Susanna ordered them to separate, which was her word for ending a fight. Susanna told Teagan to sit down, but Teagan pushed past Charlie and ran for the barn. Susanna said, "Don't," when Charlie started to go after his sister.

By the time she walked back in the house, Teagan was ready to apologize to her mother. When she went to look for her, she found Charlie, who hadn't gone over to his friend's house. He stood up from the couch, where he'd sat frowning at the TV. He started to say something, but Teagan turned her back on him and went to find her mother. Susanna was in the basement sorting laundry. Teagan hovered in the doorway.

"You didn't say where you were going," Susanna said, noticing her. She continued to toss clothes into one basket and another. Teagan thought this was a strange thing to say. In her mind, there was only one place for her to go. "Mom, I'm sorry," she said.

Susanna dropped a shirt and looked up. "What you don't realize is that I'm doing the best I can."

"I do realize. I know," Teagan said.

It seemed like the conversation was at an end, but it was

Susanna's turn to get angry. "I'm only one person. I can't stop horses from acting like horses," she said, her voice rising.

"I know that," Teagan said.

"I can't stop them kicking each other. Do you want me to sleep in the field?" Susanna was yelling now. She balled a shirt and threw it in the basket.

"No. Mom. I said I was sorry."

"Just because things don't go the way you want them to. I do everything for you, Teagan. Everything. What else do you want from me?" Susanna glared at her daughter and threw her hands in the air in a strange, uncontrolled gesture.

Teagan retreated. "I don't want anything," she said from her distance.

Footsteps came down the stairs.

"You think I haven't done everything for that animal? The money I've spent on him? Walking him around day after day? You think I have all the time in the world to nurse a horse, take care of cats and dogs, and a house, and a farm, and two children? You think it's easy?" Susanna screamed.

"No. I don't think anything," Teagan said.

Charlie was yelling for them to stop. He held an arm in front of Teagan and with the other gestured to his mother to calm down.

"Charlie, do not tell me what to do," Susanna said, turning on him.

Charlie gave Teagan's shoulder a shove and in a low voice ordered her to go.

"That's right. Go feel sorry for yourself. Don't worry about me," Susanna yelled after her.

Teagan ran out of the house.

Remember

I remember the news from the vet was that Zephyr was blind. Zep hadn't avoided a kick to the face from Duchess because he never saw the blow coming. I couldn't argue with my mother when she said she could not care for a blind, lame horse. She told me not to be there when the horse was put down, but I wouldn't hear of it, so we gathered in the cold, in the late afternoon. Jason Brill, our neighbor, led our slow, limping Appaloosa up the ramp onto the horse trailer, and stood outside the door, holding the rope. The vet, in an efficient manner, prepared the hypodermic needles and administered the shots. After some minutes, the horse's legs buckled, and the trailer rocked when he fell. I sat down on the ground. My mother wailed. My brother held her in his arms.

TWO

Hunting Hill

Julie, who was pale with strawberry blond hair (she admitted she dyed it), held out an opened one-pound bag of M&M's. Teagan took it and poured a mound into her hand. She gave back the bag before funneling the candy into her mouth and crunching the pieces into a chocolate froth.

"This will be the food drawer," Julie said, twisting a rubber band over the bag and putting it away. Julie had interesting things. She had a plastic three-drawer tower, with a plastic frame. The top drawer was now the "food drawer," the middle held pens and markers and a compass and other school supplies. The bottom drawer held Julie's hair clips, extra bottles of shampoo, lotion and tampons, and other bathroom stuff. Teagan had never seen a tower of drawers like that. She thought drawers had to be wooden and part of bulky dressers, or built into kitchens, beneath counters.

Julie had a shoe rack, a hook that fit over the door of the closet, and several rectangular Tupperwares that didn't look as though they had ever held leftovers. She stowed groups of things in these and stacked them on her side of the long, shallow closet. Teagan sat cross-legged on her twin bed and watched Julie organize. She had made some effort with her own things, more than she ever had at home. Her new collared shirts hung from hangers, and the khaki pants were folded on a shelf provided in the closet. Her jeans and T-shirts were folded, too, in stacks on the closet floor. Her hairbrush was on the ledge of the small window in the bathroom, and her toothbrush stood upright in a built-in toothbrush holder. Her shampoo bottle stood just outside the shower door, so it wouldn't be in Julie's way when she showered. Teagan's schoolbooks were stacked on the provided desk, and her other books were stacked within reach under her bed. She'd even run the cord of her new desk lamp behind the desk to keep it out of the way. It was her way of being polite to her roommate, a formality, like shaking hands.

She hoped Julie didn't expect these standards to last, though. They would have to relax once the year got going. Teagan couldn't be bothered to pick up every book off the floor, or sort and fold her clothes on a daily basis. She expected Julie felt this way, too. Her neat, putting-things-away routine was rudimentary politeness. Teagan expected the room would feel more lived in as the days passed. A few books and some clothes and shoes tossed on the floor would help them settle in.

She was only a little suspicious of Julie's plastic boxes, stacked and with tight-fitting lids. Julie seemed more of a girl-girl than Teagan. She even had a velvet pouch of earrings, gold hoops, no less. (Gold-plated hoops.) And she had makeup. Teagan spotted the tubes and small, flat containers, lipstick and mascara and eye shadow, going into the boxes. She was glad she'd moved in ahead of Julie, so she didn't have to reveal her lack of earrings and makeup. Teagan could claim one girl item, a bottle of floral-scented perfume, although she wasn't sure when she would wear it. She got it out to show Julie and let her try it. It let Julie know that Teagan understood something about being a girl, even if she didn't have mascara, not even one color of eye shadow, and had never owned a tube of lipstick.

Susanna and Charlie had gone. Teagan was to call when she was ready for a weekend at home. Susanna would come pick her up. She felt relaxed, removed from the turmoil of her house, the unsettling absence of her father, her brother's interminable silence, her mother's sad face and pretense that life was going on as usual. There wasn't anything usual left at Blue View Farm. The atmosphere in the house was morbid. It was as if the three of them were marching in a long funeral procession, and the coffin was never lowered into the ground, or maybe there wasn't a coffin at all. No one had died. Teagan knew that her father was alive, somewhere. But it was as if he had slipped through a portal. He was living a different life, in a different place, at the same time that Teagan and Charlie and Susanna were living their same life, an old life, the one Robert had simply disappeared from. She understood that her father's leaving had something to do with a woman, who they all knew existed, but who he tried to pretend didn't. But it was all backward and turned around. Robert and the woman were real, somewhere, and it was as if Teagan had ceased to exist. Teagan and Charlie and Susanna, and the thing they had called their life, had evaporated, faded like the milk bowl of clouds that sat in the hollow of the field some winter mornings, before the light and heat found them and made them rise up.

There was no point telling any of this to Julie. It was all unimportant to the life Teagan would live here at the school. An uncomplicated, scheduled existence that included classes, her room, and roommate. These things encompassed Teagan, and she could trace the shape of her life.

After finishing up their room, Teagan and Julie decided there was no reason to wait any longer for supper, which started at five-thirty. Julie wondered if she needed to wear a collared shirt into the dining hall, but Teagan argued that it was Sunday, and there wasn't a dress code except for going to class. Julie hesitated and fingered some shirts before settling on wearing the T-shirt she had on. It had small horizontal stripes in two colors of blue, and Teagan thought how her mother would consider that kind of T-shirt "nice." Teagan wore a soft, faded yellow one with HOBOKEN written on it, although she didn't know where Hoboken was and she'd found the shirt at a thrift store. They stopped in open doorways to learn the names of other girls on the hall and collected a tall, freckled redhead named Sarah. Sarah asked Teagan if she was from New Jersey, and Teagan said no and didn't ask why Sarah had thought so. Julie said that she was from Oklahoma. Sarah was from Delaware.

"Dela-*where*?" Teagan said, but Sarah and Julie just looked at her.

Sarah asked if Teagan was a day student, and Teagan explained that her mom lived far enough away that she would be a boarder.

"Most of us are boarders," Sarah said. "My mom told me that."

"What facts did your dad tell you?" Julie said.

"Um. Not much. I think he told me to study the periodic table," Sarah said.

"That's a weird goodbye," Teagan said.

"He didn't drop me off. Just my mom," Sarah said.

"I didn't see your dad today," Julie said to Teagan.

"Yeah," Teagan said, as if it were an explanation.

"Dads don't go in for that kind of thing," Sarah said.

"What kind of thing?" Teagan asked.

"Dropping us off here."

"Oh," said Teagan. She had no idea what Sarah was talking about. "Where was your dad?" Teagan directed the question at Julie.

"My dad died when I was twelve."

"I'm sorry," said Sarah.

"Thanks," Julie said.

Teagan was surprised by Julie saying "thanks." It sounded strange. "That sucks," Teagan said.

"So where was your dad?" Julie said.

"He and my mom aren't together," Teagan said.

"I'm sorry," Sarah said.

Teagan didn't say anything.

"I wonder what's for dinner," Julie said.

Teagan realized that she didn't know if her parents were divorced. She didn't think they were somehow. It didn't matter anyway. They wouldn't be getting back together, even though Grace said they might. Thinking of Grace made Teagan feel a little guilty for talking with these girls who would be her new friends, and then she felt a little mean for knowing that these girls wouldn't measure up. Her other thought was that girls who went to boarding schools had missing fathers, and then she realized that it was a stupid thought. She let her train of thought end and broke the awkward silence that had fallen on them.

"I hope it's good," she said.

"I'm hungry," Sarah said.

The path they walked was lined with old flagstones. The stones were mostly swallowed up by the grass, and only gray shapes remained, sunk in the ground. Nearer to the old brick building that was the dining hall, the stones got bigger and closer together. The path seemed to emerge from out of the grass as she walked toward the dining hall and dissolve into the ground when she walked toward the old building that was her dormitory. It was as if time ran forward or backward, depending on which direction she walked, the path coming into being or eroding into a diminished version of itself.

They saw some girls sitting around a wooden picnic bench on a painted wooden porch. Behind them a screen door let out the noise of people talking and eating. They stepped up on the porch and said hello to the older girls.

"New Girls," a stocky girl with short blond hair said.

"Freshmen," Teagan said.

"You're called New Girls. We're seniors, and you are on our senior porch."

"Okay," Teagan said.

"When you're a senior, you can sit on this porch," said a lean girl with straight, dark brown hair and fashionable glasses.

"That's nice," Teagan said. She saw that Sarah had stepped off the porch.

"So for now, get off," the blond girl said.

Julie stepped off the porch.

"Okay. We're just trying to go to dinner," Teagan said.

"Get off the porch, now," the blond girl said.

Teagan stepped off the porch and walked away.

"It's the door around the side," said the fashionably bespectacled girl.

Teagan kept walking. Julie said thanks, softly.

"I hope I'm not such a jerk when I'm a senior," Sarah said.

"They must feel really special about their porch," Teagan said.

Sarah and Teagan laughed.

"I think it's part of tradition," Julie offered.

Sarah and Teagan stopped smirking, but Teagan didn't think she was going to care much about traditions. The dining hall smelled of cooked potatoes. It turned out to be country fried steak, green beans, mashed potatoes, french fries, corn off the cob, and dinner rolls. It was like the menu at a buffet steak house. Sarah asked Teagan what country fried steak was, but Teagan had never tried it. They grabbed green trays and loaded them with thick, white ceramic plates of the industrial dining variety; plain, stainless-steel knives, forks, and spoons; and thick, unbreakable, short drinking glasses. The actual glass glasses, and real plates, and the color of the trays were all a novelty for Teagan, who was used to the plastic drinking glasses and flimsy orange trays of public school. A young black man stood behind the glass-fronted counter and loaded up plates as the girls said what it was they wanted.

"New Girls," he said when the three were in front of him.

"So we've heard," Sarah said.

"Hand over your plate, and don't miss out on the cookies. They go fast," he said.

Sarah collected her full plate, and at the end of the line they saw a large tray heaped with soft chocolate-chip cookies. They each took three. Teagan put one in her mouth immediately. It was good. She learned later that, to get the cookies, she had to get to dinner in the first hour, otherwise there was no luck, especially since the older girls took big handfuls whenever they passed the pile.

The dining hall itself had more surprises. The tables were

round with tall-backed metal chairs with padding on the seats. There was a refrigerated dispenser of three varieties of milk, nonfat, full-fat, and chocolate. Most of the sophisticated-seeming seniors drank the nonfat, Teagan noticed. She went for the full-fat and the chocolate, especially when washing down her scavenged supply of chocolate-chip cookies. There was a napkin holder, like the kinds in fast-food restaurants, on each table. On a stainless-steel table, pushed against a wall, were plastic-sleeved loaves of bread and stainless-steel tubs, one for peanut butter and the other full of strawberry jam. Teagan cut a little corner off of the chicken fried steak, which turned out to be a piece of steak fried in batter. She wasn't sure she liked it. She ate the green beans and the mashed potatoes. Julie was over by a rack filled with what looked like hot dogs.

"You're having a hot dog?" Teagan asked.

Julie laughed at her. "It's not a hot dog."

Teagan looked closer and saw that the top was covered in chocolate. "What is it?"

"Dessert," Julie said.

"It's an éclair," a girl said, popping one onto a plate and walking away.

"It's a chocolate hot dog," Teagan said.

She and Julie sat down again.

"What is that?" Sarah said.

"A chocolate-covered hot dog," Teagan said.

"Really?" Sarah said. "You're going to eat it?"

"It's an éclair." She bit into it. "It's cream-filled. Sort of a long doughnut."

"I'm getting one," Sarah said. She sat down with two and gave one to Teagan.

"I don't know," Teagan said, but bit into it. It was cold as if it had been recently frozen.

A stream of new girls was heading out the double doors.

"Is something going on?" Julie asked.

"We've got to go to our house meeting," Sarah said, balling her paper napkin.

"How do you know that?" Teagan said, getting up.

"It's on the schedule," Sarah said.

"I didn't know there was a schedule," Teagan said.

"In your room, on one of the desks, sitting next to the handbook," Sarah said.

Julie looked at Teagan, who assured her that she hadn't seen a schedule.

"We didn't need it at dinner anyway," Teagan said, feeling that Julie might think she was irresponsible. "What's the handbook?" Teagan asked Sarah when they were on the disintegrating path.

"Rule book. School codes and that kind of stuff," Sarah said.

It sounded ominous to Teagan. She would let Julie have the handbook.

Their common room was full of girls all talking at once. Teagan and Julie found a place on the floor to sit down. They seemed to be waiting for someone, and then Teagan noticed a woman who was not much taller than any of the girls. She had light blond, almost gray, short wavy hair and wore a white cardigan. After a minute she motioned for everyone to quiet down.

"For those of you I haven't met, I'm Ms. Ganski, and I'm house mother for North Dorm. My apartment is at the end of the ground-floor hall, and if you ever need anything, you can knock on my door. Tonight we're going over some of the dormitory rules. Does everyone have the handbook?"

A few yellow spiral-bound handbooks went into the air.

"If you don't have yours, it should be on one of the desks in your room, or come to me and I will get you a copy. Everyone is expected to have a handbook and to be familiar with what it says. The academic and holiday schedule is printed at the back, and all of the campus phone numbers and faculty and staff names are listed, too. We have an internal phone system, so all you have to do to call anywhere on campus is dial the four-digit extension number. Do you see those pages?"

Teagan and Julie looked around at people flipping pages. A girl with light brown skin and long brown hair offered to hold hers so Julie and Teagan could see.

"Julie forgot ours," Teagan said.

Julie pinched Teagan's arm.

"Okay, some other important things. Lights-out is at eleven o'clock. No new girl may have lights on in her room after eleven. The morning bell rings at seven A.M. from the schoolhouse, but it's a better idea to use an alarm clock. If you don't have one, I'll see about getting one for you. You may request late lights every other night, which will give you half an hour extra time, and you must do your studying in the common room, so as to not disturb your roommate if she is sleeping. If you find that you're needing to request late lights often, you might think about getting your homework done earlier.

"North Dorm is all new girls, except for your prefects, who

I will introduce in a moment. I need to explain study hall. All new girls start by having proctored study hall. After one week of successful proctored study hall, you may move to studying in your rooms. There is no music or talking during study hall hours, which are seven to nine P.M. If you have finished your homework before study hall, you are still required to be in your room, and you may do quiet activities like reading. Is that clear? Okay, let me explain room inspection."

There was a murmur through the crowd.

"Room inspection," Ms. Ganski said again. "Each day after you leave for classes, I will look at your room. Your beds should be made, everything should be off of the floor, and your closets and desks should be neat. If you don't pass room inspection, you will not be eligible to request late lights. If you pass inspection every day of the week, you earn a skip pass." She held up a stiff piece of yellow paper with a hole for a doorknob. "Hang this on your door and I will not inspect your room that day, and I will collect the pass. Each pass is good for one use."

There was another, more hopeful murmur.

"Prefects?" Ms. Ganski said.

Two girls made their way to the front of the room, smiling and waving.

"This is Sen, your junior prefect, and this is Erin, your senior prefect. I expect you to show them the respect you would show me. They are living in North Dorm to be of help to you, and they can also enforce rules and write reports, if necessary. Tomorrow, Sen and Erin will be in front of the schoolhouse at eight-fifteen to help you locate your classes. They'll be wearing blue sashes, so you can locate them."

A girl raised her hand.

"Yes?"

"What if we have a free period?" she said.

"You probably won't have a free period your first semester, but it's a good question. If you have a free period, I suggest you use your time responsibly. The library is a good place to study, and on nice days many girls read on the lawn. Also, if you need to change for your gym class or other gym-credit classes, like dance or riding, you may come into your room and change, but if I find you are staying in your room during the school day, I will ask you to leave. I think that covers the basics. Sen? Erin?"

"Sign-out for weekends," Erin said.

"Right. Sen, why don't you take that?" Ms. Ganski said.

Sen explained that for special activities on the weekends, a sign-up sheet would go up on the common room notice board in advance. Activities included plays at the Kennedy Center in Washington, D.C., and sometimes other things such as concerts. There were also social activities with other private schools, dances, sports events, and picnics.

"Okay. You have some time before lights-out. Please remember to do all of your bedtime preparations, brush your teeth, wash your face, before lights-out. Tonight Sen, Erin, and I will be coming around and knocking on your doors to remind you. You are free to go." Ms. Ganski smiled.

"What's proctored study hall?" Teagan asked Julie. The girls were filtering out, but Teagan noticed the girl who had shared her handbook lingering to talk to Ms. Ganski. A few other girls were lingering, too. Teagan hesitated and heard someone ask Ms. Ganski to tell the story of Miss Guinevere.

Ms. Ganski glanced at the clock and hesitated. "How did you hear about that?" she asked.

The brown-haired girl said her mother had gone to Hunting Hill and had mentioned the story.

"Not tonight. It's getting late. Maybe another night. Remind me," Ms. Ganski said.

Ex

Teagan woke up on Saturday morning with an excited feeling, like on the morning of her birthday, when she knew, sometime that day, there would be presents and cake. She looked around the rectangular room. Julie was turned to the wall, her yellow and pink plaid blanket tucked around her shoulders. Teagan was alone. Her mother, and her brother, and her friends were far away. Julie was sort of a friend. They would become friends, she knew. It was just that Julie was new, too. Everything was. The view out the window was new, her plain blue blanket was new, the clothes in her closet were new, her books and backpack were new. She realized, of course, that at some point, soon, all of it would not be new to her anymore. Right now it was, and she liked that. Even her hairbrush and toothbrush were new. She'd picked out a kind of shampoo she'd never used before and decided she was letting her hair grow long. She was new. Nothing old had come with her. Her horse was supposed to have been the familiar thing.

Her father's horse wasn't gone. He's gone, she had to remind herself, but not the horse. He had once ridden the horse, when the puzzle pieces fit: horse in the barn, father in the house, she in the yard, walking in one direction or the other, finding one or the other in his usual place. They seemed to form an equation, but, as she was never attentive in math class, she couldn't think how to order the problem, or what to solve for. At her old school, what she had noticed in math class was that her teacher was younger than her other teachers, and she had a tattoo that sometimes peeked from the cuff of her long sleeve. Grace had been brave enough to ask what the tattoo was. Their teacher had pulled back her sleeve to reveal words. Teagan had expected numbers. The words said, SOLVE FOR X. Grace seemed to think that the tattoo was funny, in the way that Grace found really smart people to be funny. Teagan wanted to know what x was, then she'd know what to solve for. But she hadn't been thinking about math. She'd been thinking about a horse. She'd been thinking about her father. If she knew where he was, she could figure out how to find him.

This Has Never Happened

I dreamed that in front of me were steamed fruits like the shells of snails. I cut one open and found a thick white worm. I saw a chef, standing on a lawn littered with the fruits, all cut in half, all revealing worms. He seemed desperate. He said to me, "This has never happened before."

Infinite

She was hungry, but Julie said she had to call home. Julie had promised her mom she'd call her that first weekend. "After breakfast," Teagan complained, but Julie wouldn't wait.

In the patch of grass outside the dorm, Teagan walked back and forth. Stopping at a point on an invisible line, she turned nonchalantly, as if trying to disguise that she was pacing. She didn't think it was a polite thing to do—pace—but it felt good. At one end of her invisible line, instead of turning, she began to walk an invisible circle. Instead of completing the circle, she followed a diagonal line, then traced part of a circle at the other end, picked up the diagonal line and, finding herself at the opposite end, turned, traced part of a circle, walked the diagonal line, and continued the pattern. She slowed her steps and walked deliberately, as if she were measuring distance, a step for each yard. (She remembered a story her grandmother had told her: when her grandmother was a child in a math class, the teacher asked, *How many feet in a yard?* Her grandmother asked the teacher, *How many people are in the yard?*) Teagan held her shoulders back, her back was straight, and she traced the figure eight.

The horse trotted evenly, his movement lateral through his back, not up and down. His head low, slightly flexed at the poll (the point between his ears), so that even his neck muscles were engaged; every part of him worked as a whole, and he was graceful across the flat ground, like a dancer transformed into a horse by a spell. She sat still on his back, her legs stuck to his sides as if attached to the long muscles of his back, and though she was still, her calf and thigh muscles burned, tiring but compressing, flexing against the horse's sides in rhythm with his trot, as if she were pulling him up from the ground, helping him suspend in air for a fraction of a second when he pushed off the ground with a hoof; her shoulders were back and her back was straight; she gripped the reins; in her flexing fingers she held his heavy head; her arms ached holding his constant momentum; they traveled in a symbiosis of motion, appearing to float; the effort frothed the horse's sweat into a white lather across his chest; her hair was damp under her helmet and her pores leaked salt, but rider and horse held the flow unbroken through the half circle, down the diagonal, around the half circle, back down the diagonal; the figure eight; then, finally, she stiffened and closed her fingers on the reins and the horse halted and the rhythm ended.

"Oh my god, what are you doing?" Julie said.

Teagan had her hands in front of her as if gripping invisible reins, and she'd been loping the figure eight as if she had been a horse, and she'd momentarily lost sight of her surroundings and looked up as if woken from a dream. She managed to look at Julie and laugh.

"You know, there are real horses on this campus. Maybe you need to sign up." Julie said.

"Shut up. Let's go," Teagan said.

Versus

They had a few minutes before they had to be in the common room for their last proctored study hall. All of the other girls had been given early permission by Ms. Ganski to study in their rooms, because the common room was too small and they had to crack the windows to keep it from getting too warm. But, when Ms. Ganski left the room, Julie had balled up a piece of paper and flung it at Teagan. Teagan had the bad luck to wing it back at Julie just as Ms. Ganski returned.

"I can't believe we still have to do this," Teagan said, stuffing books into her backpack to carry them down the hall to the common room.

"Well, if you hadn't gotten us in trouble," Julie said.

"You threw first!" Teagan said.

"Yes, but I didn't get caught, did I?"

"I guess you win then. But we're still in stupid proctored study hall," Teagan said. "How long?"

"Five minutes," Julie said, glancing at the slim gold-colored watch on her wrist.

Teagan looked at Julie's books and folders in a neat pile on the floor. The top folder said ARMY on it. She remembered something about Julie's dad. "What did your dad do?"

"He was a captain."

"In the army?" Teagan said.

Julie looked at her. She was wearing a gray sweatshirt that said ARMY in black letters. "What does your dad do?"

Teagan had to think about this. Her dad was a high school

principal. He was one, but now? She didn't know where he was or what he was doing. "He's a high school principal," Teagan said.

"Where?" Julie asked.

She had to ask where, Teagan thought. "I don't know. He's looking for another job."

"Where is he?" Julie asked.

"I don't know exactly." It was the truth. "He'll let me know when he decides where to work," Teagan said. It was a lie, and she thought it sounded like one. She was embarrassed. She didn't mean to lie to Julie, and she didn't want Julie to think she wanted to. She didn't know what to say, and then, she wasn't sure what made her say it, she crossed her arms and said, "You know, Navy is way better."

"Why do you say that?" Julie asked. Her tone was too sincere.

Teagan said, "It just is. I mean, obviously. They have boats."

Julie had that look on her face that Teagan was getting used to seeing. It was a flash of anger that turned into something else. "No way. Army wins," she said, with a little toss of her head that flipped her hair over her shoulder.

"Navy," Teagan said, folding herself onto the floor.

"Army is going to kick Navy's ass."

"Yeah? First you have to reach us. We're out on the ocean. You'll have to swim," Teagan said.

"We'll just fly our helicopters onto your boat," Julie said.

"What are you, Air Force now?"

"You just wait until you come on land. You won't feel so pretty then," Julie said.

"We might never land," Teagan said.

"Then you'll die on your stupid boat," Julie said.

Teagan laughed. "My boat's not stupid!"

"We have to go," Julie said, scooping up her things. The horrible fuzzy-sounding bell buzzed to signal the start of study hall. Julie whispered, "Army."

Teagan whispered, "Navy."

Red Filly

The old brick pump house next to Miss Guinevere's Garden had been converted into the snack kiosk and mail room. Every morning after first period they had a fifteen-minute break, and the girls swarmed the mail room to open their little boxes with keys. The first Monday, Teagan's had postcards in it from her mother, Charlie, and Grace. She knew her mother had arranged that, getting the mail sent in time so Teagan would have it on her first day. The cards were generic and didn't say anything interesting, but she recognized the effort.

It was Friday, and finally she wouldn't have proctored study hall. She didn't see the point of study hall on a Friday anyway. Sen had explained to her that sophomores didn't have a specific study hall and juniors and seniors didn't have a specific bedtime, and they could sometimes get single rooms. Prefects always had single rooms and their own telephones and mini-fridges. Teagan had begun to see the benefits of being a prefect and had asked Sen how someone became one. Sen had said that prefects were nominated by current prefects. Teagan had raised her eyebrows at Sen, and Sen had laughed and said, "And you have to be a good student, of course."

In her little mailbox was a blue piece of paper with some check boxes on it. A check was ticked in the box next to "Day." On some printed lines at the bottom of the paper was some handwriting that said, "Susanna French, Saturday 11 A.M." Teagan thought it was a little bit cryptic, but then realized that her mother would be coming to pick her up on Saturday morning. It was only a day visit. Teagan was glad for that. She wasn't ready to be away yet, and on Sunday there was an orientation meeting for girls who wanted to sign up for riding lessons. She had decided to go. She knew it was an extra cost, but she could already buy anything in the school bookstore, or snacks from the pump-house mail room, or sign up for an off-campus play at the Kennedy Center, and her mother would be billed for it. Teagan thought that that was a very convenient system. She hadn't actually bought or done anything that cost extra yet, but she figured that if she signed up for the lessons, she and her mother could discuss it after Susanna discovered the bill.

Someone's shoulder bumped hers, hard. She turned to see Sarah smiling at her.

"Ow," Teagan said.

"Have you seen *Phantom of the Opera*?"

Teagan was glad that Grace had a CD of the cast recording from the musical, or Teagan wouldn't have known what Sarah was talking about.

"No. I've heard some of the music."

"Everyone's heard the music. There's a trip to go see it on Saturday. I'll sign you up with me. Should I sign Jules up? I'm trying to get a bunch of North Dormers to go."

"Okay," Teagan said, still holding her blue piece of paper.

"See ya at lunch. Sit with me," Sarah said and walked out of the dark little ex-pump-house mail room snack kiosk.

"Wait!" Teagan yelled. She twisted the key in her mailbox and ran after Sarah. On the brick walk she grabbed Sarah's wrist. "My mom's coming for lunch on Saturday."

"Lunch? So what? The bus leaves at four."

"Four," Teagan said.

"Afternoon," Sarah said. "Plenty of time. Gotta go. Geometry."

The bell rang to end their fifteen-minute break. Teagan ran past Sarah and pushed her. Sarah didn't have a chance to push back. Teagan was taking the stairs two at a time.

After the school day was over and she was back in her dorm room, Teagan was glad to pull off her khakis and polo shirt (she thought polo shirts looked dumb) and pull on her old, soft jeans and an older, softer T-shirt. Her mother had told her the story, many times, of how, as a little child, Teagan had complained and fussed about wearing the cute outfits her mother bought for her, and she only wanted to wear her older brother's hand-me-downs, boyish pants and shirts. Susanna sighed when she told the story, as if it still exasperated her, or as if she was remembering something she hadn't accomplished that had been a goal at one time. Teagan, without really considering it, said to her mother that her brother's old clothes had been softer. Julie, and Teagan couldn't understand it, wore her khakis and collared shirts all the time, even on weekends, as if she liked them. Maybe she didn't bring her other clothes, Teagan thought. Susanna would have liked for Teagan to dress like Julie. Teagan sighed. She went to her closet and pulled out a pair of khaki pants and a collared shirt. She looked at them and put the pants back. She hung the shirt on the outside of the closet door and sat down to do her homework. Her weekend was already full.

"You look so nice, Teagan!" Susanna said.

Teagan was wearing the collared shirt and sandals. She'd pulled her hair back with a borrowed (without Julie's knowledge) elastic.

"Are you letting your hair grow?" Susanna stroked Teagan's ponytail.

It was a matter of weeks since she'd seen her mother, but it seemed longer. Susanna looked tired and thin, and she moved in spurts of activity, like she had just remembered to do something. She hugged Teagan, kissed her, looked her over, cupping Teagan's elbow in her hand, a gesture left over from when Teagan was smaller, and then she was digging in her purse for her keys and glancing at her watch and throwing five questions at a time at her daughter. How did she like it here; how were her classes, her friends; what were her activities (Susanna was thrilled that Teagan had signed up to go see a play); did she like the food, her roommate; should they have invited her roommate to lunch? Another time, Susanna quickly answered herself. Teagan didn't ask where they were going. They climbed in the car and drove the tree-lined road that traced a creek with steep banks all the way into the sleepy town.

"You must have gotten up really early this morning," Teagan said.

"I stayed here last night."

"Last night?"

"Yes. I got in late. Too late to bother you," Susanna said.

Teagan wasn't sure how to feel about that. Her mother had been close by last night and she didn't know it. She hadn't even called Teagan. Teagan had to think about whether this bothered her or not.

Susanna parked the car on the street and they walked down the quiet sidewalk.

"My room was nice. Here it is."

"Your room?" Teagan said.

"It's a B and B over a restaurant. Cute," Susanna said.

An antique-looking sign hung from a beam. It had a ridiculous horse on it, dramatically prancing. In engraved letters it said RED FILLY.

"What do the Bs stand for?"

"Bed and breakfast," Susanna said. A bell jingled when she opened the black door.

Dickensian, Teagan thought, repeating the term her English teacher had used. They'd been studying *Oliver Twist*.

They sat on red plaid cushions in a wooden booth and ordered sandwiches. Teagan ordered a ginger ale (old-fashioned, she thought) and Susanna an iced tea, unsweetened, and then she put some artificial sugar in it and two lemon slices, squeezing them first over her fork. Some of the lemon juice sprayed onto Teagan's face. She wiped the wet off but didn't mind the sharp lemon smell.

The food looked and smelled good. Teagan ordered a tuna melt, and it came open-faced with a big pickle and a pile of salty potato chips. She bit the crisp pickle, then she crumbled some potato chips onto her sandwich.

Susanna smiled weakly. "Your father taught you to do that."

"The chips? I made that up myself," Teagan said.

Susanna nibbled one of the little pretzels that had come with her BLT.

The first half of the sandwich was sitting nicely in her stomach, and Teagan was preparing to eat the rest, for the pleasure of it. It didn't smell like fried food or green beans. The restaurant was quiet.

"One reason I wanted to see you was to explain that your father and I are officially separated."

Teagan looked at the sandwich and knew she wasn't going to eat it anymore. Couldn't her mother have waited to talk after they had eaten? She picked up a potato chip and nibbled it.

"And, he was having an affair. I think you have a right to know," Susanna said.

Teagan did not care.

Kennedy Center

The bus was the kind that she had only ever seen from the outside, overlarge, with tall cloth-covered seats with headrests and footrests, and, at the back of the bus, a little bathroom that smelled putrid. For the evening, she had voluntarily put on a black and white flower-patterned dress that she wore for all occasions that required a dress. Seeing a play in the city seemed one of those. Sarah wore a red V-neck shirt of some silky material and a pair of black pants. The black pants were a revelation to Teagan. She'd never thought of wearing dress pants before. Her floral dress went down to her ankles and tied behind her waist. She suddenly wondered if it was a little girl's dress. She'd always worn this style dress, always long, always tied in the back, whenever it was dresses she had to wear. She thought the black and white was more grown-up. At least it wasn't lavender and pink. Also, she would be with other Hunting Hill girls, and, really, it didn't matter. There was no one who expected her to dress any particular way, and no one to make an impression on. She stretched out her legs in her cloth seat and felt just fine. She hoped *The Phantom of the Opera* would be scary and sad, like the music.

When they got off the bus, Julie held her hand and dragged her along, as if she thought Teagan might get lost. Mr. Adams, the history teacher, was one of their chaperones. He casually handed out the tickets and said, "Everybody here?" without checking a roll. Teagan was glad he didn't call out roll in the middle of the big hall hung with flags from different countries. She linked arms with Julie and Sarah, and walked with her head back to look up at the flags, while they guided her. They entered another long hall carpeted in bright red. There were sculptures along the hall with no rope or case around them. There was a statue of a man's head that looked like it was made out of clumps of mud. Teagan didn't think it was very complimentary. She wouldn't want her skin to look like that. They got in line at the concession stand and bought overpriced candy and Cokes. They ate what they could before the lights blinked and they needed to find their seats. Teagan liked the musical. It was creepy enough.

The lights came on at intermission and Sarah prodded them

to go so they could have time to explore. They grouped with other Hunting Hill girls and lots of girls said the musical was "good," and then they all turned and followed someone who knew there was an outdoor balcony. The air was cool and damp. It had rained while they watched their musical. Teagan suddenly thought that she'd been here before. The balcony was familiar. She had come here with her parents for something. She couldn't remember what. She'd have to ask. Whatever it was hadn't stuck in her memory, but the balcony and the wide view of the city, she was sure she'd seen them before. It was more than a balcony—a terrace? It stretched the length of the building and looked to be made entirely of gray marble. There were long shallow puddles on it from the rain. Teagan wanted to run and splash through every puddle.

Out of another door came a group of boys wearing rumpled button-down shirts and khaki slacks. Some of them had poorly tied neckties hanging crookedly. They were loud and kept looking over at the Hunting Hill girls. Some of the HH girls went near the group and started talking to them.

"Let's look over the edge," Sarah said.

Teagan took the distraction. They put their hands on the wide, flat stone wall and peered down into darkness and lights.

"Don't fall," said a voice.

Teagan looked to see two of the boys there.

"Like we're that stupid," said Sarah.

"Are Hunting Hill girls smart?" said the boy. He was taller than Sarah and had the kind of haircut that was short grown long, and his bangs flopped across his forehead.

Teagan and Sarah looked at each other. "It depends." Sarah laughed.

The other boy was a little bit shorter than Teagan but broad-shouldered. He had very short hair, and he stood squarely. He was looking at Teagan, and she frowned at him.

"Where are you from?" Sarah said.

"Roxbury."

"Where?" Teagan said.

"It's in Massachusetts," the broad-shouldered boy said.

"And you came to D.C.? Aren't there plays in Boston?" Sarah said.

Boston is in Massachusetts, Teagan thought, glad to pin something down.

The floppy-haired boy shrugged. "There's a trip every year," he said. "I'm Doug." He held out his hand. Sarah and Teagan both shook it. Teagan had never shaken hands with someone her own age. She congratulated herself for not laughing at him. Doug put his hands on his friend's shoulders and introduced him as Clay. Sarah and Teagan shook hands with Clay, too. Sarah wasn't smirking anymore.

"So, you like the play?" she asked the boys.

People started filing back in the glass doors. The lights inside blinked.

"Time to go back in," Teagan said.

"I was wondering if you wanted to sit with me," Clay said to Teagan.

"I can't. I don't think," Teagan said, surprised.

"Here, we can switch tickets. Sarah, you sit with me," Doug said.

Teagan realized that this had probably been the boys' plan all along. Why did Clay-from-Roxbury want to sit with her? He couldn't possibly like her after two minutes. She didn't even have an opinion about him. "Um," she said. Her ticket stub was stuck like a bookmark inside her program because she didn't have any pockets in her dress. Sarah snatched Teagan's ticket from the program and handed it to Doug, and Doug handed his ticket to Clay.

"Meet us by mud-man after," Sarah called.

Clay offered his arm. Teagan looked at him. Clay looked awkward and put his arm down, but then Teagan slipped her arm through his, and they quickly walked back inside. Clay's shirtsleeve was rough against Teagan's arm, and she wondered if people would laugh at them, walking arm and arm like in an old movie, but no one at all noticed. This boy had wanted to sit with her. She thought it was dumb; they didn't know each other and would never see each other again, she was sure, and she didn't like that he and his buddy had planned on Teagan and Sarah switching tickets. But maybe it was nice that he wanted to sit with her. He had noticed her. He had complimented her dress, and Teagan had the sense to keep from saying it was a stupid dress that she'd had forever. In the dark the orchestra swelled into sound and a thrill of electricity went through her. Maybe he would hold her hand.

The second half of the play was good, too, but she thought the Phantom was too sorry for himself, and she didn't see why he had to wear a mask. Mostly, Teagan concentrated on telepathically communicating to the boy to reach over and hold her hand. A couple of times she put her hand lightly on her own knee, where it would be easy to reach. Finally she gave up. She was deciding that the Phantom's actual name was something like Augustus Clementine when Clay shyly curled his fingers over hers, but all she felt was disappointment. The play was about to end.

Accident

On a cool Saturday morning, Teagan woke in her small dormitory room and pulled the covers over her cheek. The heat was on in the building, but there was no separate thermostat for her room, and the air outside her bed felt cold. She stuck out a hand and saw that her alarm would ring in five minutes. She turned it off. Julie's head was turned to the wall, her covers pulled up, too. Teagan spent a few moments enjoying the warmth of her bed, then threw off the blanket and got out. The wood floor was cold on her bare feet. She shivered a little and rummaged through a pile of clothes in the closet, pulling out some jeans and thick socks. Her coat was the only organized thing of hers in the room. Her gloves and scarf were stuffed in one pocket, and a winter hat in the other. It hung on a brass hook that a previous occupant of the room had fixed to the wall of the closet. By midmorning she wouldn't need a coat, but she shrugged it on for her early-morning walk.

Outside, her breath clouded. She was too early for breakfast, so she took the loop road down to the barn. The warehouse-size doors were open. She walked in. The long rows of stalls were quiet, though most of them contained a horse. Halfway down the concrete hallway, a dusty black radio sat on a wooden bench. Country music was playing, one of those songs that sounds like a love story but is about a father and a daughter. She'd been here before. In her lessons, she sometimes rode a dapple gray horse who was kept on this aisle. The barn was enormous. A building more than a barn. She thought of barns as wooden, snug, smaller. This building had two wings; stalls built back-to-back faced into four hallways. If the halls had been built in the form of a cross, it would be a cement cathedral, she thought, full of horses and hay, the Eucharist stored in the tack room next to saddles. There was also an indoor arena, and Teagan had only ever seen one at large showgrounds. This one was big enough to have a group of horses at either end, each involved in a separate lesson, and there were dusty mirrors along one wall, to check one's form, like dancers do, she thought. She felt little in the huge facility, which was more the word for it; it seemed to be for riders in a class in which she wasn't. She didn't like seeing herself in the long mirrors and compared herself to the numerous riders she passed every day along the cement halls. She was more used to fields. The building alone seemed to make her experiences useless.

The hall was empty of people. She walked past the metal stall doors, peering through the thick bars at the warm dark figures at the backs of their boxes. One delicate head of a small Arabian horse looked at her closely. She wanted to pull open the door and stroke the face but felt she wasn't allowed. The stalls were fairly big, but the cement-block walls and barred fronts made them seem imprisoning. (She'd only seen prison cells in movies. She wondered if there were people in prisons who had only seen horses in movies.) Toward the end of the hall was a door big enough to drive a car through. The cold hung around this entrance. She realized that the hallway was warmer than outside. The heat of horse bodies raised the temperature. She heard the low grumble of a truck and someone shout. She stood on tiptoe and looked out of a dusty inset window. A multihorse trailer was backing up to the barn. They must be unloading, she thought.

She could hear the impatient or nervous stamp of hooves from inside the trailer. She looked down the hall and saw that several stalls were empty. The new occupants must have just arrived. She noticed that the stalls had names on them, written in blue on pieces of masking tape. She read the names, taking her time walking back. She would have liked to see the horses come in, but she knew she wasn't supposed to be in the barn except during her allotted hour for lessons. Her stomach grumbled and she thought of breakfast. There was usually a bucket of apples in the tack room. She would take one and eat it while she walked back up the hill.

The fourth stall with masking tape on it said TEAGAN. She stopped. A coincidence, she decided. There must be another Teagan at school. Or, maybe, she was going to be assigned the horse for her lesson. She went and picked a fresh-looking apple from the tack room. As she came out she had the apple to her lips. She froze. A woman in blue coveralls was leading a dark bay Thoroughbred horse down the hallway. Teagan bit the sweet flesh. She walked down the hallway.

The woman in the coveralls slid the stall door shut. She was short and sturdy looking. Her cheeks were smooth, but the crow's-feet by her eyes gave her a crinkled look.

"The barn isn't open to students right now," she said, but she didn't sound angry.

"Okay. I'll leave. This is—" She almost said "an accident." "This is Obsidian," she said.

The woman read the masking tape on the door. "You're Teagan. I'm Shirley."

She hadn't proffered a hand, but Teagan held out hers. Shirley shook it.

Teagan peered in at the large horse. Obsidian. Ian. Her father. Her father's horse.

"You want to give him the apple?"

Shirley slid open the stall door. Ian tried to walk out, but she casually blocked his way with her body and clipped a rubber rope across the opening. It pressed against his chest when he moved forward and he stopped. "There you go," she said.

Teagan held out the apple, looking at the horse, the white blaze down his face, his flop of black wire mane, the soft brown on the side of his nose. He ignored the apple. His ears were forward and his head erect. He was looking at something she couldn't see.

"Takes 'em a few days," Shirley said. "Did you keep him turned out?"

"What?" Teagan said, her arm stretched out with the apple in her hand.

"Is he used to a stall?" Shirley said.

"Yes. I mean. No. I mean, he lived in a field."

"It'll take him a few days," Shirley said. "I'll keep an eye on him."

"Thank you," Teagan said.

Shirley smiled and coiled a canvas lead rope and disappeared down the hall to the other wing.

Ian turned in a circle. Teagan took a step back. Then he resumed his stance with his head up, ears forward. She reached up and put a hand on top of his nose. He didn't react. She tried to pull his head down, but his neck was rigid. Then he whinnied. The sound echoed off the cement walls and she covered her ears and dropped the apple. It rolled into the stall. Ian looked at what had fallen. He swooped his head down and picked up the apple and crunched the whole thing in his mouth. Foamy slobber spilled from his lips. Teagan took a deep breath. She crossed her arms and looked at him. She pushed his shoulder and began pulling the metal sliding door shut, forcing the horse to pull his head in. She looked at him through the bars. He made another quick circle and stood with his long face almost pressed against the bars, his pointed ears forward. Teagan walked out of the barn and up the hill.

Definition

Accident: a thing that happens; an event that is without apparent cause; chance; fortune; an unfavorable symptom; a casual appearance or effect; an irregularity in the landscape.

Obsidian, Ian, came to me by accident. I was living at a boarding school; the girls' school had a horse facility. I had said that I wanted to go. It wasn't an accident. The wrong horse was sent, I thought. My father's horse. My father was gone, and that might have been an accident. I used to ride a horse without a saddle or bridle (I could have had an accident) and only a cotton rope clipped to the halter.

Halter: a headstall for leading a horse. A head harness, made from nylon or leather; a thing for leading horses by the head. Possibly the etymology of the word is traced to an English woman saying to her German husband about a horse, "Darling, mightn't you need something to halt her?"

At first a thing seems to have no apparent cause. There are irregularities in the landscape. The horse steps through them. The human rides over them. The landscape was shaped by fortune. The hills and gullies seem to roll over the humped backs of whales; an ocean turned to stone.

Call

Teagan wasn't sure how to call home. Finally she picked up the dirty white phone in the hallway and dialed the area code and her mother's number. Susanna answered and accepted the collect call.

"Hi, Mom," Teagan said, not able to keep her voice steady.

"Teagan! Sweetie, I've been thinking that I need to send you a calling card," Susanna said.

Teagan could almost hear the kitchen. The hiss of the coffeepot, and Barker sighing and plopping his head down on the linoleum.

"Ian is here," Teagan said.

"Oh good. You've seen him already?" Susanna said.

"I didn't know."

"Didn't know? That he was coming? I guess I should have given you the date, but I wasn't sure myself. Shipping him was more complicated than it needed to be. They couldn't give me an exact date."

Teagan didn't know what to say. She was surprised to realize she was about to cry.

"Baby? Are you okay? Are you unhappy?"

"No," Teagan said. She didn't want her mother talking to her like she was a child. Neither Susanna nor Teagan said anything for a minute. Teagan concentrated on her breathing to suppress the urge that was pushing on her chest.

"I said you could take a horse. Ian is the horse I had to give you."

"I know," Teagan said. "Thank you," and she covered the mouthpiece and gasped.

"Do you want me to bring him back?" Susanna's voice was strained.

"I don't know," Teagan said.

"He's yours now. It's your call," Susanna said.

She Knows Everything (About Riding Horses)

Weeks passed without another visit to the barn. Teagan was busy. She had more reading to do than she'd ever had, and more writing. Every teacher gave writing assignments. Her English professor assigned the recitation of a poem in front of the class. They drew names out of a box to see who would go when. Teagan had four weeks until it was her turn. She'd chosen "Mending Wall" by Robert Frost and then wished she hadn't picked such a long poem to memorize. She'd liked the line " 'Stay where you are until our backs are turned'!" She and Julie began study hall in their room in the usual way, trying to sabotage each other's homework. Julie had hidden Teagan's algebra book behind the toilet. Teagan had made annotations on the poem Julie had to memorize, "My Heart Leaps Up" by William Wordsworth. They finally settled down, but when Julie looked at her poem, she started laughing and Teagan did, too. They heard footsteps in the hallway. Quickly they opened their books. Ms. Ganski opened the door and asked them if they were studying quietly. They said of course they were.

On a Friday afternoon, Teagan looked at her watch and quietly slipped out of her history class. She had told her teacher she would, because of riding tryouts. A new block of lessons was beginning, and she was expected to try out on Ian so that her instructors could decide where to place her. It was amazing to her that riding could take priority over classes, but it was treated like other team sports, soccer or field hockey, and students were expected to fulfill obligations to their team practices as well as keep up with their studies. She had changed into her britches at lunchtime and wore them to class. She carried her tall boots in a duffel slung over her shoulder and would change into them at the barn.

On the loop road she caught up to Ellen, another new girl and a rider. They didn't discuss tryouts but talked about riding. Teagan realized that she hadn't ridden Ian since he'd arrived, and then she realized that she could remember riding him only once, ever, the day she rode with her mother and Hope. She was about to try out on a horse she didn't know. Briefly, she wondered about sending him back home and asking to ride the school horses, which would probably be docile and dulled from years of work with different riders, but she knew she wouldn't do it. Susanna hadn't done the work of sending him just to have him sent back.

Teagan was quiet a moment, and Ellen asked her what kind of riding she did. Teagan had to think about this. She might have said English, but the whole barn seemed to do English-style riding, so there was no point in distinguishing that. She didn't have a name for her riding. It was just something she did.

"The horse I have is a foxhunter, so I'm really hoping to go foxhunting," Teagan said. She wasn't sure this was true, but after she said it, it seemed to make sense.

"I've never been foxhunting. Do you like it?" Ellen said.

Teagan said, "I haven't done a lot, but the times I've been, I liked it," not adding that this was twice.

"I do hunter seat," said Ellen.

Teagan thought that Ellen probably showed. "Do you show a lot?"

"I've done the circuit up to three-three and I'm hoping to get to four."

"Three. Three?" Teagan said.

"Three feet, three inches. The different divisions have different jump heights," Ellen said.

"Oh. That's cool," Teagan said and decided not to reveal her further ignorance and ask what a circuit was. She had never thought about competition based on the height of a jump. To her, a jump was more something to get over when it was in front of her. Ellen stopped at the message board to find out which horse she'd been assigned. Teagan went into the large tack room. It was lined with riders' trunks on the ground, saddles and bridles on the walls. A table sat in the middle, with hooks hanging above it, like upside-down Triton's staffs, for hanging bridles for cleaning. Below them hunks of yellow glycerin soap sat in grimy wooden dishes. She located her saddle and gathered the rest of the tack and her box of brushes. She looked in the apple bucket, but it was empty.

She led Ian out of his stall and tied him to the metal loop bolted into the cement wall. He could just see out of the small, high window, and he held his head up, looking. She wondered if he'd been out of his stall in the past days. She realized that maybe he hadn't. Not all of the horses got turnout. It took her longer than usual to tack up. She adjusted the bridle and then noticed an extra piece of tack. It was a large leather loop with two straps coming from it. A martingale. She held it, wondering if it was necessary. A martingale limited how high a horse could raise his head. She remembered Ian throwing his head back and almost hitting her in the face when he had wanted to jump and she had tried to hold him. She put the martingale on him, unhooking the girth and tucking it through one strap and unhooking the noseband of the bridle and tucking it through the other.

She was late. Riders had stopped walking horses past her and the aisle seemed quiet. She needed to get into the indoor arena. She walked Ian down the aisle, his hooves clopping on the cement seeming to echo, and turned to the arena. The wooden gate was shut.

When she looked in over the gate, there were about forty horses inside. A group was in the center of the sand arena, listening to something the instructor, Miss Jessie, had to say. The other horses were walking in lines moving in opposite directions. Horses going to the left (the rider's left shoulder was nearer the center of the arena) circled the arena on the outside, and horses going to the right (the rider's right shoulder toward the center of the arena) passed on the inside.

She pushed the wooden gate open, waited for a space, then walked Ian across the sand, asked him to stand, and she mounted from the ground. Then she urged him to go forward to join one circle or the other, but nothing happened. He stood rigidly, his head held up to the limit of the restraining martingale. Teagan squeezed him as hard as she could with her legs, but her horse didn't budge. She pulled a foot from the stirrup, swung her leg back, and booted him in the flank. He lunged forward. She hauled on the reins and stopped him, and got her foot back in the stirrup. She wondered what he was doing. He seemed startled and confused. Then she realized that maybe he'd never been in an indoor arena before.

She let him stand a minute, and she looked around. In front of her, girls were bobbing up and down in posting trots, their horses moving nicely forward, relaxed, or girls had their horses at polite canters, the horses themselves looking collected, their tight canter strides only a couple of yards long. She watched a pigeon flutter to the sand and watched a horse and rider ignore it, as the pigeon got out of the way of hooves. This happened repeatedly. The pigeons jostled each other off the high rafters under the peaked tin roof, their flapping only slowing the descent to the sand, where they were almost run over by unflappable horses, and then the pigeons flapped to launch themselves again.

Teagan needed to join the line. She saw a clipboard in Miss

Jessie's hand. She asked Ian forward and he went, trotting, which she didn't ask for, and then he stopped suddenly, raised his head as high as he could, and whinnied, his body trembling to make the sound. The sound carried around the arena, but he got no whinny in return. She didn't know what he was doing, maybe looking for an ally, but the horses continued under their riders' hands, doing what they were directed to do.

She was feeling a little desperate now and wanted to get him to the wall and moving around the arena. His thousand-pound horse flesh seemed rooted to the spot. She tried to turn him and couldn't. He whinnied again, shaking her in the saddle. She slipped her foot from the stirrup and booted him in the flank three times, which did nothing. Finally he took a step sideways, and she pushed him in that direction, and he fell into a trot. She directed him toward the wall, but then he stopped again so suddenly that she lurched forward in the saddle. She recovered. The other instructor, Miss Brenda, called all riders to the center. Teagan saw her chance. Ian would move with the other horses. As they turned and walked, passing him, she pushed him forward, and finally he went, walking with the group.

Standing next to the other horses, Ian turned his head to sniff a horse's neck. Teagan patted him, glad he seemed calmer, but the rider glared at her. She pulled Ian's head around. The instructors explained that the trial would consist of walking, trotting, and cantering in both directions, and then they would be jumping a small course. Not hard, Teagan thought. Basic stuff. No problem.

When the horses went to the wall again, she made sure she moved Ian with them. She stuck to the horse in front of her, keeping a polite enough distance. She finally had him along the wall, moving to the left at a trot. Miss Brenda called out that it was too crowded and half should go the other way. The horse in front of Teagan turned, and without her asking him, Ian followed the horse. She pretended that she'd meant to go. At least he was still in line and trotting forward. She was on the inside now, the other line of horses passing her on the left. Ian was agitated. He seemed startled again.

He stopped, she wasn't expecting it, and the horse behind her had to stop quickly. She muttered an apology and the rider passed her, and she got Ian moving again. His trot turned into a canter, and when she tried to put him back in the trot he gave a small buck and tossed his head. She swore. She slowed him, and it seemed as if her body would break with the effort it was taking to keep Ian at the trot. She was trying to keep a polite horse length between her and the rider in front of her, but Ian kept wanting to put his nose right up to the tail of the horse.

Teagan finally caught on. Ian was foxhunting, or at least he was trying. Keep up with the horse in front, move as a group: go all together, stop all together, turn all together, a herd of horses—not individual horses with individual riders who give individual commands. She could give him only a second of sympathy, because she wanted him to trot when she asked, stop when she asked, and keep a polite horse length between himself and the rider in front. How hard could that be for him, really?

It was hard. Ian was confused. She had no time to teach him, no time to adjust. She had to perform and he was the horse and he was supposed to listen to her. Fat chance. The corners were the worst. Around the short end of the arena, Ian couldn't tell that the horses were simply moving in a line going the other way—he thought the horses were coming right at him, and he tried to move to the side, or back up, and he would shudder against Teagan's straining legs and arms, and kick out of self-defense or desperation. It happened at both ends of the arena. Fortunately the arena was large, and so it took a good minute or two before she reached the ends, but then she felt him shudder and balk again, and knew the kick was coming. She started drifting out of the line, trying to move him away from oncoming horses, which meant that she messed up the distances in her line, and the horse behind her had either to slow down or pass her. She was about to give up when Miss Jessie called them all again.

Teagan knew that she and Ian hadn't been any good. She wondered what was written on the clipboard. At least Ian could jump. He was a natural jumper. He would have no problems. She watched as each girl left the line, trotted up to the white cavalletti jumps, took her horse over the little jumps, one, two, three, and cantered away in a straight line, then trotted her horse to the back of the group. Teagan had this. This was cake.

Ian didn't have it. It was not cake for him. He apparently found it terrifying to be the only horse moving while the others stood still. It wasn't right. It wasn't foxhunting. They were all supposed to move together, to approach the jump as a group and separate for the briefest of moments to take the jump, then group up again. Ian moved slowly away from the group, even though Teagan was pushing him with all her strength, and he weaved toward the jumps, his head turned back, looking for the other horses to follow. She finally got him somewhere near the first rail. Her approach was completely off, not straight at all, and then she asked him to jump. She didn't care where they were. She didn't care if the jump was beside them and he had to go over it sideways, she just wanted him to go. At the last moment Ian seemed to see the jump, and he casually humped his large frame over it, then sped across the next two and was at a flat gallop at the other side, racing to get back to the herd standing in the center.

Teagan stopped him at the back of the line and tried not to look at anyone.

She jumped the line two more times before she was dismissed. Each time was bad. Ian didn't understand leaving the group, and he wanted to get the jumps over with as fast as possible so that he could get back to the other horses. She struggled with him, and he ignored her. She hated him.

A select group of girls stayed behind while the jump heights were raised, but Teagan was told to leave along with the other, average, sort-of-good riders. She knew Ian could jump the higher jumps. He could do it with his eyes closed, if there had been a fox and some hounds around. In the field he would have been perfect. Stupid horse.

Teagan walked by herself up the hill to the dorms. She was relieved to find Julie in the room. Julie played piano and knew nothing about horses.

"How were tryouts?" Julie asked.

Around Town

Teagan stuffed the blue slip from her mailbox into her backpack and went to class. When the bell rang to end the third period, she looked down at the page in her notebook and realized she hadn't written anything down. At lunch she found reasons to keep getting up from the table so she didn't have to talk.

"Why don't you get your food all at once?" Sarah complained after Teagan bumped her arm for the third time.

"Teagan likes courses," Julie teased.

Friday night she didn't want to watch the movie in the common room.

"It's really scary," Aleah said, excitement in her dark eyes.

"I'll have nightmares," Teagan said.

Sen linked arms with Sarah. "You'll change your mind," she said and they left.

It was rare to be left alone in the room. All the new girls had similar schedules, and they moved from place to place in groups. Julie and Teagan's room had become the hangout for their friends, who walked in all the time without knocking. Teagan hoped the other girls were too interested in the movie to stop by. She thought she might read. She sat cross-legged on her bed with a novel held limply in her hands. When Julie ducked into the room for her warm slippers, Teagan was asleep.

In the morning, she stayed in bed while Julie got dressed and ready to go to breakfast. She nodded briefly at Julie's offer to bring back toast. Teagan fell asleep again. When she finally got out of bed, she felt exhausted. There was a stack of cold toast on a paper napkin on her desk.

Later that afternoon Julie ran across the lawn and threw her arms around Teagan. "Where the hell have you been? I checked the infirmary. Sarah said you probably ran away."

"Ran away? Where to?"

"Did you go for an extra-long walk or something?"

"My dad picked me up."

"Your dad?"

"I guess I forgot to tell you." She saw the look on Julie's face and said, "He lives about an hour from school. I thought you knew that."

The truth was that Teagan hadn't known it. When her father had picked her up, she felt she wasn't able to look him in the face. They went to the Red Filly for lunch, and Teagan kept quiet about having been there before. She ordered a grilled cheese and barely tasted it. Her father told her about his new job.

Afterward Robert wanted to walk around the little town. Teagan stifled a yawn as they walked. Robert landed a weighty hand on her shoulder and rested his palm on the back of her neck. "Yawning?"

Teagan glanced at his face. "I went to bed late."

"You stay up as late as you want?"

"On weekends. We watched a movie."

Her father was her father, the man she remembered, but she

was having trouble with how she felt, standing next to him. He had hurt her mother. He had left them. She'd known about the other woman. She thought of Charlie. He and her father were alike. She pictured Charlie alone at Blue View. She felt stunned with the extra realization that her father had left Charlie, too. Her father's hand was hot on her neck.

"Are you riding?"

"Yes. Lessons."

"They have horses at your school?"

"I have Ian," she said.

"You do?" He turned her head toward him. Teagan shook her head to get him to let go. He seemed big to her. Looming. She couldn't distance herself from him. He had spoken the words as if he was playing a game with a baby—his voice overly happy.

"I do." She wanted to stop herself from asking, "Do you miss him?"

"He's a great horse. You'll have a great time." Robert was strolling on. The buildings along Main Street seemed to thin out. Set back from the road was a slatted wooden fence, and beyond was field. In the middle distance was a small red barn. "Looks just like Blue View."

Teagan thought it didn't look anything like it. "Yep."

"We're looking for a house. Lisa doesn't ride, but I found a great piece of land. It has a shed we could turn into a barn. You could keep a horse there."

Her thoughts seemed to crash. She wondered if she should point out that she was his daughter, or simply that she had no idea what he was talking about. She just looked at him, his mouth moving, saying things that made little sense to her, and the purple and green skin under his eyes. She felt she could have been anyone, a ghost. He was still talking.

"I hated mowing all that grass. Every weekend, god. A farm is so much work. One thing after another. There was always something falling apart."

My mother, she thought, and she remembered her father on the blue tractor in the field.

Thought

Same as it was. The same getting up and lying down. Same days and same doings. (Don't you know?) Same comings and goings. (Could have said it yourself.) The tasks, the exact motions of fingers and hands. What is described? Riding a horse. (No.) Just that. (Liar.) Think about this, the metal buckles, nylon soaked with sweat, dust, dirt (once soil) under the nails. Smells of grass and flatulence. Something is poignant, like the point of a fur-lined ear. (Feathered.) (Almost pointed.)

Robert Bought the Horse
(Because It Bit Him on the Arm)

Teagan led Ian out of his stall and tied him. She stepped back and looked at him for so long that he swung his big head around and looked at her. His eye was large, round, dark. His ears flicked toward her, then one flicked backward toward the sound of a sliding stall door, the hollow thump of a plastic bucket. He lifted his head and strained to see out the inset window. His ears flicked forward again. She knew he spent every day, twenty-four hours, in the stall. He wanted outside. He, the horse. Her father's. Not her father's anymore. Not her father, maybe. He didn't seem to miss her, much. He didn't want his horse. So he was hers. This animal. This big man's horse. The horse didn't seem to care about her, much. He seemed to be looking out, all the time. Looking for someone other than her. Waiting for his owner, his rider. She thought, I'm what you get. And then she thought, You're what I get.

She picked a brush out of her bucket but crossed her arms and kept looking at the horse. He didn't need brushing. Shirley groomed him. But she was used to routine and felt odd about tacking him up without first running a brush over him. Ian grabbed at the rope with his floppy soft lips. He held it in his mouth for a moment, then let it drop. Teagan thought how bored he must be, looking at cement walls. It was the first sympathetic thought she'd had for him. She. He. Her "he." She'd have to figure him out; there was no one else to relieve him of his cement box. She thought, Because you are left behind.

The brush pulled easily over his well-groomed hair. Down both sides, working away from the spine, down all four knobby legs, a swipe at the long feathery hairs at the back of each hoof, no dust there, no field to pick it up from, she worked around the large body. At his head she lightly held the leather noseband of his halter, keeping his head low to brush it. When the bristles edged his nose, he grabbed for them. She held the bristles for him to sniff. He smelled the brush and lost interest. Just him. She stroked his long face and leaned her forehead on his face and breathed in his horse scent. She wanted to be comforted. After a moment he tossed his head and his bony jaw knocked her temple. She rubbed the place, tossed the brush in the bucket, and wiped her eyes.

He didn't need his hooves picked out, but she lifted each one anyway, briefly scraping the soft underside. She yelled and dropped his leg and swiped at the empty air behind her. He'd nipped her on the butt. She turned around. His head was forward; he made no move toward her. She looked at his big dark eye. He blinked his long eyelashes. The nip hadn't hurt her; it had surprised her. She turned again to lift his hoof and sensed his head come closer, but when she straightened and turned, he had looked away. This was not behavior she liked. "Oh good," she said, "You bite."

Ian moved quicker than she could react. His blunt teeth caught the skin of her arm. He let go immediately, and she raised a hand to hit him in the face, but the horse threw his head up high, the dark eye rolled back in the socket and the white showed, and his head trembled against the rope that tied him. Her hand in the air, she watched this and realized he was afraid of her. She dropped her hand. He dropped his head. Slowly, she reached for his halter. He lifted his head again, not as high, and she caught the halter and tugged. He struggled for a minute but she held, the muscles in her arm tightening, and then he stopped pulling. With her free hand she reached to stroke his face. With both hands she worked his head toward her until the tension left his neck. She pulled his nose to her body and spoke softly. He lipped the loose hem of her shirt. She moved his nose away.

"How about this: I won't hit you if you don't bite me," she said, knowing he wouldn't keep his end of the bargain. As an experiment, she turned and lifted his hoof as if to clean it, and sure enough, she felt him turn toward her. She reached a hand behind her and waved it around, coming into contact with the soft side of his retreating nose. She turned back around and stroked his long face. Maybe he thinks we're both horses, she thought, thinking of times she'd seen horses in the fields use their mouths to nip and annoy each other, and sometimes to itch each other's backs. He's being a horse, she thought.

She figured out that, along with his horsey strength, he was perceptive and sensitive. One spoken word was enough to get his attention. Her hand on his side could direct him from the ground. She could get him to back up with a hand against his chest. She became a quieter rider and began to realize why her mother and her father had liked the horse. He was good and he was experienced. When she found the right way to ask him, he could do anything. She could speed him up or slow him down with lightly given commands. A little pressure from her leg or lifting the reins told him what to do. He could maintain a canter at different speeds. If Charlie had let her drive his manual-drive car, she would have likened the horse's paces to the gears. The only things that worried her a little were his limitless energy and the times he looked toward the fields, when he could see them, and she felt as if he might bolt, run flat-out, jumping whatever fences he came to. She thought about what she would do if he did run away with her. Hold on, she decided, and not fall off.

After a ride, when she untacked him, his behavior was bad. He would grab for ropes or her hands with his mouth. He stained her light brown britches with bright green grassy slobber when he pulled at the fabric with his teeth (she had been pulling off his saddle and wasn't quick enough to shoo him). There was something about that part of their rides he didn't like. And when she backed him into the stall and slid the door shut, he ignored his hay and stood stock-still, staring at her, until she walked away.

Persimmon

"Dogs eat poop," Sarah said.

"That's disgusting. They do not," Julie said.

"And hoof clippings," Teagan said, reaching behind her and playing with the fringe of the sad old carpet on the common room floor. Some threads came off in her hand.

"My family's always had dogs and they've never eaten poop," Julie said.

"They love horse poop," Sarah said.

"Especially if it's fresh," Teagan said.

"And they roll in it," Sarah said.

"What kind of dumb-ass dogs do you have?" Julie made a face and hugged a pillow.

"Any dog," Teagan said.

"Any dog in a barn. I don't care if it's the prissiest poodle; it'll eat and roll in horse poop," Sarah said, her long arms stretched out over some pages of notes. She twisted a pencil in her long fingers.

"And hoof clippings," Teagan repeated.

"From where?" Julie said.

"When the blacksmith trims the hooves, the dogs steal the clippings and go chew on them," Sarah explained.

"Right there. Right after they clip it?" Julie said.

"As soon as," Sarah said.

They had been studying, mostly successfully, for midterms, but had come to a point of inertia. Julie tried to start them on their English study guides, but Teagan didn't feel like she needed to study much for English and would do it later, and Sarah said that she was officially brain-dead. Julie wasn't hungry yet, so they didn't go to dinner. Sarah didn't want to watch TV, and Teagan for once didn't want to go for a walk, so they had slumped in their states of complete inactivity and were there twenty minutes later, talking about whatever. Teagan thought she could fall asleep, lying on her back on the rug, her feet propped up on the couch.

"Sarah," Teagan said, then paused inordinately.

"Yes?"

"I can't believe that you kept from us that you're famous."

Sarah gave a feeble laugh.

"Yeah, Sarah. Why don't you have your hundreds of blue ribbons hanging in your room? You could wear one every day," Julie said.

"I don't want to brag," Sarah said. She had finally confessed to them that she'd first applied to Hunting Hill for the riding program. She had been a National Champion of Tennessee Walking Horses and had gone as far as possible in the levels. Just before the start of school, she had admitted to her mother that she didn't want to ride anymore. Her mother had tried to convince her to keep riding and competing, but Sarah was done with it. Her top-level horse had since been sold. When they'd asked her why she'd stopped riding, she said she'd been doing it for so many years already, and won everything she could, and wanted to do other kinds of stuff. Julie had said, "If I were a national champion of Tennessee Walking Horses, I wouldn't just quit." Teagan had called Julie the Champion of Annoying, and then Julie hadn't spoken to her for an entire day, which was a punishment Teagan was learning to predict. "I've spent enough time in a barn," Sarah added.

"With puppies eating poop," Teagan said.

"Our dog did try to eat a bird once," Julie said.

"I think dogs can eat anything they want," Teagan said.

"And then he threw up," Julie said.

Teagan and Sarah made the appropriate *ew* noises, which seemed to satisfy Julie.

"Horses can't throw up," Sarah said.

"And lightning bugs have glowing penises," Julie said.

Teagan laughed. "Good one, Jules."

"No seriously. They have no ability to throw up. Ever," Sarah said. "There was this horse who gorged herself on persimmons, and the seeds wouldn't pass out of her stomach, and they were stuck. She couldn't throw them up."

Teagan tilted her head, finding the energy to be somewhat interested. "Colic," she said.

"Really bad colic," Sarah said.

"Isn't that what babies did in the seventeenth century?" Julie said.

Teagan pointed a finger at her. "Julie. No references. This is a study break."

"It's the same thing. Digestive-tract blockages. It's dangerous in horses," Sarah said.

Julie interrupted, holding up a hand. "Wait, I forgot to ask what a persimmon is."

"A fruit," Sarah said.

"Kind of orangish, purplish," Teagan said.

"Kind of wrinkled, golf-ball-size," Sarah said.

None of them knew enough to make jokes about testicles.

"Sounds gross," Julie said.

"They are," Teagan said.

"They get really sweet when they're ripe," Sarah said.

"Do you eat them?" Julie said.

"You could," Teagan said. "Our dog does. Loves 'em. Eats them off of the ground." She pictured Barker lying next to the gray, scabbed bark of the persimmon tree, happily chewing.

"So this horse at the farm where I kept my horse, she had persimmon trees in her field. None of the other horses went for them, but apparently she spent an entire day under the trees, just eating and eating. Persimmon seeds are big. About as big as an almond, and the seeds piled in her stomach."

Sarah went on to explain how everyone at the barn took turns walking the horse continually to keep her from lying down, which would make her situation worse. When the vet finally came, Sarah stayed with some of the others to watch him stick a rubber tube down the mare's nostril, into her stomach, and pump out some of the seeds.

"Well now I'm hungry," Julie said.

"Horses are fragile," Teagan said. "One thing goes wrong and they just go downhill from there."

"Horses sound like a lot of trouble," Julie said.

Sarah and Teagan agreed this was true.

"But worth it," Teagan said. She didn't see Julie look at Sarah. Sarah only smiled. Teagan thought about Ian, standing by himself in his stall day in and day out.

"Let's go to dinner," Sarah said. "You slackers aren't worth anything right now."

Teagan stretched and yawned. "Glowing penises," she said.

Turn Out

Everyone was somewhere. At the dining hall for lunch; sitting on the stone wall in Miss Guinevere's Garden, reading letters; in the library getting started on research papers; in the computer lab, finishing assignments before afternoon classes. The hallways of North Dorm were empty. Teagan sat in her room with the door shut. She should have eaten lunch, checked her mailbox, gone to the library or the computer lab; she had over-due homework. She didn't do anything. She didn't want to go anywhere. She felt like she would fall asleep. She wondered how much trouble she'd be in if she didn't go to her afternoon classes but couldn't think of any reason not to go. It was just that she felt tired, but feeling tired wasn't the same as feeling sick, and she didn't have the energy to fake an illness. She expected Julie or Sarah, or maybe Aleah or Sen, or even Ms. Ganski, to open the door and ask her why she was there. The door stayed shut. The clock told her she needed to start walking to class in fifteen minutes. Lying on her bed, she thought of Ian at the barn, and her thoughts turned to her father. She didn't know his telephone number. She'd forgotten to ask. He was distant, and, like in her nightmares, it was as if the people around her could move but she was frozen, unable to move or speak.

She thought about the word *nightmare* and separated it into *night* and *mare,* and thought of a night mare as a cold, ghostly horse who carried her through vivid and terrible dreams. On the night mare she was helpless; she couldn't control the horse, not its pace or where it went.

Her father always told her what to do; he did not ask her for her opinion. Whatever he ordered, she either did or didn't do it. Maybe now she wouldn't do it. What it was she wouldn't do, she wasn't sure. Nothing. Anything. Maybe she would lie on her bed and do nothing, and not do anything. Maybe she would never sleep again, and then there could be no mare, no night, no loss of control.

She pictured the house at Blue View and what might be going on inside it. She wondered where her mother was, where Charlie might be. She thought of Grace. Teagan hadn't talked to her in a couple of months. She wondered if Grace knew she had Ian with her. They'd see each other over the holidays. Maybe Teagan would teach her to ride Ian. She thought, I want him out of that goddamn cement box.

Shirley said he'd started kicking the door, knocking a front hoof against it, repeatedly, rattling it in its sliding track. When Teagan took him out for her riding lesson, his legs below the hock were stocked up, puffy and swollen from standing still. After the lesson, the heat in the legs went down some. She made herself late for class by staying to wrap the lower part of his leg, binding the long band of cloth around, wrapping from the front of the leg to the back, careful not to put too much pressure on the long tendon. Shirley said she'd take the wraps off after a few hours. Teagan couldn't be late to class after every lesson. She didn't want Ian to need the wraps. He'd never needed them before now.

Susanna would keep the horses in their stalls the night before a foxhunt. She'd pile the stalls with clean straw to keep the horses clean. In the cold, early morning, Teagan would help wrap the horses' legs; it kept them clean and also kept them from getting scrapes and cuts from riding in the trailer. After the hunt, the horses were hosed off, cleaned up, and Susanna would turn them out into the field, where they could walk and wander and take a good roll in the dust.

In the stall, overnight, Ian might have anticipated what was coming in the morning; the squeak of bucket handles and heavy wooden doors at dawn; the shaky ride in the metal trailer; the smell of fifty horses and fifty hounds; the huntsman's horn and the hounds' song; and then the animals begin to run.

Teagan untacked her horse and led him into the wash stall. She sprayed his neck with the hose to let him get used to the cold water. When done, she squeegeed the excess water from his body and rubbed a towel over his back, digging in with her palm to massage the back that carried her. She rubbed the towel on his face to scrape off the sweat that stuck under his bridle. She fed him an apple and absentmindedly stroked his neck while he chewed. She did what she knew how to do for him.

"Maybe get him one of those big plastic apples," Shirley suggested.

"What does he do with it?"

"Tie it inside the stall. Some of them will play with it."

Teagan said she would get him one, but she knew he wasn't going to play with it.

"If he starts anything else, weaving, you might want to think about turnout," Shirley said.

"What's weaving?"

"They sway. Side to side. Sometimes they're bored."

She felt sick at the thought of finding making the insane motion inside his stall.

"He needs turnout," Teagan said.

"It's extra," Shirley said.

"He needs it," Teagan said.

Shirley nodded.

Teagan looked at the clock by her bed. I'll go to class, she thought, and I'll get Ian out of that stall, or I'll send him home. Maybe her dad would pay for Ian's turnout. She thought better of it.

Manners

Miss Jessie was thin, with short, feathery gray hair, and had a pinched, thin face. Teagan hadn't seen her on her hall before. While she tacked Ian for the lesson, Miss Jessie stood and talked with her. Teagan tried to pay attention to two things, responding to whatever her teacher was saying, and tacking up, trying to remember all the pieces, especially the martingale. Miss Jessie hadn't acknowledged Ian in any way; in a barn full of horses he was another horse. Maybe he didn't like being ignored, because he lunged at Miss Jessie's arm. She didn't waste a second and smacked him across the nose, yelling, *"No."* Ian threw his head in the air, his eyes rolled back. Teagan had seen it before. She reached for his halter and stroked his long face, pulling his nose to her chest, *Easy, now.* She was shocked at herself and embarrassed, even while she coaxed the horse, because she was defying, as if Miss Jessie had done the wrong thing. She had done the wrong thing; the horse didn't need the force of the blow, but her teacher didn't know that. Teagan was surprised how fast and hard she'd struck. She didn't really like Miss Jessie, but still fought a familiar urge to cry.

"I'll see you in the arena," her teacher said and walked away.

When Miss Jessie was gone, Teagan put her arms around Ian's neck and hugged him tight. He tossed his head but otherwise didn't fight her. As a horse, he thought horse thoughts, and maybe he tolerated being loved. She let go, and he lipped her arm with a soft mouth, leaving slobber on her skin.

Troll

Teagan cinched the girth. "Goin' out today," she told him.

He looked at her with one big eye. She led him outside to the mounting block. His ears were forward and his head high, but he stood nicely while she climbed on the block, stepped up on the stirrup, and sat lightly in the saddle. On Saturdays girls were supposed to ride in pairs. Teagan spotted a rider a ways off in the grass. The grass was a large oval area, fenced in. She was planning on using the ring, a fenced circle within the oval. Walking up the hill, Ian's stride was long, forward. He liked *outside*. She felt him start to veer toward the yellow, scrubby field, a little farther off, and she pressed her leg against his side to steer him toward the ring. His energy seemed to subside, and then he halted. He did not want to go to the ring. She pushed him forward. *Come on.* She didn't like the ring either, but their terrible performance during tryouts had stuck with her, and she felt she needed to ride like the other girls, and that meant controlling him in the ring. At least they were outside. They could, at least, have that.

She walked him into the loose sand of the ring. He was resisting her. She felt like he was making himself heavier, and she had to work hard to push him forward with her legs. With every fiber of muscle she had, she kept him going around the ring at a trot. She was feeling tired after just a few minutes of riding, as if she was doing all of the moving for him. When he faced the gate, *out,* he would speed up and she'd have to slow him down. Once they'd passed the gate, and he knew they weren't going *out,* he would slow down and she'd have to work hard to speed him up. *A couple circles at an even trot. It's not much to ask for,* she complained to herself, although part of her agreed with the horse; the ring was boring. *Gimme this and we'll go out to the grass,* she bargained with him in her mind.

A pile of white painted poles lay on the ground just outside the ring, under some narrow trees that didn't give much shade. After some circles, at an irregular tempo, at the trot, Teagan slacked off a little bit; she was getting tired, and just as they passed the pile of poles, Ian shied. He jumped sideways and broke into a canter. Teagan tipped forward over the saddle and hung for a moment with her bottom up in the air, struggled, couldn't regain her balance, and fell. Ian stopped when she was off, staring at her on the ground as if he didn't understand how she'd gotten there. She quickly dusted herself off and grabbed his reins and got back on. She was angry. Her horse wasn't young, about seventeen years old, a seasoned animal, desensitized to the detritus of barns, of ropes and saddles and buckets and trailers and fences and jumps and parts of jumps. She had three thoughts: that maybe the combination of the poles under the trees bothered him, but he was too experienced to let that startle him, and her last, creeping feeling, which she knew was probably true, was that he had done it on purpose.

One chance to prove me wrong, she thought, and walked

him over to where the poles lay inert on the ground. A young horse might have needed to see, and smell, and run away and come back, and see, and smell again, to understand. Ian just stood, his ears pricked up at the other horse over in the grass. *Big faker,* Teagan realized. She put him back on the circle, and in her inexperience didn't know her mistake of giving him the distance of two-thirds of the ring to prepare to act up again. They reached the poles, he leapt away; she stayed in the saddle and put him back on the circle. He did it again, and she was able to hold him a little more and get him back on track faster, but after several circles, and she was close to tears, she couldn't get him to move past the place without reacting. Finally, she toughened and rode smarter. Approaching the poles that lay to their right, she slipped her left leg out of the stirrup and held it against his flank, as far back as she could. She shortened up on the left rein and prepared to pull. The right rein she held steady against his neck. She felt him start to leap and pushed with her leg against his flank, keeping his back end in place, while she held his head to the left. With his head turned away from the poles, and shoving his hind end to the right, she forced his right shoulder toward the fence. He fought her, but she mustered her strength and held him, keeping his body moving straight ahead.

Around the top of the circle, she relaxed and he continued forward at the trot. At the poles, again, she held her left leg farther back and prepared to fight him, but it wasn't necessary. She'd won, or, at least, Ian didn't find the game interesting anymore. He trotted dolefully in a circle. She brought him into the middle of ring and halted. She patted his neck, exhausted.

———

He didn't entirely give up the game he'd invented, which Teagan called troll. Whenever he was bored with their exercises, Ian would suddenly "see a troll" peeking out from behind a tree, from a shadow on the ground, or from behind a fence post. He would shy away or halt suddenly, his ears forward, his nose forward, and he would snort at the perceived thing that frightened him. Teagan learned to stick to the saddle, to pat his neck, as if to say she called his bluff, and get him moving forward again. He never saw the same troll twice. But when they were *out*, even on the oval of grass traced by a fence, Ian was a different horse. He moved with energy, his stride long and easy, his ears lightly forward, his neck soft and body relaxed. Like Teagan, the horse seemed happiest moving along a horizon.

Tall Boots

What I liked about Hunting Hill: the big windows in the classrooms that looked out on the lawn with old trees; the large grass riding area with its wood-rail fence; that my dorm was at the edge of campus, where the woods began; how simple it was for me to slip into the trees and run the network of pine-needle-covered trails; the worn flagstone path that dwindled into the ground as I walked from the dining hall to my room. My favorite things were not my classes, or even my friends. I liked carrying my tall, black riding boots to class with me in a canvas bag. It had a strap I would sling over my shoulder. Carrying them meant I would be riding, soon. I wore tennis shoes until I was at the barn, when I would pull on my boots. It was a little ritual I had that meant I would see Ian, who liked me.

Sleeping Over

The narrow, blue, standard slip of paper in her mailbox informed her that her father was signing her out of school for the weekend. She wondered if she was allowed to refuse. During lunch, she sat on the low stone wall of Miss Guinevere's Garden, plucking withered phlox and destroying the blossoms in her palms. The petals crumpled easily. She wasn't allowed to pick the flowers. She had missed her father, after he was gone. And now, so suddenly, he was back. And every time she saw him, every time he took her to lunch or wanted to walk to the barn with her to pat Ian and feed him an apple, she felt that she didn't want to see her father anymore. He didn't seem to notice her, even when they walked together. She wasn't sure why he was visiting. It seemed, to her, that maybe he wasn't sure why he was visiting. Maybe he felt obligated. She felt obligation, to give him a hug and receive his kiss on her cheek. She said she loved him, too, but it was as if she was pretending to be a daughter, and he was pretending to be a father. She wanted something to be real, something to be as tangible as a horse, even if it was the wrong horse. A horse that was her horse. So it couldn't be the wrong horse, if it was hers.

Julie practiced piano in the afternoons. Sometimes Teagan listened while Julie played from Wagner's Ring Cycle. Julie explained the cycle and Teagan thought it sounded like it would take a long time to play. Today, Teagan didn't see Julie, didn't leave her a note. She packed her duffel bag and sat on the steps of her dorm and watched her father's car come down the school road. The silver BMW was gone. This car was black. They ate a late lunch at the Red Filly, and then her father drove through the countryside, passing old farmhouses and fields, barns and hillsides dotted with fat, docile beef cattle. The view out her window was lovely and lonely, and Teagan was afraid. Her father had sipped his glass of white wine without smiling. He had purple sagging skin under his eyes. Teagan tried telling him about the play she'd seen, but after a few sentences she stopped, because Robert was looking over the waitress as she refilled Teagan's 7 Up. He didn't seem to notice she'd been talking or had stopped talking. He tried to interest her in ordering dessert, but she didn't want any.

The radio station played "Don't You Even Try."

"This is the Everly Brothers," Robert said, singing along.

Teagan didn't like the song. She thought the harmonies sounded eerie. Sarah had introduced Teagan to Tori Amos, and Teagan tried to hear the singer's drifting voice in her head, the music that sometimes crashed and poured, but the even notes of her father's song pushed out that other music, and she looked at her father's large, rough knuckles gripping the steering wheel.

The apartment was a narrow hallway above an outbuilding on a farm out in the countryside, somewhere. At one end of the hall was a bedroom and a bathroom, at the other was a small kitchen.

"Do you want dinner?" Robert said.

"No," Teagan said.

"We ate a late lunch."

"Yeah."

"I rented a movie. Do you want to watch a movie? There's not much around here."

"Okay."

In the kitchen was a narrow cot with a patchwork quilt and a pillow on it.

"That's okay for you, right?"

"It's fine," Teagan said.

"Let's watch the movie," Robert said.

She sat at the little table while he opened a bottle of wine and poured a glass. "Want anything? I have orange juice."

"No," she said.

"The TV is in the bedroom since there's no living room," he said.

He set the bottle and his glass on the spindly bedside table. She crawled over the double bed to lie near the wall, her head propped up on musty-smelling yellow quilted decorative pillows. The bedspread had a pattern of blue and white squares. The mattress sank when he lay down, his bulk taking up most of the bed. He held the remote and started the movie, and refilled his wineglass. The movie played. She didn't say anything and he didn't say anything. At a funny part they laughed. She didn't look at him. His big muscled arm lay near her. She could tell he was different from the wine. She kept her hands folded across her stomach. Susanna had always preapproved the movies Teagan watched, nothing too violent or too sexy, no R-rated films. The main characters were having sex. The man grunted and the woman moaned. Teagan kept her eyes glued to the naked bodies and did not look at her father. He lay very still. When the movie ended, she said, "Excuse me," and Robert got up so she could get off the bed. Teagan brushed her teeth and said good night to her father. She didn't change into her pajamas, and, wearing her jeans, she lay on the narrow cot and spread the damp-smelling quilt over her and curled up. She stayed awake most of the night. Her father came into the kitchen once and rinsed out his glass, and dropped the bottle in the plastic trash bin. She heard it clink against other glass. In the morning, she accepted the coffee he offered her and picked at her scrambled eggs. She said she didn't want to miss her Saturday riding time slot and lied, saying it was at eleven. He drove her back to school, and she returned his kiss on her cheek, and she said she loved him, too.

In her bed in her dorm room, she slept until three and went to take her riding time at four. Ian's glossy coat felt familiar to her hands. He stood when she told him to stand, trotted when she told him to trot, cantered when she told him to canter, halted when she drew back the reins. She patted his neck, and he lowered his head and walked easy and comfortably back to the barn. She hosed him off, dried him with a towel, secured the straps on his wool blanket, and led him outside to the small paddock he shared with a little Morgan horse. The little horse came over to greet him and the two horses playfully nipped at each other, then grazed the sparse grass.

Omit

The Foxtail Inn had green plaid tablecloths and flowers on the tables, and the menu was long. Teagan said she didn't want to go to the Red Filly, and the Foxtail was the only other choice. Susanna said she didn't mind treating Teagan, and even handed her a little ribbon-tied box. Inside was a large pin that looked like a stretched-out safety pin.

"It holds your stock tie. It's real silver, so don't lose it."

"I don't have a stock tie," Teagan said.

"I got you one, and I have my old hunting jacket for you, in the car. You'll be all set to take Ian hunting in the fall."

"Fall's over," Teagan said.

"Next fall," Susanna said.

Susanna ordered the salmon and Teagan copied her.

"I didn't know you liked salmon," Susanna said.

"I've never had it." Teagan shrugged.

"That's an expensive dish if you don't like it. You could try some of mine."

"I'll eat it," Teagan said.

The green and white interior of the restaurant was soothing. She was hungry, and the fish melted in her mouth as she steadily ate. Susanna did most of the talking, telling Teagan what Charlie was up to, that he was playing football and had a nice girlfriend; she said she'd gone to dinner at the Penns', and Grace said to say hello, and Leta had baked Teagan cookies (Susanna forgot to bring them), and that Barker was finally acting like an old dog and didn't come on as many walks, and the roof of the house needed repair because it was leaking, and Susanna was volunteering at a homeless resource center, and what a great experience that was. Teagan told her mother what she was studying in her classes and made it sound more interesting than she really thought it was, and she told her that things were going well with Ian, but she left out falling off of him and the problems she sometimes had with him; she told her mother about her friends, Julie, Sarah, Sen, and Aleah, and how at Hunting Hill she'd met girls from all over, from Saudi Arabia and Japan and South Korea and New Jersey and Oklahoma; she didn't talk about how she wasn't hanging out with her friends as much, maybe because she felt tired so often lately, and was constantly having to catch up on homework; and she said she was taking French but didn't mention that it didn't make sense to her, and she was having trouble memorizing the verbs that everyone else got right away; and she didn't mention that she felt more homesick instead of less, and she was too embarrassed to say she wanted to come home.

"Did you know your dad is living not far from here?"

"How do you know that?" Teagan said.

"He finally called and gave me his address and phone number. Can you believe he waited this long—anyway. I bet he'll come take you out to lunch if you call him. I'll give you his number." Her mother's voice was even, positive, as if she was happy, as if she wanted this to be good news for Teagan.

Teagan couldn't believe that her mother wasn't angry, wasn't upset, wasn't telling Teagan to stay away from her father because he was— She couldn't think exactly what. She knew her mother was pretending that everything was okay, for Teagan's benefit, as if Teagan didn't know, as if everything wasn't wrong, and Teagan ordered the biggest dessert on the menu and ate it all.

She didn't mention that she'd seen her father, that she knew where he was living.

"You must be stuffed," Susanna said, signing the bill.

"Thanks, Mom," Teagan said.

"I was thinking we could do some shopping. Are there stores here that you like?"

"I don't need anything. Let's go back to school and you can see Ian," Teagan said.

"Sure. I'd like to see him and the barn," Susanna said. "But you don't want to explore the town a little bit?"

"No. There's nothing here," Teagan said.

Out to Lunch

Ian was hers; she had taken him from her father, she felt, and made him her horse. He looked for her; he whinnied when she called his name; he listened. She was a different rider, more confident, stronger. She was a different girl lifting the saddle to Ian's back, engaging in a silent conversation with him as they covered the available ground at a controlled canter. She was a different girl in her classes, opening to chapters in textbooks she had failed to read; she was distracted and tired, uninterested. She was staying up late to study, cramming for quizzes and writing sloppy essays. She skipped breakfast to do homework at the last minute, and in the afternoons she would ride or take long walks, her books stacked on her desk, untouched. She was no longer synchronized with Julie and saw her only briefly between classes. Teagan often ate a quick lunch and then walked back to the dorm, finishing an assignment before her next class. During study hall, Teagan pretended to read, but her eyes glazed over the words, and she practiced perfect circles in her mind, directing Ian with a light contact.

During break, Teagan noticed that Julie didn't wait for her in the hallway, and she didn't see Sarah either. Aleah waved from down the sidewalk but kept walking. Teagan checked her mailbox, and the only thing in it was a blue slip of paper. She bought peanuts from the snack kiosk: breakfast.

At eleven on Saturday morning, Teagan was walking to the barn. She didn't want to wait on the steps of her dorm, watching the black car winding along the school road, toward her. She didn't want to admit that she was running away, and knew it was childish. Maybe he would give up and go away. She would delay so much they would run out of time. She was being ridiculous. The barn doors were closed, and she went around the side to the doors that opened into Ian's hall. One was open and a blue wheelbarrow full of straw sat halfway through. She edged around it. Ian was outside, in the paddock. She went to the barn office, a little corner room, concrete like the stalls, with a desk stacked with papers and clipboards, and a few stray lead ropes. Miss Jessie had her back to the door and was looking in a filing cabinet. Teagan knocked on the open door. Miss Jessie turned around and frowned.

"Teagan? The barn is closed right now."

"I know. I'm sorry. Um, I wanted to let you know that . . . I think I lost my riding crop."

"When's the last time you had it?"

"I think yesterday." Teagan knew her bat was in a bucket in the tack room.

Miss Jessie opened a metal locker and pulled out a bucket and shoved it toward Teagan, and told her to look through the ones in there. Maybe someone had turned it in. Teagan took as much time as she reasonably could, picking out the bats and putting them back in. Some had colored handles, blue or green, some were falling apart, the nylon weave along the length worn through, showing a plastic rod.

"It's not here. Could I go up to the grass and look? I might have dropped it."

"You didn't have it with you after the lesson?"

"I don't remember," Teagan said.

"Are you riding this afternoon?"

"Four," Teagan said.

"Can you look for it then?" Miss Jessie asked.

Teagan stood for a moment. She hadn't thought of that.

"Make it quick," Miss Jessie said.

"Thank you. I will," Teagan said, and outside she jogged up the hill to the riding area. She bent down and swiped the grass with her fingers, pretending to look. She walked a little and brushed the grass with the side of her shoe, and kept doing it every few feet, as if she were expecting to unearth something. She was involved in her search for nothing and didn't recognize the purr of the car rolling along the gravel near the riding area, and looked up to see her father walking toward the fence. He rested his hands on the top rail. She looked at him and smiled, not for him but because she imagined turning and running as fast as she could into the woods. She saw him glance at his watch. She walked over.

"Your roommate said you were here."

Teagan had a flash of anger toward Julie and then realized Julie had probably guessed at the places Teagan would usually be. The barn was likely.

"I lost my riding crop."

"Did you find it?"

Teagan's game was over. He wasn't interested in waiting while she looked for nothing.

She ordered a BLT at the Red Filly, and her father ordered a rare hamburger and a glass of wine. She wondered why he wanted to see her. He didn't talk much, and he finished his first glass quickly and seemed irritated when he didn't manage to signal the waiter right away for another.

"How are you?" Teagan asked. The words were foreign in her mouth, and she was embarrassed. She noticed he didn't look well, but she didn't mean to ask how he was. He was supposed to ask her.

"Lisa wants kids. I don't know if I want kids again. I've done that already."

Teagan felt chilled.

"And she wants to buy a house, and I don't have the income for that at the moment. Divorce is expensive. And we already have to pay for a wedding. It won't be a big wedding, but she's invited her family. I hope you and Charlie will come. It's in three weeks. I'll send you an invitation."

Teagan sat very straight with her hands on her knees. Her father wasn't looking at her. He was looking at his plate, sipping his wine, picking at his french fries.

"My job is good, but not really where I want to be. It's a small county, but I have to give them at least a year, really two, before I could move on from there. And I have to find someplace to store all the things from Blue View. Nothing will fit in my apartment. You saw it. It's way too small."

Teagan stopped listening. She looked at the prints of stylized horses in dark wooden frames on the walls of the restaurant. They were horses with skinny necks and spindly legs and bulging eyes, centered on a backdrop of muddy yellow-green grass and blue-gray sky. There were some black-and-white photographs of foxhunts, the dark jackets of the huntsmen were really red, she knew. Everything in the restaurant looked old. The floorboards were stained darker in some places, and large knots in the wide pine boards stood out. She looked at her sandwich on her plate and felt sick.

"Excuse me. I have to go to the bathroom," she said.

"I had yours wrapped up," Robert said when she got back, and he handed her a little square Styrofoam box. She cradled it gently in her lap on the drive back to school.

Girls' School

Rule: Guide, manage, control, moderate, restrain (oneself, one's desires, actions).

Rules, exactly worded in handbooks, are guidelines for a girl, to influence her to manage her behavior, and to control her choices, so that she moderates her time, and restrains from a desire to act in conflict with guidelines written down in a handbook. Girls' schools are imbued with rules to keep a girl doing what she should, and not what she shouldn't, but if she hopes to make a Discovery: the action or an act of revealing something secret or not generally known, then she acts on her desire.

Night (Memory)

I remember when Sarah wanted to go smoke a cigarette, because she had gotten some, somehow, and she had revealed the valuable contraband to me. I didn't smoke, wasn't a smoker, but when she asked me to help her sneak out of the dorm, just before lights-out, I was honored to be chosen as sidekick, and I did my best. We couldn't go out the front door, so I suggested the window, and maybe impressed her by taking out my small pocketknife, and slicing the edge and bottom of the screen, as precisely as I could manage, while she hovered near the door, to be a distraction in case my roommate walked in.

When the cut was large enough to admit our bodies, slim enough to pass through, I peeled back the screen. The room was on the first floor, at ground level. There was still enough of a drop that going headfirst wasn't a good option. I remember that Sarah came up with the way to do it. She turned around, put her hands on the floor, and propped a toe on the window sill. For a moment she balanced on her stomach, smiling at me, then dropped out of sight. I copied her. I recall a feeling of suspense when I was upside-down, my feet poking through the screen, because I was hoping that Julie would not walk in at that moment, and, by some luck, she didn't.

There was a door on either side of the dorm, and although it seemed unlikely that anyone would walk by, we tried to keep to shadows. Looking out of place, a tall black streetlamp glowed above the grass. Beyond the poor lamplight was the corrugated side of the gym building. Beyond the gym was the School Road, a paved narrow road that looped the campus. We would have to wait for the white security Jeep that cruised the loop after dark to pass by on its round. Where we wanted to get to was to the fields beyond. One field was mowed, but the other was still covered in tall wheat. What we did: we slid through the lamplight to the corner of the corrugated wall and waited, listening. The Jeep with its silent blue strobe light creeped past us. We backed against the brick wall. When it was too far away to cast light back to us, we ran as fast as we could for the field. Cold air slapped my face, the hem of my T-shirt rose up my body. I felt the brush of coarse stalks; heavy heads of wheat tipped and swayed as I moved among them. We lay down on the ground, wrapped in heavy smell of sweet grain, and looked into a deep black sky with stars flickering white, our cigarette smoke curled upward, the ghosts of doves.

One Night

Teagan and Sarah convinced Julie and Aleah to come with them, now that they were good at sneaking out. Sarah suggested the simple goal of walking as far as possible without being seen. She put Teagan in charge of keeping track of time because she wore a watch with a face that glowed when she pushed a button. The four of them made it all the way to the barn. Teagan wanted to see Ian, but the barn doors were padlocked. It was nine-thirty, and cold, and they were excited to feel out-of-bounds, even though they could have taken the same walk in the daytime and not been in trouble. Julie said they should walk back, since there was no place else to go, but Teagan put a foot on the fence that bordered the field and made up a game: they would all line up on the other side of the fence and run across the field in the dark, and whoever fell over last was the winner. Sarah laughed out loud at the idea. Teagan appreciated what a good sport Julie was, really, because she climbed over the fence, too. They spaced themselves along the fence, leaning forward, each in her own ready-to-run position, with one hand touching the top rail. Teagan said, "Go."

The ground was uneven, and each time Teagan almost stumbled she leapt, trying to outdistance her own inevitable fall. She had impressions of the others to either side of her, and then a tangle of grass caught her toe and she went down, rolling over to her back and laughing. She could hear the others laughing and shouting. Aleah had run diagonally and ended up far away. Julie found this hilarious and kept laughing while trying to wave at

Aleah in the darkness. No one could say who had stayed on her feet the longest, although since Aleah seemed to have ended up the farthest away, they named her the winner. They jogged part of the School Road and made it to the dorm in plenty of time, and although they burst in, breathless, cold, and full of energy, no one asked where they had been.

A Ghost

Julie and Teagan were sitting on Julie's bed, looking at her photo album. Aleah knocked on the door, even though it was open. Her curly dark hair was pulled back. It was close to bedtime, but she hadn't taken off her usual bright lipstick, eyeliner, and mascara. Aleah sat with them and looked at the pictures for a minute. Julie pointed out her sister and mother, her dogs, her yard in Oklahoma.

Aleah said, "Let's go ask Ms. Ganski to tell us the story about Miss Guinevere. Remember she said she'd tell us? I just saw her in the common room."

"You mean you'd rather do that than look at my photos?" Julie said, shutting her album.

"The woman Miss Guinevere's Garden is named after?" Teagan asked.

"She's supposed to haunt the school. Come on," Aleah said, standing up. They followed her and collected Sarah along the way.

"Why does she haunt the school?" Teagan asked.

"Maybe she likes it," Julie said.

Ms. Ganski was sitting at the table, talking with the prefects, her gray-blond hair in perfect curls, her wire-frame glasses folded and tucked into the neck of her sweater. She didn't hurry to finish her conversation, but then she turned in her chair and gave them her attention.

Aleah was their self-appointed spokeswoman. "Ms. Ganski, we were wondering if you had time tonight to tell us the story of Miss Guinevere?"

One of the girls at the table was Sen. "Oh, they're excited. Look at them."

"Don't you want to hear it?" Sarah asked.

"I already know it," Sen said.

"Why didn't you tell us?" Teagan said.

"I don't remember you asking." Sen said.

The other senior prefect, Erin, pushed back from the table. "I already know it, too. Good night, everyone."

Teagan muttered good night with the others.

Ms. Ganski smiled at Sen. "Why don't you tell it?"

"Me? Okay."

The girls settled on the floor in a half circle, facing Sen, like little girls who knew they had to be still and not talk before they would be told the story. Sen leaned forward in her chair, her hands clasped on her knees, playing the part of the storyteller. "Before Hunting Hill was a school, it was a private house and property, owned by a wealthy man. He fought in the Civil War."

"Was he Union or Confederate?" Teagan asked.

"Think about where we are," Julie said.

Sen hushed them, holding up one finger. "After the war, he returned to live with his wife and children. In the house also lived a maid."

"That was Guinevere?" Teagan asked.

"Shut up, Teagan," Julie said.

Teagan shrugged at her.

"Something happened. The wife got sick, and so did the maid, who was Miss Guinevere. The story goes that the maid lost her mind, and so she was locked in an attic room, and maybe she was even chained there. Whatever happened, one day Miss Guinevere ran out of the room, fell down the stairs, broke her neck, and died."

There was a small silence from all of them.

"Sick with what?" Teagan said.

"Is she buried here?" Sarah asked.

"Shh," Julie hissed.

Sen continued. "I'll tell you that part, too. In the early nineteen hundreds, a day school for girls was founded by a couple."

"A couple of what?" Teagan asked, turning up both palms.

Aleah laughed.

Sen narrowed her eyes and regained her audience. "A husband and wife," she said.

"Herbert and Clarissa Knowles," Ms. Ganski interjected, softly.

Sen said, "Herbert and Clarissa Knowles moved into the house. They lived upstairs and the downstairs rooms were used for classrooms."

"Which house is it?" Sarah asked.

"It's not here anymore, right?" Sen asked Ms. Ganski.

"It burned," Ms. Ganski said, in her quiet voice.

Sen continued. "One day, Clarissa was upstairs in the house, and she saw a woman standing in front of the window, but she could also see the view out of the window, through the woman."

Sen paused and looked at them.

Teagan and Julie grabbed each other's hand, and Sarah and Aleah scooted closer together.

Sen and Ms. Ganski laughed.

"Maybe it was her own reflection in the window?" Teagan suggested, hopefully.

Sen ignored her and said, "Clarissa researched the history of the house and discovered that a maid who had lived in the house had died young. Clarissa also found out that she had been buried on the property."

"There wasn't a tombstone?" Julie said.

"Shh," Teagan said.

Julie raised her eyebrows at Teagan in disbelief.

Sen said, "Clarissa figured out where Guinevere might be buried, and when she and her husband and some older students dug in that spot, they discovered human bones inside an old leather trunk."

The girls gasped.

"That's gross," Sarah whispered, with her hand over her mouth.

Aleah frowned. Teagan wondered how Guinevere would fit in a trunk, but she didn't want to ask.

Sen continued. "They found the skull with a hole in it. Clarissa sent the skull away to be examined, and it was determined that the hole was made by a Civil War–era bullet."

"She didn't fall down the stairs," Teagan said.

Julie said, "Obviously. Who shot her?"

"Do you want to hear the rest?" Sen demanded.

They were quiet and looked at her.

"Clarissa had Miss Guinevere's remains reinterred at Hunting

Hill and had a grave marker made for her. And she's still buried here." Sen sat back and looked at Ms. Ganski, who smiled.

"What's re-entered?" Teagan asked.

"It means she was buried again," Ms. Ganski said.

"She was buried in a trunk," Sarah said. She made a face.

They were all quiet for a minute, then Julie sat up straight and said, "Aleah, you have a trunk."

"Let's see who fits in it," Sarah said, scrambling to her feet.

"Me first," Teagan said.

They ran for the door, Aleah waving at them, saying, "Wait, I have to unpack it."

Ms. Ganski's voice stopped them. "Girls, the bell is in fifteen minutes."

"We can make it," Teagan said.

They all hurried down the hall.

In bed with the lights out, Teagan whispered to Julie, "We forgot to ask where the grave is."

Julie didn't respond.

"Do you think Miss Guinevere really haunts the campus?" Teagan asked.

"She only haunts you," Julie said.

Teagan felt a little strange. Hearing the story of Miss Guinevere seemed to make her real. Drifting into sleep, Teagan tried to imagine Miss Guinevere. She wondered if her family had known that she had been killed. Teagan tried to picture an old attic room and saw that it looked down on the school barn. She turned in her bed and felt she had summoned a ghost: a light-filled figure, wordless.

Grave Site

Julie wasn't speaking to Teagan. Teagan had discovered that Julie owned a pink bra, and as a joke she pinned it up on the message board in the hallway. The bra was a real bra. It was padded and had underwire. Teagan's bras were plain white cotton things, with no padding or wire, so the pink bra was a thing of fascination for her. She never guessed that Julie would be so sensitive about her underwear. Teagan was pretty sure no one had seen it anyway. Teagan had simply slipped the thing under the hem of her shirt and walked down the hall. As soon as she was back to the room, she suggested that Julie go look at the message board, because someone had left her a message. Julie was furious with Teagan, but Teagan considered that maybe Julie was really just disappointed that there hadn't been a real message.

Teagan came back from the barn in the afternoon and found Julie reading on her bed. She tried to apologize, but Julie wouldn't even look at her. Teagan thought she was taking it too seriously. She left her alone and went to search for Aleah. Her roommate said she'd gone to a friend's for the weekend. Teagan knocked on Sarah's door, but there was no answer. She thought maybe she was at the dining hall, eating late. It couldn't hurt to walk over, especially since Julie didn't want her around and she didn't feel like doing homework. She found Sarah walking and eating a cheese sandwich.

"You missed dinner?" Sarah asked.

"No. I was looking for you."

"What's up?"

"Julie's mad at me again."

"Is she often mad at you?"

"I stuck her bra on the message board."

"Why did you do that?" Sarah asked.

Teagan was surprised that Sarah hadn't laughed. "It was funny." Teagan shrugged.

"Maybe not that funny."

"Yes it was. Do you want to look for the grave?"

"You found it?" Sarah said.

Teagan had gotten her attention. "No, that's why I said let's look for it."

"I don't think I want to," Sarah said.

"Why not?" Teagan stopped her with a hand on her shoulder. "Sarah?"

"It's creepy. Why do you care about it?" Sarah pushed past her and they kept walking.

"We're Hunting Hill girls. I think we should know where Miss Guinevere's grave is."

"Ms. Ganski probably knows," Sarah said.

"But she's not telling us. We have to find it ourselves. I think you're supposed to."

"And then what?" Sarah said.

"And then we know."

"You want to see the ghost, don't you?"

After a moment Teagan said, "I wouldn't mind, really."

"If you start being haunted, I'm not hanging out with you anymore," Sarah said.

"I think Miss Guinevere is probably pretty nice," Teagan said.

"What, you think she's going to do your homework for you? Make your bed?" Sarah said.

"Maybe. Maybe she looks after Hunting Hill girls."

"Like she's Mamma ghost?"

"Maybe," Teagan said.

"I don't want a Mamma ghost, thanks."

"But you want to look for the grave, don't you?" Teagan said.

"I'll go with you, but I'm not touching it," Sarah said.

"You don't have to," Teagan said.

It took a little persuading to get Julie to talk to Teagan again. Teagan thought it was ridiculous that anyone would hold a grudge over underwear, but she finally made Julie laugh by wearing her own underwear on her head and walking up and down the hallway right before bedtime, when lots of girls could see her. Julie seemed satisfied, so they finally picked an afternoon to go looking for the grave.

"It could be anywhere on campus," Sarah said.

"We're not actually going to find it," Julie said.

"So why are we looking?" Sarah said.

"Hunting Hill," Teagan said.

"Very good. You've learned the name of our school," Julie said.

"No, the actual Hunting Hill," Teagan said.

"That's right. There is an actual Hunting Hill," Sarah said, tossing up her hands. "Behind the barns, where the foxhunts always start from."

"Horse people are weird," Julie said.

"I bet you anything it's there," Teagan said.

"So instead of flowers on her grave, Miss Guinevere gets horse poop?" Julie said.

Teagan gave her a look but didn't say anything because she had just won Julie back and didn't want to lose her again.

"Horse poop makes flowers grow," Sarah said, standing up. "If we're gonna go, we better go," she said, swooping her arm to get them to walk through the door.

They walked past the barn, and Teagan blew a kiss to Ian, who was out of sight in his stall inside. They paused at the fence line they were not supposed to cross, looking conspicuous. They didn't see anyone nearby, so they climbed over, walking the path they'd stumbled along in the dark.

The small group stopped together in the field. Hunting Hill was an obvious rise above them. There was nothing built there, no marker to designate it, but it had a look of having been used. The grass was short and the weedy plants were sparse. On the far side was a small, bushy tree.

"That's the Hawthorn," Sarah said.

Julie and Teagan looked at her.

"Biology class. Mrs. Wade told us. It was a gift to the school."

"That's got to be it, then," Julie said.

"That is it," Teagan said.

"Wait, do you already know where it is?" Julie said.

"Teagan has been communing with Miss Guinevere behind our backs. She wants Miss Guinevere to be her ghost mother," Sarah explained.

Teagan shrugged.

"What's this about?" Julie said.

"Ask Teagan," Sarah said.

"She'd be better than my real parents," Teagan said.

Julie and Sarah didn't say anything.

"C'mon," Teagan said, and she started running up the hill, and they all ran, the way horses sometimes will gallop up a hill for no apparent reason, except that they can.

Teagan crossed the summit at a run and slowed to a trot near the Hawthorn. Sarah and Julie pulled up beside her. Julie pushed her hair out of her face. Teagan began walking around the little tree.

"Here it is," she said.

Sarah put her hand over her mouth.

"Are you shitting us?" Julie said.

"No, it's right here. Come look," Teagan said. She knelt down and reached under the tree. The thorns on the branches caught her skin. "Ouch," she said.

Sarah half-screamed and jumped back, and Julie laughed at Sarah.

"This tree has thorns," Teagan said.

"Did Miss Guinevere get you?" Julie said.

"Julie, really, shut up," Teagan said.

For once, Julie did not retort.

Teagan brushed leaves and standing water off the raised letters of the square stone plaque set in the ground. "Can you see?" she asked. And she read the words aloud for them anyway.

HERE LIES MISS GUINEVERE

DIED 1866

HER GHOST HAUNTS HUNTING HILL

"I didn't think we would find it," Sarah said.

"Well, we did. So now let's go," Julie said.

"She's real. She's right here," Teagan said.

"Teagan, if you start acting any creepier, I'm changing room-mates," Julie said.

"Did you all think she would really be here?" Teagan said.

Sarah said suddenly, "Teagan, you touched the grave."

"So what?"

"Now you're cursed," Sarah said.

"Isn't that what she wanted?" Julie said.

"What do you mean?" Teagan said.

"If you touch the grave, you're cursed. That hand is going to get mangled somehow," Sarah said.

"That's not true. That's just a thing to make people not mess with her grave."

"You messed with it," Julie said.

"The curse isn't real," Teagan said. "It's just so people will leave her alone."

"Teagan knows," Sarah said.

"Miss Guinevere has adopted Teagan," Julie said.

"You guys are stupid. Let's go," Teagan said. She walked away, but she felt that if she looked behind her, she would see Miss Guinevere standing by the Hawthorn in her long skirt. Teagan had summoned the ghost and the ghost had arrived. Teagan did not look back. Julie trotted to catch up with her, and she linked an arm around Teagan's.

"I'm so sorry you're going to lose your hand," she said.

Late at Night

Julie said Teagan couldn't do her homework at night in their room anymore. The light and the rustling kept Julie awake. She told Teagan to get her work done during the day. Teagan felt she couldn't concentrate in study hall. She couldn't think with other people thinking around her. She tried to explain this to Julie, but finally she just made Julie agree not to tell on her when she snuck into the common room to do her homework. After everyone had gone to bed, and the only light was a slim yellow bar under Ms. Ganski's door at the end of the hall, Teagan walked the hallway softly, closed the common room door behind her, and turned on a lamp in the furthest corner. If Ms. Ganski walked in, Teagan was prepared to pretend it was the first time she'd stayed up late to do her homework.

After several nights, when Ms. Ganski did not discover her, Teagan began to rely on the quiet of the half-dark common room, even if she still found it difficult to concentrate on her work. She urged her tired brain to read, to memorize, to string sentences together in some semblance of an argument. Her essays often had the same comment from her teachers, "What are you trying to say?"

Because she was so tired, and failing at her work, and alone, Teagan summoned Miss Guinevere to sit with her, to keep her company, to silently praise her for trying, at least, to be a student. Teagan imagined that Miss Guinevere knew that she spent so many nights alone in the common room, and so she joined Teagan in her walk down the dark hallway, keeping anyone from finding her out. She imagined Miss Guinevere stayed with her while she surrounded herself with books, and barely read them, while she reviewed her notes, even though she seemed to forget them by morning. Miss Guinevere had been alone, too, away from her family, and she had not been treated well, and she had died strangely.

Teagan sympathized with her, and she created the person of Miss Guinevere in her mind, a young woman who appreciated Teagan's sympathy, who looked out for Teagan and saw that she came to no harm, because Miss Guinevere wanted to protect Teagan, as she had not been protected. Teagan made up the story without meaning to. It simply wrote itself in her mind over sleepless nights, bit by bit, until Teagan and the ghost were both in the room, near the lamp in the furthest corner.

And Teagan wasn't afraid, because she knew she was half-dreaming, and she also knew that whoever Miss Guinevere had been, she was not bad. So, when Teagan could no longer keep her eyes from closing, and she was afraid of falling asleep on the floor and being found out in the morning, she would gather her books and pages, and as she closed herself into the safety of her room, just before she shut the door, she would whisper good night.

Wedding

The basement classrooms were all science labs, with big black tables with little sinks and faucets in one corner of each, and cabinets along the walls, full of beakers and trays of glass tubes, dissection kits, and bottles of chemicals. The room had a chemical smell. Teagan sat at one of the big tables with Sarah. She tried to remember not to lean her arms on the table. It always seemed a little sticky. The tables were wiped down at the end of class, but there still seemed to be layers of various substances on their surfaces. The bell rang and Mrs. Wade started her lecture on the respiratory, digestive, and circulatory systems.

"When we consider the internal workings of the body, there is one necessary thing that we might not always think of. Can anyone guess?" Mrs. Wade asked, pacing in front of the class.

No one raised a hand to answer oxygen or blood. These were obvious.

"Blood can't circulate without compression. Compression is essential."

Teagan thought about blood pushed through stringy veins and bigger arteries. She wrote down the words she heard Mrs. Wade say: *alveoli, peristalsis, ileum, coronary, atrium.* The words sounded like places to Teagan, parts of a large and complicated house, and she had to memorize the sequence of the rooms, the organization of the doors; it seemed endless. When the bell rang her hand felt stiff from so much writing, and the verbal dissection of the body made her feel nauseous. She was glad to leave.

At break the pump house post office opened. Teagan opened

her mailbox and found three hand-addressed envelopes inside. On the first two she recognized handwriting from Charlie and Grace. The third envelope had her address printed evenly in the middle of the envelope, but it had no return address. She didn't have time to read any of them, so she shoved the letters in her backpack.

In French class she repeated the verb *to be*, chanting with her classmates:

Être:
je suis / nous sommes
tu es / vous êtes
elle est / il est / elles sont / ils sont

Teagan was thinking about the letters in her bag.

"How would we introduce ourselves to someone? Teagan," Miss Thomas asked.

Teagan was unfocused. She looked blankly at Miss Thomas for a moment.

"My name is," Miss Thomas prompted.

"*Je m'appelle* Teagan."

"And how would we say, 'I'm pleased to meet you'?" Miss Thomas smiled impatiently.

"I don't remember," Teagan said.

Miss Thomas turned away. "Cierra?"

"*Enchanté,*" Cierra answered.

"Very good. *Très bien,*" Miss Thomas said.

Très bien, very good, thought Teagan. She wasn't very good.

She hadn't looked at her French book last night. Miss Thomas didn't call on Teagan again. When the bell rang, Teagan picked up her bag without looking at anyone and headed for the library.

It was a pretty library, with a winding staircase. She wondered why she didn't come more often. She walked up the stairs and into a long room with yellowish light coming through tall windows. She chose an empty table and sat down, pulling the letters from her bag.

Dear Teagan,

I hope you are enjoying your new school. I'm proud of you for making the transition. Work hard and keep your nose clean.

Love,
Charlie

It surprised her. Then again, she thought, she'd never read a letter from her brother. He sounded more parental, less friendly, than she'd hoped. Maybe he was more of a grown-up than she'd realized. Maybe he was feeling alone at their old school. She missed him and suddenly realized that she hadn't just left Grace behind; she'd left Charlie, too. She wondered how he was and felt selfish. It was harder, after Charlie's short letter, to open the one from Grace. She and Grace had never had to write letters to keep in touch before, but she could still hear Grace's voice in the words she wrote. Grace mentioned something about goals for the new year, which was funny, but Teagan's attention was already straying toward the third letter. She studied the handwriting. A woman's, she thought. She opened the cream envelope and pulled out a stiff, embossed card.

It took her a moment to understand that it was a wedding

invitation. She'd never seen one before. Robert French was getting married to the woman she had seen in a closet, who wore a purple suit. Teagan guessed that the purple-suited woman had addressed the envelope. She dropped the card onto the table. She couldn't believe that her father had not addressed the envelope himself. The least he could do was to address it himself. Teagan didn't like that purple-woman had written her name.

Her next thought was clear; she wouldn't go to the wedding. There was no way she would go. She needed to tell someone. She needed to tell Charlie that she wasn't going to go so that he wouldn't go either. Or maybe they would go and rescue her father. Wasn't there a moment in a wedding where someone in the audience was allowed to object? She'd seen it in a movie. She would stand up. She would object. And Charlie would try to pull her back into her seat, and her father would turn and look at her. She wouldn't be able to stop herself, so she wouldn't go at all. She picked up the envelope and a smaller card fell out. It read "The favor of your reply is requested." She ripped it in half.

Attend

There's no way I'm going. Don't go, Charlie. Don't do it. He doesn't want us."

"He's our father," Charlie said. There was a quiver in his voice.

"Charlie, if I go, I'll stop the wedding. I can't sit there. Don't go. Please, Charlie."

Invitation

Teagan wasn't sure what she wanted, but Susanna said that she wanted to be with Teagan for the weekend of the wedding. If Teagan had had time to figure out her thoughts, she would have come to the conclusion, as she did much later, that she would have preferred not to mark the occasion at all. Then again, when she knew she would see her mother, she was glad.

Hunting Hill's guesthouse was decorated in exactly coordinating shades of yellow, green, and pink. It made Teagan feel as if the only thing out of place was her. She hadn't realized that the school had a guesthouse until her mother explained that she was staying there, and then suddenly, on a hill Teagan had surely seen before and walked past several times, was a small pale yellow house with a shingled roof and a white door. It even had a name, the Stirrup Cup, which referred to a silver cup offered up to riders on horseback before a foxhunt.

When she mentioned this to Julie—that her mother was coming up for the weekend because her father was getting remarried, and that there was a guesthouse on campus called the Stirrup Cup and her mother would be staying there—Julie gave her a blank look and then said, "What the heck is a stirrup cup? You horse people are weird." As a rule, Teagan would never tell Julie that she was right about anything, but this time she admitted to herself that Julie was right about two things: Teagan was a horse person, and horse people were a little bit weird. She was beginning to see this.

Susanna arrived and called Teagan's dorm to say that she

had. Teagan heard the soft shuffling of feet outside her door and opened it to find Ms. Ganski taping a note to the door. Ms. Ganski smiled and handed the note to Teagan without saying anything.

Teagan went into the bathroom. She splashed her face with water and, just because, she brushed her teeth. She laced up her clean blue Tretorn sneakers and briefly checked the pocket of her coat. The invitation was in there. She walked to the guest-house. Inside the house, Teagan stood in the living room, or sitting room, which looked as if it were cleaned every day and no one ever sat in it. She looked at the brightly flowered couch, curtains, and rug, the rose stems of the lamps, and the green interior of a little bowl that sat on a yellow side table. It all made her feel sleepy and hungry. She went up the staircase, which she was now able to recognize as old, having been in a number of old buildings since living on Hunting Hill campus. The stairs seemed too small, narrow, and steep. Upstairs was a balcony hallway, and old, unevenly fitted white doors had little black numbers painted on them. She knocked on door six. Susanna opened it and pulled her daughter into a hug. Everything in the room was blue, yellow, and white. Teagan sat on the yellow striped bedcover and watched her mother unpack her few things and line up some toiletries on the top of the dresser. Teagan thought it was strange that the room had a sink under a mirror. She'd never seen a sink in a bedroom before, but it kind of made sense.

"How are you?" Susanna said, hanging up a skirt in the narrowest closet Teagan had ever seen.

"Fine."

"Really?" Susanna said, now fishing out a tube of lipstick from her purse.

"Yes. How are you?" Teagan said.

"Well, it's surprising, isn't it?"

Teagan didn't know what to say. She thought that if she were her mother, she would be at the wedding right now, ripping flowers from their vases or throwing dead birds at the purple woman. She didn't know where the dead bird image came from; maybe they were doves. Her mother's I'm-in-control voice made Teagan want to lose control. How could her mother be so calm? How could she not be crazy with anger? Seeing her mother in the perfectly decorated room felt surreal. She felt as if her life had frozen since she'd come to school.

"I have a puppy," Susanna said.

Teagan listened to the words. She didn't say, "*We* have a puppy."

"I brought a picture. It's a black Lab. I shouldn't have, but I did," Susanna said. She produced a color photograph of Barker looking, Teagan thought, suspiciously at a black blob on the kitchen floor.

"I went to a horse show that Hope was riding in, and a woman brought these puppies. I held this one in my lap for about an hour. It was a bad idea, but there you go," Susanna said.

Charlie shouldn't get to have a puppy without her, Teagan thought. "What's the name?"

"Max."

"Oh."

"Charlie named him," Susanna said. She sat down on the bed beside Teagan. Teagan didn't want her that close. Her mother's "made-up" smell was familiar, a mixture of perfume and waxy cosmetics.

"Do you want to see the invitation?"

"You have it?" Susanna said, unable to hide her shock.

Teagan rummaged through her coat on the bed for a minute. She pulled out the cream envelope. Her mother took it and slid out the card without hesitation, with practiced fingers that had opened a hundred such pieces of mail over a lifetime of invitations. The ripped halves of the reply card fell onto the bed. Teagan snatched them up and crumpled them in her hand.

Susanna looked over the words on the invitation. "How do you feel about this?" she asked Teagan. It was as if someone had told her to say it.

There was still time to go to the wedding. "I want to burn it," Teagan said.

Susanna looked at her daughter. Teagan could see her struggle.

"A cleansing," Teagan said. She didn't know where she got the words from. Then she remembered. In Sunday school, they'd written down what they were giving up for Lent on strips of paper and then burned them in the sink. The fire and smoke had made Teagan realize that church was something real, something that had secret power in rituals.

"All right," Susanna said. She was smiling with the corners of her mouth turned down, a look Teagan reflected in her own face. "We need matches."

There were no matches anywhere in the clean, prim bedroom. Teagan hunted through the pink and green sitting room, opening drawers that didn't even have a layer of dust to be disturbed. She circled the room. Didn't anyone in this house ever need to light anything on fire? A plain white door set into the white wall caught her attention. She went toward it and it opened onto a galley kitchen. Bingo. She opened drawers of mismatched knives and serving spoons, and finally found little books of matches, the kind the girls who smoked seemed always able to produce when someone asked for a light. She climbed the stairs with one concealed in her hand, although no one was there to see. In the room her mother was timidly opening the drawers of a little dressing table.

"Got them," Teagan said.

Susanna looked up. "You found—?" she said.

Teagan was worried for minute that her mother would back out, say they shouldn't.

"We'd better put it in the sink," Susanna said, and she lifted the card and envelope from the impeccably made bed and dropped them in the white porcelain sink.

Teagan handed her the matchbook.

"Do you want to say anything?" Susanna said.

"It's not a voodoo doll," Teagan said.

Susanna laughed. The first match was a dud. The second lit. Susanna lifted the card and held a corner of it to the flame. It caught and she dropped it into the sink.

While it blackened and curled, Teagan felt mollified. Then the smoke alarm went off. In the small room the noise was immense. Teagan clamped her hands to her ears and her mother did, too. They looked around the room and Teagan pointed at the round wart of the alarm casing over the doorframe. She shoved the blue silk–covered chair over toward the door and Susanna stood up on it, Teagan holding on to the back of the chair and on to her mother's leg to steady them both. After a minute Susanna got the plastic cover free and pulled the hanging battery from the wires. The beeping stopped.

There was a knock on the door. Teagan and Susanna looked at each other.

"Answer it," Susanna said.

Teagan pulled open the door as far as it could go, with the chair blocking it. A small blond woman wearing yellow glasses frames slipped inside.

"I'm next door. I heard— Is everything all right?"

"There's no fire," Susanna said.

All three of them looked at the smoldering ashes in the sink.

Teagan steadied her mother as she descended from the chair. In plain language Susanna explained that her ex-husband was getting remarried and that she and her daughter had decided to burn the wedding invitation, as if this was what one did. Teagan stayed quiet.

The blond woman, as if trying to convince herself that she didn't need to call the police, explained that the house had caught on fire once; that fire was a problem in old wooden houses.

"We're done burning," Susanna said.

The woman looked flustered and on her way out offered that, if they needed anything, she'd be happy to call the school for them. Susanna assured her that they did not need anything at all. Teagan smiled and gave a little wave to the blond woman, who, looking worried, closed the door.

Image

It didn't matter. Teagan walked into the bathroom and splashed water on her face. The towel was soft against her eyes. She wanted to sleep. She couldn't sleep. Teagan leaned her head against the cool of the painted cinder-block wall. She looked at the opposite wall, and the collage that she and Julie had spent about a week's worth of afternoons making. They'd found all kinds of pictures in magazines and carefully cut them out and arranged them and taped them to the wall, overlapping images of models and cities and the interiors of fancy restaurants, jewelry and clothes, makeup and shoes, coats and purses, landscapes of Italy and Arizona, beaches and cute dogs, sunglasses and horses, all favorite things, or things they liked or secretly admired and wanted; as if the collage was an amalgamation of what successful adulthood might look like, or feel like, or be like; it was what Teagan thought she was supposed to want. In her sleepy, irritated mood, she suddenly hated the collage.

What she wanted to do was rip it down, and especially all of the smiling faces, the languid landscapes. In her sleep deprivation, the images seemed to move a little in front of Teagan's eyes to shift. Teagan wanted to suppress those flickering motions; like a cat, she wanted to pounce. She placed both of her hands flat against the large area of thin, glossy magazine clippings, and then she curled her fingers, making claws, and the paper under them ripped a little, and then she swiped down, and the tearing sound was extremely satisfying. She ripped more and more, the cutouts settling around her feet.

Teagan didn't notice Julie right away; her roommate was standing, looking surprised, in the bathroom doorway. When Teagan noticed her, Julie turned to face her. Teagan was breathing heavily, as if the ripping of the collage had been tough physical work. When Julie said, "Teagan, what the hell?" Teagan simply brushed past her and crawled into her own bed, pulling up the covers. She could feel Julie standing over her. She could sense Julie's anger almost like heat.

"What the hell was that for? I worked on that for a long time. So did you," Julie said.

Teagan curled tighter in her blankets.

After a moment, Julie went back to her own bed, but Teagan knew that the damage was done. Even if, after a while, Julie stopped being mad, there was no repairing the collage, and even as she tried to keep her crying to herself, muffled in her pillow, Teagan knew that they wouldn't make another one.

Reinterred

Teagan walked to the Hawthorn after supper, without trying to hide from anyone. Students and teachers must have seen her go, but no one stopped her. She wondered if they thought she was so strange that they were no longer going to bother her. She was failing in her classes. Julie wasn't ignoring her, entirely, but she didn't have time for Teagan either. Teagan seemed to have slipped into a different version of Hunting Hill, one where she no longer existed. She went to class, she went to meals, she went to her dorm, but none of it seemed very real to her anymore, and she was so tired all the time. She was too tired to talk to anyone, and she was too tired to explain why she hadn't done her homework.

The ghost of Miss Guinevere was annoying her. She didn't want a ghost for a friend anymore. She felt the ghost was pestering her, telling her what to do, telling her to do all the homework she was behind in, telling her to be a better Hunting Hill girl, even though Teagan felt that she could not be a better Hunting Hill girl. She simply could not. So, she walked to the Hawthorn. She climbed the actual Hunting Hill behind the barns, and she stood at Miss Guinevere's grave again.

"Go away," she said. "I don't need you. I want you to leave me alone."

Teagan walked away. As she passed the barns she saw that the side door was open. She went inside and along Ian's hallway. The horses were munching their evening feed. There were sounds of eating and a sweet smell of grain, and a warmth from every stall containing a horse. She went to Ian's stall and unlocked it and slid the door open. He turned to her and nosed her and smelled her, but he was also interested in his food, and he kept eating. She stroked his sleek neck and pressed her face against it and breathed in. He was real. The horse was real and Teagan felt real when she was with him. She also knew that she wasn't supposed to be in the barn in the evening, so she kissed his nose and slid the door shut.

Funeral

The dream I had, when I woke up feeling so scared. Mourners gathered in a graveyard, and I was in the coffin. I looked up and saw the faces looking down. My parents were there. Charlie was. Grace was. They were surprised I'd died so young. I wasn't dead, but I couldn't move and I couldn't speak. Couldn't they see that my eyes were open? They were burying me alive. A minister began the funeral. I was running out of time. There was no time. I wanted to tell them they were making a mistake. I couldn't believe they were going through with it, and I had no way to stop it.

Lesson

She was glad to see Ian. He did everything she told him to do and seemed happy to do it. She tacked quickly, because she wanted a few minutes to ride by herself before the lesson started. She rode along the fence line, trotting at an easy pace, absentmindedly gripping a lock of Ian's dark mane. She heard a shout behind her and knew what it meant. She turned Ian and trotted to where the lesson was assembled. Miss Jessie was standing on the ground in front of the other riders on their horses. Teagan was glad Miss Jessie couldn't hear her thoughts. She didn't like

Miss Jessie. Today she had the girls trot in two-point position (which was jumping position) in both directions, then they took turns going over a low cavalletti, and Miss Jessie called out her critique of each girl's performance. Teagan felt removed from everything. She didn't care about the exercise, the jump, the other girls, Miss Jessie's instructions or her comments. Teagan let Ian do what he wanted. He was as bored as she was. When it was her turn, Teagan pointed Ian in the general direction of the jump. Her muscles did all the things they knew to do. She could have been watching herself. She had a feeling of detachment. Ian seemed to obligingly do what he knew to do, which was to trot, jump, trot, and then fall into his lazy walk, which, because he was a big horse, looked purposeful, even though Teagan could feel he was hardly making an effort.

Miss Jessie turned to the group. "Girls, that was a perfect example. Teagan, come do that again and I want everyone to watch," Miss Jessie said.

Teagan was uninterested. Ian was uninterested. They both knew what to do and did it. "Beautiful," Miss Jessie called out and signaled the next rider to move forward. She approached Teagan's horse's side at the end of the lesson and praised them both for their work.

"Thank you," Teagan said, and when she was sure Miss Jessie was finished with them, she loosened Ian's reins completely and let him walk at his own pace. She hitched up her leg and reached down and loosened his girth while he walked. After she'd rinsed him off and wiped him down, she led him to his paddock. He began to graze the sparse grass, and Teagan walked up the hill.

Psychologist (Vampire)

It was a betrayal that her mother had set up the appointment. Ms. Ganski informed her that on Thursday afternoon she would be driven into town. Teagan waited for the Hunting Hill van in front of her dorm. She was furious, but had no one and no thing to take it out on. A shriveled old white man sat behind the wheel. Teagan sat in the back on a bench and didn't pretend that she would talk, to him or to anyone. In town she walked into a gray stone building with a black shingled roof. It had once been a house, and she was tired of old houses. She had to fill out a long questionnaire and she made up the answers. Finally she was ushered into an office that had a large shiny wooden desk and two leather armchairs with brass buttons seeming to bolt them into shape.

The furniture wasn't so strange, but the man himself was. He was a vampire. His dark gray flannel suit had a thin white stripe to it, and he wore a black silk tie. His face was pale and sharply featured. And his hair was in a pompadour. She'd only seen Elvis with hair like that. The vampire's dark hair had a single wide white stripe running down the middle of it, like he wore a skunk curled sleeping or dead on his head. The only thing that confused her was that it was daylight, and she didn't think that vampires could be out in the daylight. Maybe he'd treated the windows with something.

He offered her a scone. She thought about this for a minute. Why a scone? Was he going to have a scone? No, he wasn't, he was only offering her one. It was obviously poisoned, or it would knock her out, so he could drink her blood. Why had her mother sent her to a vampire? To Teagan, this seemed to signal that her mother was out of touch. How could she not recognize a vampire when she saw one? The vampire walked around to the front of his dark, shiny desk, which Teagan knew was hiding a coffin, and he perched there and twisted his long, gray fingers together. "Do you believe in God?" he asked.

Teagan thought about this. "Yes," she said.

"Then pray to God for comfort," he said.

She thought, Don't tell me what to do.

Hide

It was the most childish thing Teagan could remember doing. She walked to the barn and went into Ian's stall. No one came down the hall. Ian kept turning away from his hay and nosing her to make sure, again, that she wasn't hiding an apple or a carrot from him. He didn't seem to know why else she would be there, and her presence in his stall seemed to bother him. She wished she could communicate to him to play along, but she wasn't sure what the ruse was. She finally realized that she needed to be seeming to do something, even though there was nothing she needed to do. Ian was groomed, fed, turned out, and brought back in by Shirley, who would normally tack the horse before lessons, but Teagan had bargained with her, promising not to be late to her lessons if she would let Teagan tack up.

It had always been part of her routine and she was just used to it. Shirley seemed to understand.

Her brushes, unused, were in her trunk in the tack room. Teagan could grab some brushes and then pretend she needed to groom Ian, and then she would come up with a reason why. She left the stall, walked down the hall to the tack room, and ran into her father.

"I've been looking for you."

"Hi," she said.

"Your roommate said you might be down here." He was frowning.

"I had to do some stuff," she said.

"I was going to take you to lunch," Robert said.

"Ian wants to see you," Teagan said, hearing herself talking like a little girl.

Robert relaxed. "He does?" he said, in a voice that was meant to entertain her.

"Down here," Teagan said.

The hall seemed long. They didn't talk. Teagan pulled back the door and stood to the side, watching her father and the horse together. Ian didn't seem to show any specific sign of affection, although he did nose Robert's shirt and let Robert stroke his long face, and he didn't let anyone but Teagan handle him like that as far as she knew. She was glad that there wasn't a happy reunion between her father and Ian, just familiarity.

"He's a good horse," Robert said.

"He is," Teagan said.

Robert slid the door of the stall shut. "How about lunch?"

Teagan looked at her hands. "Dad, I have a lot of stuff I have to do."

There was a silence, during which Teagan could hear Ian chewing hay.

"I came here to see you," Robert said.

"Sorry," Teagan said.

"Okay." Robert walked down the concrete hallway, his hands balled in fists.

Teagan slid into Ian's stall and sat there. Ian looked at her, chewing hay.

Another Visit with the Vampire

He seemed to be wearing the same gray flannel suit with the white stripe and the black silk tie. Teagan guessed that he slept in his clothes, in the coffin behind the desk. As always, he had slightly inclined his head with its dark roll of hair with the white skunk stripe and offered a scone, but Teagan had immediately put up her hand and said, "No, thank you." The vampire must have read somewhere that humans really love scones and will eat them at any point in the day. She never expected him to eat a scone, because they were not blood scones, and she didn't know if vampires could eat baked goods. She had the idea that maybe it was the same scone, proffered day after day, for months or years, unless someone actually took the scone, but she couldn't imagine that anyone would. Through the session, Teagan tried to say as little as possible. The things she did say, she tried to make sound uninteresting, and to contain as little information as possible. The vampire perched in front of his desk. Teagan thought he did this to guard his coffin. She looked at his gray, unlined, undead face.

Then the vampire said, "How is your relationship with your parents?"

It was a good question, one she had to think about, and one that would require self-analysis to answer, and she was not about to put that much effort into it. She cast around for a one-word response that would appear to have substance to it, and she said, "Complicated." The moment she said it she knew it was the wrong word to have chosen. She had veered too close to actual feeling.

"Complicated in what way?" the vampire asked.

He had countered well. She thought about her next move. She would relay fact, with no emotion attached. "They're divorced. They live in different places," she said.

"And that's hard for you?" the vampire asked.

What kind of a question is that? she wondered. How could it not be hard for her? But maybe he meant that it was unimportant? No, he's out of touch, she thought. He has lost his connection with human lives, and he's pretending to understand that her beating heart means more than circulating blood; that it means she experiences emotion, even though she was doing her best not to.

"I'm okay," Teagan said.

"It seems that you are here because you're not feeling okay," the vampire said.

Teagan thought, I'm here because my mother is making me take these appointments. She decided that the question did not deserve an answer. She considered offering him the scone.

"How are you feeling about your parents?" the vampire asked.

She decided that he was probably trying to figure out how he could hypnotize her and drink her blood. She wouldn't look him in the eye anymore. She looked at her knees instead and replied with fact, again, trying to keep her information as straightforward as possible.

"I'm moving back with my mom," Teagan said.

"You're leaving your school?" he asked.

She realized he was probably noting that he would have one less potential blood bag in his office.

"There are other schools," she said.

"And what about your friends?" he asked.

"I have other friends," Teagan said. It was true.

Run

Girls were supposed to ride in pairs during their free time on the weekends. Teagan trotted over to a girl on a small, light brown horse. She was feeling unusually friendly. The horse was a school horse. It had an overworked look about it, and the saddle and bridle seemed frayed and mismatched. The little horse looked spry enough, though. The weather was crisp. It was the middle of November. Smells of rotting leaves and a hint of snow carried through on the breeze. The girl introduced herself as Claire.

"Is he a warmblood?" Claire asked.

Teagan stroked Ian's neck. "No. All Thoroughbred as far as I know."

"He looks big for a Thoroughbred. They're supposed to be

fast, aren't they?" Claire said. She was reining in her little horse, who was trying to trot.

"Yes. I've never let him go flat-out. Want to race?" Teagan said.

"You know we're not supposed to," Claire said.

"I know," Teagan said. She wouldn't push, but she would do it if the girl would.

"Okay," Claire said.

It wasn't a fair matchup. If Teagan had thought it through she wouldn't have suggested it in the first place. They didn't have a course; they just let the horses run. Little horses are surprising in how fast they can be, and at first Teagan thought Ian might be beaten, but then she realized that he was just keeping pace with the other horse. A sickening feeling went through her when she realized that Ian had gears she didn't even know about. She let the reins slide, loosened her seat in the saddle, and Ian took off.

She didn't know where the little horse was except that he was behind her. The cold air hit her face so sharply her eyes blurred. She willed Ian to slow down because she couldn't make him. He did finally slow, feeling her stiffen and pull back on the reins, and the tears fell out of her eyes and she could see again. She stroked his neck and patted him and stroked him again. She circled him back to speak with Claire, who was a good sport, even if she seemed dispirited. Teagan's horse had won.

Return

A new prepaid calling card in hand, Teagan stretched the white cord of the hallway phone into the cleaning closet. She crouched, her back to the wall, surrounded by mops. She punched in the series of numbers and waited. She was glad Grace answered the phone.

"Hi, Grace, it's Teagan."

"What's up? How's your school?"

"Okay. Okay, it's not so good. I'm going to leave." Teagan felt a huge relief, telling Grace that she wanted to come home. She breathed heavily.

"Oh. Are you going to come back?"

"I think I will. I mean, I am," Teagan said.

"Great. We'll be in school together," Grace said. There was a pause. "You were kind of stupid to leave."

"Yeah." Teagan laughed and her eyes teared.

"You're coming back—soon?" Grace guessed.

"Yes. I'm coming back for next semester."

"Great," Grace said.

"Great," Teagan said.

The silence was awkward. "I'll see you soon, I guess," Teagan said.

"Call me when you're back in town."

"I will." A mop fell sideways and hit Teagan on the head. She made a noise.

"What's that?" Grace said.

Teagan said, "Mop."

THREE

Ian (Obsidian)

The horse comforted her. She stood in front of him and used the soft brush on his face. She put her nose right up to his big velvet nostril and exchanged breath with him. She pushed the stiff brush over his hair, making it glossy. She lay her cheek against his warm neck and felt the wire hair of his mane. His impatience kept her moving and working. If she lingered too long, leaning on his round side so that she could feel his big ribs lift with his breath, he stepped away from her, or tossed his head, or sometimes stamped a hoof. She cuddled him needlessly anyway, wrapping her arms around his broad neck to hug him until he tried to shake her off. When he was really annoyed, he tried to nip her.

She got to work, checking his hooves, untangling knots in his long tail, pushing dust off his back with the brush, breaking up dried mud on his shoulder with a currycomb. When she fit the bridle on his head, she made sure that each strap of leather lay flat, that the skin around his ears wasn't pinched and that the browband settled in a way that wouldn't pull his mane. She slid the saddle into place so that his hair wouldn't be rubbed the wrong direction. When the girth was cinched she picked up each front hoof in turn and stretched the leg so that the loose skin of his armpit wouldn't pinch. If the tack fit comfortably, then he would go better. She led him into the yard and cinched the girth one more time once she was in the saddle. She liked to start out with a loose rein, letting him walk out and stretch his legs and long neck, before she gradually began to gather him, taking more weight in her hands through the reins, fitting her calf tightly against his side, until they were one total package so that she followed his movement and he responded to the signals she gave him, as if they spoke to each other.

On the Bit

Now that she was home, Teagan started training with Hope again. Hope suggested that Teagan prepare for a combined training event and found one that offered dressage and cross-country. Teagan agreed to enter. She would not miss the third phase, stadium jumping. She felt she could do without jumping in an arena altogether. It was technical and she didn't have the horse for it. Ian was used to taking jumps at stride, launching himself in a long arc over a wooden coop. In foxhunting, jumping was a means of getting from one field to another. The setting-up that jumping in an arena required, the way a horse needed to carefully balance in order to make a tight turn and jump within a limited number of strides, made Teagan anxious. She worried that she would make a mistake. Jumping in the ring meant it was her job to ride technically, to be aware of her next move so that she could help Ian set up for each jump. She hated

hearing his hooves knock against a pole when they didn't jump
well. The sound was louder than the stroke of a hammer. In the
hunt field, Ian never made that kind of mistake.

Riding in the woods, Ian was always eager, but Teagan knew
that he wouldn't make the same effort in the ring. The difference was obvious. Riding out, Ian felt light and powerful, as
though the reins she held connected her to a perfectly tuned
engine. In the ring, Ian could feel so slow and clumsy it was
as though he had forgotten how to walk. Teagan had to keep
pushing him forward, and sometimes he would even stumble, as
if he was dragging his feet, which she guessed he probably was.
She knew that the moment she turned him toward the gate, his
head would lift. In the field he would move forward so readily
that Teagan's work became to hold him back instead of push
him forward.

In the lessons with Hope, they focused on dressage, because
Teagan and Ian needed more practice in it than in cross-country.
Teagan knew that if Ian could choose his own horse life, he
would not mess with dressage, but she had begun to appreciate
the focused work. For all of Ian's resistance, she noticed that,
through practicing dressage, he had become more flexible, and
stronger on his left side. He had always favored his right side
because he was stronger to that side.

Dressage built Teagan's strength, too, and taught her to be
a quieter rider. The biggest challenge for Teagan and Ian was
learning how to collect. Hope had offered the metaphor of a
tightly coiled spring. She also talked about putting a horse in an
imaginary box that traveled around him as he moved. *Don't let
him run out the front, or fall out the back,* she would say. Teagan
could hear Hope's voice in her own mind, and although now

Teagan knew how to do the work, actually doing it was the hard part.

"We'll work a little bit, and then maybe we'll head out," Teagan said aloud to Ian, scratching his mane, because she wanted to head out, too. Ian made no change in his unenthusiastic plodding along the fence line. "C'mon now, you can do this," she said aloud, but she thought, Even if you don't want to. She pressed her lower legs into his sides. His head lifted and he responded for a moment, but she could feel him immediately falling behind again, as though his long torso was slipping backward behind the position of her leg. "No you don't," she said, encouraging herself, and she shifted her leg back and tried to gather him again. Ian picked up his momentum only a little so Teagan didn't have to work quite as hard to keep him going. All of this work and we're only at the walk, Teagan thought.

She wasn't strong enough to make her riding look effortless, though the goal in dressage was that the rider should appear to move very little. The movements of her hands, the use of her legs and back should be an unobservable conversation between her and her horse. It took so much effort to get Ian into proper form, her problem was that, once he was collected, moving the way he was supposed to move in dressage, or close enough, she couldn't always summon the endurance to keep him there.

When they moved together in the way they should, she had to carry the weight of his motion in her back and arms. When Ian was on the bit, which meant his neck appeared slightly arched, he was light in his steps, his powerful hind muscles were engaged, and it was as though each step carried him into the air as well as forward. He balanced between his front and back ends and didn't favor one side or the other. It took strength to maintain, and Teagan needed to be strong to keep him that way.

Hope explained to Teagan that she might carry ten to twenty pounds of pressure in her hands as she held Ian in proper form. Now, after twenty minutes of work, Ian was starting to be more engaged, and Teagan prepared to set herself against the burning in her muscles that she knew would start. It would have been difficult for her to explain to someone watching how much work she was doing, steadily supporting the weight of her horse's momentum with her own body.

Her eyes trained on a point traveling slightly ahead of them. For a matter of moments, they accomplished it and moved beautifully. Ian crossed lightly over the ground and they seemed to float. Teagan was quickly exhausted, and the relief she knew she'd feel if she let Ian abandon the work won over her wilting determination to keep on. The reins slipped in her fingers and she relaxed her back, and Ian was released. He had been going at the trot, and he quickly fell into the walk, as though Teagan had shifted from fourth gear to first, entirely skipping second and third.

She let out a breath of exhaustion, kicked out of her stirrups, and dropped the reins. She tipped her chin to the sky and reached her arms over her head, stretching. She knew they should keep working, but the shade of the woods was too tempting, and Ian's immediate switch in attitude was too joyful to ignore. Past the gate she pointed him toward the woods, and suddenly she was a lightweight passenger carried by an energetic horse who flowed forward across the field like a tide that had no ebb.

Sift

The rain made the cardboard smell even more like cardboard. The container for glass stunk with an old sweetness from soda bottles and yeast from beer bottles. The steps to the metal box were made of steel in an open weave to let water through. When the back of my car was empty, I felt damp and hungry, even though I hadn't been outside long. As I was pulling away from the recycling center, my favorite bakery came to mind like a vision.

Sift sat on a corner. I circled the block to look for street parking. I almost closed my eyes and wished as I walked in the door, and I saw they were there, the almond macaroons. There wasn't a huge pile. Other people had been buying them, but there were enough. I asked for three. I knew that if I bit into one I would eat them all, so I waited. I wanted to sit down and enjoy my little feast.

Outside the rain had calmed to a drizzle, but there was a rivulet along the curb. I walked to my car. Macaroons were a discovery for me. I did not eat them as a child.

A woman pushed a double stroller toward me. By the time she was near, I realized I should step aside because there was a low place in the uneven sidewalk where a large puddle had formed, and one end of it looked too deep to want to walk through. She was at the puddle when I crossed through the shallow end and stood by a building so that she could have an easier path.

"You didn't have to do that," she said and smiled, and directed the stroller around. I could see that the infants were the same age. Twins. I wanted to ask her which one was born first. The wheels of the stroller cut through the edge of the puddle, and there was enough water that they sent ripples to the deeper end. I watched the puddle until the surface was smooth again. A person stepped in the edge, and the surface broke again, and re-formed. The rain had stopped. The puddle wouldn't last, but it was big enough to seem a surprise. I thought of a larger puddle, an obstacle, that I once rode Ian through. There was a low wall purposely constructed so that horse and rider had to drop into water and go through, then over a little wall on the other side. As happens to me sometimes, for a moment I felt I deeply missed the horse. I was broken and then smoothed myself again.

Ponying

The day was going to be hot, but it felt less humid. Teagan didn't wake up feeling groggy like she did when the humidity was high and her room baked in the early sun. She quickly went downstairs.

"Where's Mom?" Teagan asked.

"Vermont," Charlie said.

"When did she leave?"

"Yesterday afternoon," Charlie said, looking at her and eating toast.

"Oh, right," Teagan said, but really she'd forgotten that her mom had planned the trip.

That meant she was visiting the nieces and would see her sister. Susanna and her sister hadn't kept in close touch. Teagan saw her aunt only every few years. It seemed that all of a sudden Susanna wanted to visit her. Charlie was packing up to go back to college. Teagan was supposed to get through a lot of summer reading to catch up with her class for sophomore year. There was also an optional paper. She didn't know why it was optional, so she decided to option out. She'd read a few pages of *The Scarlet Letter* and then left it on the floor of her room. It was boring.

Charlie finished his toast, took a swig of a soda, and then hefted a huge green duffel bag, a giant limp slug, onto his shoulder and carried it out to his car. He was moving to a shared house in town with some college friends. Teagan realized she hadn't been aware that he was leaving so soon.

He walked back in and took out a brown leather wallet, opened it, and handed some twenty-dollar bills to Teagan. She took them but didn't know why he was giving them to her.

"When are you leaving?" she asked.

"Tomorrow afternoon. I have to pick up keys at three."

Teagan neatened the bills in her hands.

"But I'll come back to say hi. I'm not far." Charlie smiled.

"What's the money for?"

"Food. It's from Mom. Don't spend it all at once," Charlie said.

"I can't drive," Teagan said.

"Then don't eat all of the food at once," Charlie said.

He smiled but Teagan didn't.

"Mom'll be back next week. If you need anything call Grace's mom."

"Call Grace's mom? Shouldn't I call you?" Teagan said.

"No. I'm busy," Charlie said. "You'll be fine. I'm going to go drop some stuff at Nick's. I'll bring back supper. What do you want?"

"I don't know," Teagan said.

"I'll get pizza," he said. He shut the kitchen door behind him.

Through the window she watched his car until it was out of the driveway. She was still holding the bills. She shoved them in a drawer and in ten minutes was dressed to go riding. Charlie had told her that she wasn't allowed to ride by herself while Susanna was away. Teagan had said nothing, which was her way of saying that she would ride anyway.

Her plan was to just give Ian a little exercise, working him in a forty-meter circle in the field, like she had at Hunting Hill, but Duchess came to the fence with him, as if she wasn't going to let him out of her sight, so Teagan opened the gate for them both, and the mare followed. Teagan brushed Ian, breathing in his familiar scent, stopping to lay her face against his smooth neck. He tossed his head a little. She finished grooming. She briefly went over Duchess, checking her hooves, which were clean because the ground was dry. She was not planning on saddling the mare.

Teagan took both horses off Blue View Farm, down a dirt road into a piece of woods she was pretty sure Susanna had permission to ride in. A lead rope trailed from Teagan's hand, and Ian didn't seem to mind having Duchess's head at his rump. She wore only a nylon halter. When the trail in the woods widened Teagan pushed Ian into a trot. Duchess started a step or two late and the rope jerked in Teagan's hand, but she closed her fingers. Ian, maybe because Duchess was so close behind him, began to canter, and, trying to keep hold of Duchess's rope and the reins of her own horse, Teagan couldn't get organized to slow him down, so she let him keep going, holding him at an even pace, and Duchess, cantering, caught up so that the horses were side by side. Teagan looked at the mare, bare but for the halter, keeping pace, and smiled. She reached out and briefly stroked the mare's mane. Teagan stood a little over the saddle, off Ian's back, and he kept his even, smooth, and steady stride.

The trail hadn't been maintained and was hemmed with weeds and branches on the sides. Teagan let Duchess's rope slide through her palm and the mare fell in behind Ian. The lead rope wasn't meant for ponying and wasn't very long, but Teagan clutched a bight of rope in her hand, trying to keep it from snaking out of her grip. A tree trunk, laid down across the trail for a low jump, was ahead. Teagan just sat, letting the horses decide. Ian hopped over it, and there was no tension in the lead rope as Duchess found her spot and hopped over, too.

After the low jump Teagan felt able to sit heavy on Ian's back and slow him to a trot, and then a walk. She breathed deeply. Her arms were tight with adrenaline. She'd never ponied before, and she knew it wasn't exactly safe, taking two horses on the trail, and letting them canter, and letting them jump, especially because no one knew that she was in the woods.

The horses were excited, moving in a herd of two, and their walk was brisk, and Ian kept trying to move forward into a trot; if she let him trot he tried to canter. The trail opened into a clearing. The clearing rose to a hill, and at the top, to Teagan's surprise, sat a perfectly fine coop, its weathered wood frame in good condition. The open field, and the hill, the horses running together, and the light control Teagan had of their heads; Ian took off, his powerful hindquarters propelling him up the hill, and all Teagan could do was try to hold him steady.

She hauled on Duchess's rope and felt the mare make an effort, and then Duchess was neck to neck with Ian. Teagan held both Ian's reins in one hand, and Duchess's taut rope in the other. Rising in the stirrups, her leg muscles burning, holding both the horses' heads in her hands, Teagan felt she was steering a double team, driving them like she was in a chariot.

A thrill went through her when she saw Ian's ears flick forward to the coop, and she felt him shift his weight and prepare to spring from the ground. She pressed her calves against his sides to support the leap, and to hold on, and because she had no other choice; the horses matched themselves, stride for stride; one carried a rider, and one did not, and they leapt in unison and landed beautifully, galloping on the other side of the coop.

Teagan held on, held steady, and at the bottom of the hill she was able to slow them both to the walk. Glad to be upright and whole, she slapped Ian's neck in a series of pats, good boy. She reached over and hooked Duchess's neck with her arm, pulling the mare close, giving her hard pats, ruffling the mane, "That a girl," Teagan praised her, and she didn't even like the mare that much. Seeming satisfied, the horses walked side by side the rest of the way back to the barn.

Afternoon

Teagan stomped into the kitchen, wearing her riding boots and one of the T-shirts she wore for the dust and horse-slobber atmosphere of the barn. She had an apple between her teeth and some carrots in a bag. One snack for herself, and one for Ian.

Charlie was on the phone. Teagan heard him say, "Okay."

He looked at her. "What are you doing?"

Teagan danced on a booted foot. "Going riding. Later, alligator."

Charlie didn't say, "After a while, crocodile." Instead he said, "Dad's coming to get us."

Teagan stood, surprised. She took a bite of apple and decided she wasn't going to go.

"He's taking us to lunch. You better hurry up and change," Charlie said.

"When did this happen?" Teagan asked.

"He called. Just now," Charlie said.

Teagan wanted to throw her apple at Charlie's head. Why did he always do whatever their father told him? In her own mind she was already walking out of the kitchen, to the barn, to her familiar routine where her hands would move through their rote tasks, and in a matter of minutes she and Ian would be heading toward a patch of woods, surrounded by things that rustled or sang or held still, and Ian would take her wherever she asked him.

"I'm not going," Teagan said.

Charlie stood still. "You have to."

Teagan stood, too. Two statues in the kitchen, with completely different sentient thoughts. Charlie softened his voice, cajoling. "Just do this."

Teagan shook her head. She felt that if she spoke, they would keep arguing, so she walked up to her room and sat on the bed, looking out of the window to where she could see Ian's dark shape in the field. The day was good for riding. Teagan vaguely considered how her father came and went, but how her horse was always there, in the field.

From the sounds in the hallway, Teagan imagined Charlie standing by the front door, good soldier that he was, good son. She thought she could hear the gravel crunch under the wheels of the car. She felt she knew what was said in a brief, quiet conversation at the front door, and then Charlie was going, walking to the car and sitting down on the seat.

Teagan wasn't sure if she had won or lost. Then she could hear the car engine, and the fade of it down the driveway. Then she cried, picturing Charlie sitting in the car by himself.

Closet

Susanna was away and the house was empty. Teagan didn't feel like calling anyone, not even Grace. Barker and Max were in the living room, lying in the sun. Teagan hadn't done any of her summer reading, and she had slept on the couch in the living room, again, while the dogs slept on the floor.

Teagan's own bed felt unfriendly to her. She wasn't sleeping well, maybe because she was used to having a roommate. She missed Julie but hadn't tried to call her, and hadn't written even though she'd promised she would. For something to do, she tried making coffee, remembering how she thought Susanna did it. She didn't like it and mixed some with milk and chocolate syrup, and that was a little better. There was less food in the house than she was used to, so she made herself a peanut butter and jelly sandwich for breakfast. She made a peanut butter and honey sandwich for lunch. She thought about drinking the beer she found but for no particular reason decided not to.

In a wandering mood, Teagan found herself standing in front of Susanna's bedroom door, as if her mother were telling Teagan she could come in. Teagan thought how it wasn't her parents' bedroom door anymore, it was just her mother's. She went inside, looking around as if discovering it. The bedspread was new. She looked at the things on her mother's dressing table but didn't touch anything. Her father's dresser was there. She thought of it as her father's. Teagan pulled out the drawers but saw Susanna's clothes in them. She opened the closet. Susanna's familiar skirts swung from the suck of air the door made. Teagan ran her hand across a row of hanging shirts, like stroking a horse's neck. The shirts were silky and soft until the end of the row, when her hand rested on a flannel sleeve.

Doughnuts

"Y'all drink coffee now?" Teagan watched Caroline and Grace dumping more sugar into their tall Styrofoam cups of light coffee, which they'd ordered with cream and sugar already added.

"This is what we do now. If you were here, ever, you'd know," Caroline said.

"And we don't say *y'all*, either. *Y'all* isn't a word," Grace said.

"Y'all say *y'all*," Teagan said.

Caroline shook her head slowly at Teagan. "I'll get seats."

The doughnut shop was practically empty. It was four in the afternoon. Teagan sat next to Grace across from Caroline. She sipped her sugary coffee. It was good. The sweet hit her like a drug, and she grinned. Caroline grinned back. They picked up their doughnuts and bit. The cream in Teagan's Boston cream mingled with the sweet dough and chocolate layer of icing, and for a moment she was completely happy. Everything around her seemed ordinary and comfortable, even the way Caroline delicately held her powdered doughnut, barely dusting her fingertips in the white sugar, and Grace purposefully put down her half-eaten chocolate-covered chocolate on the white napkin while she sipped her coffee, prolonging her pleasure.

"This is genius," Teagan finally said.

Grace widened her eyes and nodded. When they'd consumed all of the doughnuts, there was another little silence, and they sat as if grieving that the feast had ended, as if there were no more doughnuts to be had, even though the air was thick with the smell of frying dough. The two-part tone of the door's bell and the cash register's clink-chunk, made a tune.

Grace gave Teagan a look, but Teagan couldn't tell what it meant.

"So, how was y'all's year?" Teagan asked.

"Not very memorable. You know, it's school," Grace said.

"Nothing exciting?" Teagan asked.

"The seniors won Spirit Week. Big surprise," Caroline said.

"Oh, right. I forgot about Spirit Week. What was their theme?"

"Something to do with *Grease*. There were a lot of poodle skirts," Caroline said.

"Oh, the movie *Grease*. I've never seen it."

"It was pretty unrecognizable. They tried some plotline having to do with the basketball team; it didn't make any sense."

"What did our class do?"

"I wasn't part of it," Caroline said.

"Me either," Grace said.

"But what was the theme?" Teagan asked.

Caroline said, "Grace and I were on a committee that won the vote for doing our own version of *Spinal Tap,* but Mrs. Rackley said she would have to act as censor for the lyrics."

Teagan asked, "Who's Mrs. Rackley?"

"Our principal?"

"Oh, right," Teagan said.

"So then the theme was switched to a parody of *Cinderella,* but it wasn't good. It was mostly the field hockey team doing something incomprehensible with their sticks."

"They wore ball gowns," Grace said.

"That sounds dumb," Teagan said.

Grace nodded and sipped her coffee.

Caroline was looking closely at Teagan again. "Is that your dad's shirt?" she asked.

"What?"

"Your shirt. Is it your dad's?"

"It looks like it's your dad's shirt," Grace added.

Teagan was wearing a blue plaid flannel shirt, too big for her, unbuttoned and with the sleeves rolled up, over a tank top. She startled a little. "Yes. It's his. He left it."

Caroline glanced at Teagan and then met eyes with Grace.

Grace looked under the table and said, "Are you wearing his shoes, too?"

Teagan was. They were an old pair of worn leather penny loafers, too big for her; she was wearing two pairs of thick socks.

"They're comfortable." She began rotating her Styrofoam cup of coffee on the tabletop.

"And is that his belt?" Grace asked.

Caroline leaned forward over the table and looked at the wide leather belt in the belt loops of Teagan's cutoff jean shorts.

Teagan said, "Yes."

Cookies

In my apartment I put all three beautiful macaroons on a plate. I carried the plate to the couch and sat on one end, facing the window, and tucked my feet, and bit into the first cookie. It was chewy and soft and the smell and taste of sugar and almonds filled my nose and mouth. I had dived into sweetness. The delight of eating cookies lightened the thought that I did not have anything else to get rid of. Something was over and done with, but I was reaching for the second macaroon and smelling it and eating it; there was comfort that I wanted, and I wondered if it was because of the thought I had of Ian. And when I think of the horse I am twinned in a thought of my father, who rarely saw me ride the horse. I finished the second macaroon and was glad to have the third. I placed it on my open palm and held it so that it was framed in the light of the window. I wanted to admire it for a moment before I consumed it.

Skeet

She lived here, didn't she? She didn't see why she shouldn't go, too. It wasn't until they were all in the field that Teagan realized she had invited herself along on Charlie and Jenny's date. She'd been too interested in the guns to notice that, half an hour previously. Teagan rode in the bed of the truck with the guns. They were in long canvas sleeves, two of them. Charlie drove through the field, down the gully and up, with Jenny in the cab beside him, and Teagan looked at the guns, sleeping in their sacks.

He'd already set up the trap. It was an army-green-color skeletal thing with a seat bolted on. She stood aside, watched Charlie unsheathe a 12-gauge and a .22 shotgun.

"What's the difference?" Jenny was almost hopping with nervous energy.

Charlie laid a hand on the first gun. "The twelve is heavier. You'll probably like the twenty-two, but give them both a try."

He wasn't talking to Teagan. Jenny moved closer to the guns, and Teagan hung back and folded her arms. She scanned the woods as Charlie helped Jenny fit a leather pad to the front of her shoulder and secure it with a strap. Charlie didn't offer anything to Teagan, but he spoke to both girls when he picked up each gun in turn and showed them how to break the barrel, load the cartridges, and how to take the safety off and put it back on. "Keep it broken down until you want to shoot, and the last thing you do is take the safety off. And don't point it at me or your feet." He smiled.

Teagan felt a surge of embarrassment. It was either that the smile was especially for Jenny or that she hadn't seen her brother actually smile in some time. She realized he was happy. She wanted to walk away. She decided she didn't want to stay and shoot, but she thought she'd stay to watch them shoot one time. Charlie led Jenny to the trap to show her how it worked. Teagan lingered and looked at the guns in the bed of the truck. Charlie kept them clean and oiled. She'd forgotten he had guns. She forgot he cleaned guns. She forgot that their dad had bought him the .22. She had a vague memory of a conversation her parents had about getting Charlie a gun. She remembered something else.

Charlie looked over at Teagan. She backed up a step and raised her palms to show she wasn't touching anything. He waved her over, frowning.

Beside the trap was a big cardboard box and several little rectangle boxes. The big one was separated into six compartments, and each compartment held a stack of round disks that were black with a circle of neon orange on top of each. She had pictured something in the shape of a bird. These were the clay pigeons. The other boxes held cartridges. The 12-gauge ones were encased in yellow plastic, and the .22-gauge were smaller and encased in red plastic.

"Do we get in trouble if we shoot a horse?" Jenny said.

Charlie smiled.

Teagan frowned at him. "I put them in the barn," she said, but Jenny's attention was on Charlie.

Charlie straddled the arms of the trap and sat down. He slid a pigeon into the arm. "This will throw it up to about there." He scanned the sky and then pointed with his whole hand.

Jenny and Teagan looked up at some unidentified point in the distant sky.

"I can adjust the height," Charlie said. "Keep in mind that the longer you wait to pull the trigger, the farther it travels from you. And it's harder to hit on the way down. Now this spring arm will break your leg if it hits you, so don't let it hit you." He waved them back a couple steps and then pulled a string. With a violent clang of metal the arm swung and the disk became a little neon dot in the sky.

Jenny jumped up and down. "There's no way I'll hit that. I hope you brought a lot of bullets."

Charlie's voice was light. "It doesn't matter."

"Which gun belonged to Dad?" Teagan asked. She already knew that it was the double-barrel. She asked just to spoil his happiness a little, and maybe because she wanted to hear him say it.

"The twelve was Dad's. He bought me the twenty-two."

So there it was. She noted that Charlie didn't say their dad had given him the 12-gauge gun. Their dad had just left it behind.

Charlie got the guns out of the truck. He put a folded tarp on the grass and lay them on it.

"Let's see you shoot," Teagan said to him. She wanted to be friendly suddenly.

Charlie turned to Jenny and smiled a little and opened his hand to the guns.

"You first," Jenny said, laughing.

Charlie squeezed Jenny's shoulder as he walked past her. Teagan voluntarily climbed into the seat of the trap and with both hands tried to cock the sling arm. The heavy spring was too strong.

"This one slides to load," he said, and with the gun balanced over his left arm, he used his right hand to cock the gun and the bullets clicked into place. "Whoever's shooting stands out in front, and everybody else get back. And then I'll say pull, and, Teagan, you release the pigeon."

Teagan tried again to pull the arm of the trap back into place. She got it halfway and then she lost control of it and it flung back into place, spitting out a pigeon that trailed above the ground.

"Stop," Charlie said. He carefully fit the .22 into Jenny's hands and told her the safety was on. He pushed Teagan out of the seat and sat down himself and loaded a pigeon and the arm. "Don't touch it until I say pull," he said to Teagan. Charlie took the gun from Jenny, positioned her back a few strides, walked forward, held the gun up and sighted through it, then lowered it, clicked the safety off, and nodded at Teagan. With the gun sighted again, Charlie said, "Pull."

She pulled. The pigeon flew into the air and at the top of its arc exploded into pieces. Jenny clapped and Teagan had to smile at Charlie's perfect shot.

Teagan climbed off the trap and decided to walk back. "Good luck, y'all. Come back in one piece."

Fence

"How can there be a pond on a mountain?" Caroline said.

"Are ponds not allowed on mountains?" Teagan said.

"I thought you said it's a man-made pond," Grace said.

"It is," Teagan conceded.

"That's different," Caroline said.

"A pond can still be on a mountain," Teagan said.

"I think we usually think of ponds at low points in a terrain," Grace said.

"Yes, but, gravity," Teagan said.

"Gravity is real," Caroline said.

"I'm not arguing against gravity," Grace said.

"Good, because gravity would be mad at you," Caroline said.

They were walking across a neighboring farm. Teagan wasn't even sure who owned it, but she knew that the pond was there because she'd seen it when she had been riding on the trails. Susanna had permission to ride on the land, and Teagan knew that walking to the pond and swimming in it were not necessarily permitted by whatever agreement Susanna had with the owners, but she didn't worry about it. She'd never seen anyone the other times she'd walked to the pond.

Teagan had suggested the swim, and Grace and Caroline had agreed because it was so hot and the pond was in the woods, which would feel cooler. Plus, hiking to the pond just sounded like a nice idea. As they were walking, Teagan was trying to remember what Susanna had told her. There was something Susanna had said about the farm. Teagan couldn't remember if it had something to do with maybe leaving a gate closed, or open, or if one of the fields had been planted and they should trace the edge of it instead of walking across the middle. She figured it would be obvious to her if they came across something that was different from before.

They came to a gate that was secured with a chain wrapped three times around the post. It had a metal clip to secure it but no lock. Teagan unwrapped the chain, paying attention to the way it was fastened, and after they were through the gate she carefully repeated the wrap around the post and pulled the excess chain tight and clipped it to itself again. She thought it was unnecessary. No farm animal could open even a loosely wrapped chain, especially one clipped to itself.

They started across the field, which did not look recently planted. It didn't even look mowed, and Teagan didn't see any animals at all in the field.

"Do you know who owns this?" Grace asked.

"No. My mom does."

"Should I ask if we have permission to be here?" Caroline asked.

"I don't think we're not allowed to be here," Grace said.

"Not the same thing," Caroline said.

"Where's the pond?" Grace asked.

Teagan pointed straight ahead into the woods. "That way."

"How far is it?" Caroline asked.

"Not far," Teagan said.

She didn't know exactly where the pond was, or how far into the woods it was. She couldn't have described the way. She just knew that if she went through the gate they had just gone through and walked more or less straight across the field from the gate, there would be a wooden-plank footbridge over a muddy stream, and across that a path into the woods, and then if she followed the path, the pond showed up to her right, eventually. That was the way to the pond. It was always the same.

"Is this a gross, slimy pond?" Caroline said.

"No. Would I walk us all this way for a slimy pond? It's good swimming," Teagan said.

"You've been in it before?" Grace said.

"A few times," Teagan said. "I mean, there are frogs, but I haven't seen any snapping turtles."

"Snapping turtles?" Caroline said.

"I haven't seen any," Teagan said.

"And should I ask why they are called *snapping* turtles?" Caroline said.

"They snap," Teagan said, clapping her hands at Caroline.

"And they can take off a toe," Grace said.

"What?" Caroline said.

"I have all of my toes," Teagan said.

"I have ten toes," Grace said.

"Right now you have all of your toes, but wait until an evil turtle eats one," Caroline said.

Teagan stopped walking. The triple chain on the gate suddenly meant something to her. Susanna had told her not to cut across the field. Teagan didn't even know how Susanna knew that she sometimes did walk across the field, so she hadn't paid much attention to her mother. Grace and Caroline didn't notice that Teagan had stopped. Teagan looked all around the field. She didn't see anything, but the land dropped down on the far side.

"I forgot something," Teagan called out to Grace and Caroline.

They turned around to look at her.

"You want to go back?" Grace said.

"No. I forgot to tell you something. I just remembered."

"Is it bad?" Caroline asked.

"It's not good. I just remembered that Mom said there's a bull in this field."

"Now you tell us?" Caroline said.

Grace was scanning the field as Teagan had done.

"Is it true that a bull will chase you if you're on your period?" Grace said.

"I've heard that," Caroline said. "I've heard that they can smell you."

"Because I'm on my period," Grace said.

They stood for a moment, tense, looking around.

Teagan said, "Let's run for it."

The opposite side of the field and the fence were visible. They ran. As she was running Teagan started to feel scared, as if the bull was going to charge over the rise in the field at any moment and catch up to them. The only thing they could do was outrun it. Teagan had been behind Grace and Caroline, but she caught up to them and passed them, shouting as she went, because she had just remembered, too, that there was an electrified wire running along the top fence board. She shouted out not to touch the wire, and she slowed just a moment to plant her palms flat on top of the board so she wouldn't touch it, and she pushed off the lower boards and leapt over, not touching the wire with her leg either.

Beside her Grace was doing a similar climb, avoiding the wire. As she landed on the sloped ground, Teagan fell and rolled over and heard Caroline scream. Teagan looked up, expecting to see the bull, and expecting to see Caroline on the ground with them, having just escaped the bull, but Caroline was on the ground on the other side of the fence. Caroline screamed again.

Teagan looked around, but there was still no bull. Caroline screamed again and Teagan paid attention to her words.

"You didn't say it was an electric fence!"

"I said it while we were running," Teagan said.

"Are you okay?" Grace asked Caroline.

"No, I'm not okay. I just got electrocuted," Caroline yelled.

"Get out of the field," Teagan said to her.

"I was trying to," Caroline said.

"I'll help you," Grace said, carefully climbing over again.

"I am not touching that fence again. Where's the gate?"

"It's back across the field," Teagan said.

Caroline was on her feet. "No, where is the other gate. The one to let me out."

"I don't know. I don't think there is one," Teagan said.

"This is stupid," Caroline said.

"Like this," Grace said, and she demonstrated to Caroline how to plant her palms and press on them so that she didn't have to grab the wire, and then she showed how to get good leverage off the bottom planks to jump over.

"I think that Teagan has to get shocked, since she didn't warn me about the fence," Caroline said.

"What?" Teagan said.

"It's only fair," Caroline said.

"I told you about it," Teagan yelled.

"I couldn't hear you while I was running from a bull," Caroline said.

"That's not my fault. How about the fact that I didn't want you to get gored by a bull?"

"How about the fact that you didn't remember the bull until we were already in the field?" Caroline said.

"Is that the bull?" Grace asked.

A square, ruddy brown cow with horns had appeared on the ridge of the hill.

"That's the bull," Teagan said.

"Touch the fence," Caroline said.

"Caroline, come on," Teagan said.

"Come on," Grace said, too.

"Touch the fence, Teagan," Caroline said. She and Grace were still in the field.

"What, you're going to sacrifice Grace if I don't shock myself?" Teagan yelled.

Grace pulled Caroline's arm. "Come on."

Caroline yanked her arm out of Grace's hand. "I'm not moving until Teagan touches the fence."

Teagan looked at the bull. She couldn't tell if it had come closer. "Okay, fine. If you get out of the field first," she said.

Caroline stood still and glared at Teagan.

Teagan said, "Grace, get out of the field."

"Caroline, come on!" Grace said, putting a foot on the fence and motioning Caroline to her.

"Touch the fence!" Caroline yelled.

The bull was wandering in their direction.

Teagan slammed her palm against the wire and there was an audible sound like a *clunk* and Teagan screamed and fell down. Grace and Caroline climbed over the fence. Teagan rolled over and then pushed herself to her feet. They all looked back at the bull. It was still moving toward them, trotting a little, then stopping to stare at them. Grace took off running across the foot-bridge and without a word Caroline and Teagan ran after her.

On the narrow trail in the woods they all kept running. Grace was first, then Caroline and then Teagan. Caroline turned her head and smiled a conqueror's smile at Teagan. Teagan grimaced back and hopped over some rocks to the side of Caroline and sprinted up to Grace and then passed her. When Teagan saw the water, she didn't stop but ran straight into it. Grace's splash followed. Caroline stopped to take off her shoes.

Jonquil (Narcissus)

Teagan saw that Susanna was digging. Green rubber clogs, brown socks pulled up, shorts, a pink sleeveless shirt, gardening gloves, and a straw sunhat.

"What are those?" Teagan asked, looking at a bag of brown spheres.

"Daffodils."

"Isn't it late in the season, or something?" Teagan asked.

"You can put bulbs in the ground anytime," Susanna said.

Teagan stood and watched her. With a serrated trowel she stabbed the ground, lifted and set aside a clump of earth. She pushed a papery orb into the hole and blessed it with a handful of black compost, then fit the clump of earth back on, like a lid. She marked the spot with more compost, patting it. She moved in a rhythm, stab and lift, a ritual of dirt. Teagan looked to where she had started. A dotted line of compost mounds ran along the edge of the yard, the last just beside Susanna's left hand. Stab, lift, inter, mark.

Teagan asked, "How many are you planting?"

Susanna answered by pointing with the trowel along the smooth unturned edge of the yard. There would be a fence of flowers. The bulbs would wait beneath the ground.

"Won't it be pretty?" Susanna said.

"It will be a lot of the same thing, over and over," Teagan said, suddenly feeling inexplicably angry. She walked to the house, then looked back her mother, who kept on kneeling and digging.

Robert's Visit

Teagan was home alone when she heard her father's voice in the hallway downstairs. She'd been reading on her bed. She stopped reading to listen. She heard her father's voice call for her and Charlie.

"Dad?" she yelled.

"Teagan," Robert yelled up the stairs.

Teagan rolled off her bed and went to the head of the stairs, where she saw her father standing on the bottom step, looking up at her.

"Teagan, come down and give your dad a hug," Robert said.

Teagan walked down the stairs and awkwardly hugged her father. "What are you doing here?"

"I was in the neighborhood and I wanted to see what my kids were up to," Robert said.

"Charlie isn't here."

"Is your mom here?"

"No. I think she's at the store. I think she's running errands." Teagan couldn't remember where her mother had gone.

"Just the two of us," Robert said.

Teagan didn't know what to say. She felt that her father shouldn't be in the house without her mother, but she also didn't feel she could ask him to leave. "Do you want to go get lunch? I mean, together," Teagan said. She thought that maybe she could get him to go somewhere with her, and then when Susanna got home, she could say that her dad had stopped by to take her to lunch. That seemed easy enough. But she was surprised when Robert suggested they make lunch instead.

"Your mom keeps a well-stocked fridge. I'm sure there's plenty of things to make lunch." Robert walked through the house to the kitchen.

Teagan followed him. "I don't know. I haven't looked," she said. She opened the refrigerator and stared into it. Nothing in it registered as food to her. She picked up a bottle of mustard and turned around to see her father looking in the pantry.

"Here we go," he said, bringing out a bag of potato chips and a plastic bag of sliced bread. He held them out to Teagan.

She took them and he squeezed her shoulder as he brushed past her and looked into the refrigerator. He brought out a beer and helped himself to a glass from the cupboard. "Want one?"

"No, thanks," Teagan said, surprised that he really seemed to be offering and not joking.

"Your mom leaves you home and trusts you not to drink all the beer?" He laughed.

"I guess so," Teagan laughed, too, but she didn't see what was funny.

"You make us some sandwiches. Cheese and mustard. I'll take whatever else you find."

"What are you going to do?"

"Your mom left me a folder. Did she tell you?"

"No," Teagan said.

"Well, she probably left it in a drawer in the living room or maybe on her dresser. I'm going to look for it. You make us those sandwiches, okay? Then we'll eat together."

"Okay," Teagan said.

She watched her father walk through the house and she called out, "Mom might be home soon, and then you can ask her where it is."

"That's okay. I'll find it," Robert called back.

Teagan realized she had the bag of potato chips in her hand. She thrust it onto the kitchen counter and hauled open the refrigerator and pulled out a plastic drawer. She wanted to get the food made quickly and call her father back. She found cheese and something wrapped in butcher paper that turned out to be turkey. She gave it a quick sniff and it seemed fine. She tossed slices of bread onto the counter and squeezed mustard onto them. "Dad!" she called out. She globbed a hunk of turkey onto each sandwich and pressed the second slice of bread down. "Food's ready!" Teagan yelled. There was no answer. She walked into the middle of the house and called out, "Dad?"

"In a minute," she heard Robert call back.

"Dad, the sandwiches are ready. Can you come eat?" Teagan yelled.

"Just a minute, Teagan," her father yelled back, in a tone she had not heard in a while.

Teagan stood in the hallway. The authority in her father's voice caught her off guard. He hadn't spoken to her that way in many months. It occurred to her that he hadn't spoken to her very much at all. She felt annoyed. She walked to the hallway door and pushed it farther open. "Dad," she said. There was no response, and Teagan suddenly felt that she didn't care what he was doing. It wasn't any of her business. She walked back to the kitchen and put the unappetizing sandwiches on plates.

When she turned around, her father had a small cardboard box in his hands. "Just going to put this in my car. Right back," he said.

Teagan stood still in the kitchen and listened to the front door open and close. Then she listened to it open again. Teagan carried the plates to the table. She got glasses out of the cupboard and filled them with water. She knew her dad would want ice in his but she didn't put any in. She put a stack of paper napkins in the middle of the table.

"That looks great," Robert said with enthusiasm.

"Did you find what you were looking for?" Teagan asked.

"I did."

Robert and Teagan looked at each other. Teagan knew that neither of them wanted to eat the sandwiches. She didn't know why her father was standing in front of her in her mother's house. She realized, too late, that she should not have let him in, and she realized he had let himself in.

"I miss you, baby girl," Robert said.

Teagan said, "Thanks."

"Come here," Robert said.

Teagan felt like the wind was knocked out of her when her father pulled her tight against his chest. One arm was wrapped tightly around her shoulders, almost around her neck, and Robert was pressing his other hand hard against her, rubbing her back in wide circles.

"Dad," Teagan said, turning her head and trying to push

away with her hands, but he was too big and he held her too tightly. Out of one square of the windowpane she saw Susanna standing in the driveway, her purse on her shoulder, looking at Robert's car.

"Mom's home," Teagan managed to say.

Robert released her, smiling wide and holding her by the shoulders. He pulled her to him again and kissed her on the side of her mouth. "I love you, Teagan girl." He walked to the front door.

Teagan heard a few words exchanged between Susanna and Robert. She wiped her mouth with her forearm and pulled her shirt straight and took a few steps backward.

Susanna walked into the kitchen. "You don't have to let him come in when I'm not here" was all she said, in a soft voice.

Teagan looked at her mother's back as Susanna began putting the bread and mustard away.

Combined Training

The alarm went off at five o'clock and Teagan immediately went into the bathroom and splashed cold water on her face, as she coached herself to do on show days. She was not fully awake, but she was out of bed. She pulled on shorts and a T-shirt and shoved her bare feet into tennis shoes. Her next job was to walk straight out the door to the barn without lingering in the kitchen or stopping to get anything to eat. She knew that if she did, precious minutes would go by. She did drink a glass of water. Barker and Max happily ran past her in the yard, excited by the early-morning sounds and smells that they usually didn't have a chance to explore.

Teagan sleepily watched as Max plunged straight into a bush after some scent or small animal. Her steps felt wobbly, as if she was walking in a dream. She opened the gate instead of climbing over. She held the gate open for Barker, but Max crawled under the fence just beside the opened gate. The smell of the barn made Teagan more alert. She picked up Ian's halter and rope and went into his stall. He was still sleeping, his head hanging down. He blinked a little when she ran a hand over his neck. She walked him outside and around the driveway a couple times to get the stiffness out of his legs. On the second lap he stopped, raised his head, and flicked his ears toward the field. He snorted and took a sideways step that Teagan had to avoid, and he stopped and stared again, and snorted again. Teagan couldn't see what it was he was seeing, or maybe he could only smell it. She figured it was deer in the field. She waited until Ian stopped staring. He gave another snort, this one as though he was over whatever it was, and he put his head down to rip up some grass.

She patted his neck and led him into the barn. He was clean from a bath the day before, so she brushed him quickly and checked the braids in his mane. Only the last two had come out. She braided those again and stuffed the small black rubber bands in the pocket of her shorts and began folding each braid and securing it with a rubber band. She worked quickly. She braided his forelock and folded it as well. The braids were just for dressage. After all of the work of braiding, she would rip off the rubber bands and loosen his mane when it was time to ride the cross-country course.

She filled his grain bucket, shoving a quick handful under his nose as she passed so he wouldn't be too impatient. She broke off four flakes of hay and shook them to loosen them, then shoved them in his hay rack. She filled his water bucket to the brim, because she wanted him to drink, and she led him back into his stall, where he immediately plunged his head into the grain bucket.

Teagan checked her grooming box and added the hoof paint, some rags, and the Vetrolin, which advertised itself as an "invigorating liniment" on the handled jug. She always rubbed Ian down with it after he had worked hard. It was an emerald green when she poured it into a bucket of water and it made her hands feel good. Sometimes she rubbed some on her own arms and legs.

She placed the grooming box outside the barn door and she carried Ian's saddle, bridle, and two clean saddle pads and grouped them in the grass. She had cleaned and oiled his tack yesterday after giving Ian his bath. She took an extra plastic bucket and tossed an extra lead rope and halter in it. She broke off as many flakes as she could carry from a bale of hay and stuffed them into a net bag and tossed the bag beside the bucket. She looked around her, thinking what else she needed. She walked into the barn and picked up her helmet, her blue and white silk helmet cover for cross-country, and her Tipperary vest, which was the same color blue. The vest fit tight and was short in front and long in the back. It had horizontal blocks of padding in it and supposedly would help hold her ribs together if she fell on course. She tossed a riding crop onto the pile because she knew that Hope would want her to carry one, but she also knew that she would purposely drop the crop before cross-country, because she felt distracted holding it and the reins in her fingers. She couldn't find her gloves, and then looked inside her helmet and found them stuffed in there, along with a brown hairnet.

She walked up to the house, where the kitchen smelled like coffee and Susanna had eggs and toast and some cut-up honeydew melon ready for her.

"Good girl getting up by yourself," Susanna said. "I didn't see you and thought you had slept in, and when I went to check on you, your bed was empty."

"I'm not going to sleep in. Hope would kill me," Teagan said, sipping orange juice.

Susanna poured herself some coffee.

"Could I have half a cup? Mostly milk?" Teagan asked.

"Am I teaching you to drink coffee?" Susanna said.

"No. I'm teaching myself," Teagan said. "I actually like it."

"Don't like it too much," Susanna said.

At a quarter after six Susanna sent Teagan to get dressed and told her to meet them at the barn. Teagan had to wear white britches for dressage, so Susanna offered to pack up the trailer and the car and load Ian. Teagan pulled on the britches, tall thin boot socks, and a stiff blue button-front shirt. She secured the plain silver stock pin her mother had given her to her long white stock collar, and flung it around her neck like a scarf. She didn't know how to tie a stock tie, so she would let Susanna or Hope do that. Teagan had asked Susanna why riders wore stock collars. Susanna said that it was to look dressy and nice, but Hope told Teagan it was so riders had a long piece of cloth with them in case someone took a bad fall and broke an arm or needed a bandage.

Teagan shoved her feet back into her tennis shoes and grabbed her riding jacket in its green canvas cover out of her closet, and her tall boots in another green canvas bag, which was really two single boot bags connected by a strap. She fit the strap on her shoulder with one boot hanging in front of her and the other hanging behind her. In the kitchen she took another gulp of milk and coffee, sipped some water, made sure the dogs were there and not outside, and shut the kitchen door behind her. She looked to the barn and saw that Susanna was driving to the house. Hope drove behind in her own car.

Teagan went up to Susanna's window. "Can I ride with Hope?"

Susanna said it was fine with her, but she wouldn't let Teagan open Ian's side door and say hello to him, because she didn't want her to risk getting her white britches dirty. Teagan thought that white britches were really a stupid idea. It felt like a trick, to have to wear them and not get them smudged.

Teagan liked riding with Hope because Hope talked about the events she had ridden in, and she always had the map of the cross-country course and had Teagan study it and talk herself through it. This time Hope asked Teagan to go over her dressage test. The dressage arena was a rectangle labeled with letters. A and C were at either end. M, R, B, P, and F were along one side, and H, S, E, V, and K were along the other side. Teagan never asked why those letters were chosen. An invisible X was understood to be the exact middle of the dressage arena, equidistant between A and C.

A rider was supposed to enter the arena, halt at X, and salute the judge or judges, who sat in the judges' box just beyond C. The salute was not a requirement, but most riders did it, and if your horse halted nicely and stood still, it was considered a beneficial "introduction" to your test. The salute consisted of extending the right hand down beside the leg and a quick nod of the head.

After talking it through, Hope and Teagan decided that she would not attempt the salute, because in those few seconds Ian might lose focus and it could throw off the whole test. Hope said, as she had before, that she wanted Teagan to start riding her test before she entered the ring, meaning that it was going to take all of Teagan's effort and concentration to keep Ian moving through the test. Teagan would make the smallest of pauses at X, then move through the first element.

Hope held the test paper against the wheel. "Okay. Tell it to me," she said.

Teagan began to recite the test from memory. "Enter at A, working trot. Between X and C, medium walk. At C track right, at M working trot."

"And these are rising trots, not sitting," Hope said.

"Rising trot," Teagan corrected. She had practiced in the yard using various T-shirts, jackets, boots, whatever was close at hand, to represent the letters, and pretended to ride Ian through it, walking from letter to letter and describing to herself what she should be doing with her hands and legs, and how she should think about her next move.

"After M comes A, circle right twenty meters, rising trot," Teagan said to Hope.

Hope glanced at the paper. "Good."

"Across the ring, change rein," Teagan said.

"Be specific," Hope said. What letter do you turn at?"

"Um. I know I go through X," Teagan said.

"Letters," Hope said.

"M to K," Teagan said.

"Other way around. K to M, passing through X," Hope said.

"I knew that," Teagan said.

"Keep going," Hope said.

"Left twenty meters at C," Teagan said.

"At the trot," Hope said.

"At the trot," Teagan repeated. "Walk between C and H."

Hope said, "Now, HXF is the free walk, and this is where you could lose him. Don't be too free, okay? He should extend his neck, but don't let him entirely off the bit, if you can. He's going to think that the work is over, and you've got to get him back and finish well."

"Okay," Teagan said, although she had no idea how this was really going to go.

"What's the rest?" Hope prompted.

"F to A, medium walk. A to X, halt," Teagan said.

"Okay. Good. And do salute at the end. It's polite. And then exit the ring as quickly as you can. Turn to the right and walk off the center line in case the rider behind you wants to come in as you are leaving. They may have a lot of folks to get through before the cross-country phase."

"Okay," Teagan said. Then she remembered that Lilly was coming to the event. "My neighbor Lilly is coming to watch today," she told Hope.

"That'll be fun. Does she ride?"

"She's been taking lessons. I think she's interested in getting into eventing, but she doesn't have her own horse," Teagan said.

"It's always nice to have another pair of hands to help out, but don't let her slow you down, especially getting ready for cross-country. If you miss your time then that's it. You have to scratch. The judges aren't going to fit you in later. There are too many other riders."

"Lilly will understand. I think she's mostly going to watch," Teagan said.

After the dressage test was over, Teagan and Lilly set to work getting ready for cross-country, which was the most exciting for both of them. Teagan was looking forward to riding it, and Lilly was planning to watch at several different jumps along the course. Hope had gone to retrieve Teagan's dressage scores, which were available after all riders had completed the test. Teagan hadn't done badly, or particularly well. She was not surprised when her score was entirely average, putting her in the middle of the field.

"You're not a ribbon contender with this score. You won't be able to make up enough points in cross-country, so focus on riding well and have fun," Hope said before she went off to speak to a friend who also had a riding student at the event.

Teagan thanked her and said she would. Lilly had pulled out all of Ian's braids and brushed his mane. She pulled the removable velvet cover off of Teagan's helmet and put on the silks, and she put Teagan's Tipperary vest and riding crop next to the helmet. Teagan tied Ian to the trailer and put a bucket of water and some flakes of hay near him. Hope had said not to give him any grain until after cross-country, but Teagan snuck him a couple handfuls to thank him for not being terrible in the dressage arena.

The smell of grilling hamburgers from food tents wafted over the trailers, but Susanna brought out sandwiches and fruit. Lilly's mother, Joan, had brought homemade brownies. Lilly and Teagan ate and looked at all the other horses tied to other trailers on the hill. Teagan told Lilly that she could have any of the horses she wanted. Lilly picked out a lovely slender chestnut who was wearing a blue fly bonnet on her ears to keep off flies. It reminded Teagan to put some more fly spray on Ian.

"I'm only choosing her because Ian is taken," Lilly said.

"Of course," Teagan said.

Teagan looked out over all of the horses and told herself that she could have any horse she wanted, and although there were some good-looking horses, she found she wasn't interested in any of them. She looked at Ian. He was beautiful and probably the strongest horse there. She knew that she barely trained at all compared to more serious riders, and Ian still had enough energy to compete without getting overly tired. She was looking forward to riding cross-country, but an event wasn't made up of just cross-country, and the other phases were not as much fun for her.

She found herself wondering what Grace and Caroline were up to, and she wished she was hanging out with them. Then she rebuked herself because she knew that not every girl got to gallop a horse over jumps. She was glad Lilly had come. Having her there made the day more fun, and Lilly was interested in everything Teagan or Hope taught her. Ian would be the best horse for Lilly, Teagan thought. He's an older, seasoned horse, so he knows how to do everything. Lilly wouldn't have to train him, she could just learn from him. He's kind. He wouldn't throw her or run away with her. Teagan surprised herself by thinking, Maybe I'm finished with riding.

Hope walked up with Teagan's cross-country number. "Look how organized," she said, gesturing to the Tipperary and helmet.

"Lilly did that," Teagan said.

"She's your new groom," Hope said.

"She's an event rider in training," Teagan said.

"Well, good. I'm glad to hear it," Hope said. "Now, Teagan, you're on deck in about twenty minutes, so get tacked and trot out a little, that way, away from the trailers, to warm up."

"Teagan, change that shirt," Susanna said.

Teagan took off the blue button-down and pulled on a plain white long-sleeved polo shirt. Lilly and Teagan tacked Ian together, and Susanna tied Teagan's number around her waist, over her Tipperary.

Susanna rapped her knuckles lightly on the chest of the vest. "No falling off," she said.

"Promise," Teagan said.

Ian seemed to know that something more fun than dressage was happening. Teagan felt him lean into his stride and he tossed his head a little in anticipation. "Go easy, sir." Teagan patted his neck. She slowed him as they reached the trailers again and walked to their own trailer.

"Check your girth," Hope said.

Teagan shoved her fingers under it and then tucked her leg back, reached down, and easily cinched it up a little more.

"How do you feel?" Hope said.

"I'm fine. He's a little strong," Teagan said.

"Okay, then I want you to walk him out of the starting box. An easy trot up to your first jump. Got it? There's no reason to burst out of the gate. He'll pick up speed but you've got an entire course to cover, and you don't want to start at a gallop and then have no horse left at the end."

"What if he fights me in the box?" Teagan said.

"You don't want him to, that's true. If he jumps around in the starting box it will be a disqualification. Keep him walking until it's time to go in. Let's go now. I forgot the bit check. Hurry."

Hope walked fast up to the starting box, which was a wooden rail fence built as a square, with one open side. Two event officials in red vests were standing a little below it on the hill. Hope gave them Teagan's number and name, and Teagan was asked to drop her reins while an official checked the bit in Ian's mouth. Hope explained quietly to Teagan and Lilly that there were new rules concerning cross-country. Only snaffle bits were allowed, and chains and martingales were banned. The horse had to be able to run comfortably without extra aids.

"A crop is an aid," Teagan said.

"Short crops are allowed," Hope said.

"I'd rather drop it," Teagan said.

"You'll want it if he hesitates at a jump. You are only allowed one refusal."

"I won't remember to use it," Teagan said. She knew that Hope wasn't pleased.

"Okay," Hope said.

Teagan handed the crop to Lilly.

"How are those stirrups?" Hope asked.

"Up one on each side, I think," Teagan said.

"I agree," Hope said.

Teagan dropped the toes of her boots out of her stirrups, and Hope raised one stirrup while Lilly raised the other. "Better," Teagan said, standing in her stirrups and putting her heels down.

"You'll get a five-minute warning and then a one-minute warning. At ten seconds they'll count out loud for you. If you cross the start before ten seconds, you're disqualified, but trying to keep him in the box for a full minute might be difficult, so what I want you to do is wait to go in until you hear the ten-second countdown. That way you walk in, turn around, and go."

"Okay," Teagan said. She heard her number called and the

five-minute on deck warning. Ian was excited and Teagan walked him in a small circle, changing direction every minute, while she watched another rider enter the box, and then exit the box, her horse leaping into a full canter. There was a murmur from the audience standing nearby.

"Don't do that," Hope said.

Teagan smiled at her.

"You can circle the box," Hope said to her. "And, Teagan, don't hold your breath."

Teagan nodded. It was easy to forget to breathe on the cross-country course. She was focusing on keeping Ian moving and silently asking him to stay calm. She told herself to remember to breathe. She heard the announcer say her number and "Ten seconds" and start the countdown. She and Ian were behind the box. She didn't enter it until the announcer was at five. Teagan walked Ian into the box, paused for a moment, then turned him around to the starting line.

The announcer said "One," and then said, "Have a nice ride."

Teagan's heart was pounding, but she pushed Ian forward and was calm enough to answer, "Thank you," as Ian left the box and broke into a powerful trot that Teagan was nonetheless able to hold him to. They trotted to the first obstacle, a friendly enough tree trunk, even though it was big, and Ian leapt over and landed in a forward canter. Teagan smiled as she stood in her stirrups and patted his neck. "Good boy. Let's go," she said, as they headed for the second jump on the rise of the next hill.

Spoons

The Garretts were from another century, Teagan thought. She walked into the kitchen of the eighteen-hundreds farmhouse to see if Lilly was there. On the old wooden dining table a pie and a braided loaf sat next to homemade preserves, herbed butter, a pot of tea under a hand-knitted cozy, and a stack of soft hand-embroidered cloth napkins. All of the Garrett children knew how to make homemade things, Teagan thought, with some jealousy. Even the boys could sew. She had attended Sunday school with Lilly's brothers and remembered their embroidered Psalms were much neater than hers. In fact, one was framed and hanging on the kitchen wall. *The Lord is my shepherd. I shall not want.* Teagan couldn't remember what she'd done with hers. Lilly's mother wasn't there. The kitchen was inviting but empty at the moment. Teagan walked up to the table and looked at the food, like a feast in a fairy tale, and thought of the honey-colored table at Blue View Farm, where often it was just Teagan and her mother sitting down to supper, but Susanna kept automatically setting out four places at meals, and Teagan would pick up two place mats, two sets of cutlery, two glasses, and put them back. She looked out of the window and could see Lilly across the lawn carrying a bucket. Teagan went outside and saw everyone walking toward a small green and white barn.

She ran outside past Charlie and Susanna and paused beside Lilly's mother. Joan gave her a hug in greeting. Teagan waved to Lilly's younger brother, Paul, and her father, Jim. She caught up with Lilly.

"Hi."

Lilly saw her and looped her arm through Teagan's. "Hi."

Teagan looked into Lilly's bucket. "Apples?"

"I was picking them. There's a tree down the trail a little that has good ones."

"When did this barn appear?" Teagan asked.

"It didn't appear. My dad and I have been building it."

"That's great. What are you going to put in it?" Teagan asked.

"Dad and I are planning on getting horses. We have two stalls, and, you know, the field is big enough for turnout."

"That's cool," Teagan said. She could smell new paint.

"It's dry," Lilly said, watching Teagan press a finger to the green wall. Lilly set down her bucket and lifted the latch on the main door. The two stalls were side by side and faced out.

Jim was explaining to Charlie and Susanna how they'd gone about building the barn. Lilly led Teagan inside and showed her the small area for saddles and bridles and the new tall aluminum cans that could hold fifty pounds of grain and the hay storage on pallets at the back.

"Looks like you are all set," Susanna said.

"I think we've got everything we need," Jim said.

"Except the horses," Charlie said.

Jim laughed. "Yes. We still have to find those."

Teagan stood looking around. She was thinking, her arms crossed. Lilly liked Ian. Teagan wondered if Ian might be happy living here with Lilly. Teagan didn't want to think about Ian in the field at Blue View, with no one to ride him. It was her job to take care of him, but she was quickly feeling like she didn't want to take care of him. Not every day. Maybe there were other things she wanted.

"Where's Seth?" Teagan asked.

Seth was Lilly's older brother. Teagan had always liked the look of him. She didn't talk to him much, but she liked it when he was around.

"He took the truck. I think he's chopping firewood for the fire pit. There's a tree that fell that Dad wanted cleared."

"So, have you looked at horses?" Teagan asked.

"No. We've just been working on the barn."

"You know, Hope could probably help you," Teagan suggested.

"That would be great," Lilly said.

"I'll ask her," Teagan said.

They wandered out. Lilly slid the lock shut on the main door. On the way back to the house they all stopped to admire the new fire pit, lined neatly with pieces of slate. Paul said they would have a fire and roast marshmallows after dinner. Susanna and Joan walked inside, involved in a conversation about gardening. Teagan took the bucket of apples from Lilly, put it on a chair, and started sorting through the top layer.

"This looks good." Lilly picked one and handed it to Teagan.

Teagan shined it on the thigh of her jeans, then bit in. The flesh snapped in her teeth. Then Joan invited them all to serve themselves tea and bread and butter or jam, while she finished cooking the supper. She asked everyone to pick a glass from ones she was setting out, and a napkin, and to choose a place at the dining table. Teagan was by the table and picked up glasses and handed them out. Seth came in the door and said hello. He wrapped an arm around Teagan and squeezed. She indulged a moment in breathing in the scent of freshly split logs that came from him.

As they all gathered around the table, casually jockeying for places, Teagan made sure to be on the same side as Seth, so he couldn't her eat. It was something new for her. She'd started feeling embarrassed eating in front of people she liked too much. Somehow her hands and mouth felt too awkward and she preferred to sit where she could glance at Seth but he might not notice. Teagan asked Lilly to sit next to her. Jim tried to put Susanna at the head of the table, but she refused and insisted that Jim sit there. Charlie waited quietly until everyone else had chosen to take a seat.

When there was a big wooden bowl of salad on the table, and beautifully roasted pieces of chicken, and a bright orange mound of sweet potatoes, they joined hands and Jim said a grace. They filled plates and Charlie raised his beer. "To the cooks."

"To the cooks," everyone echoed, and Joan gestured to Lilly and Jim, who had helped.

Teagan tried her small glass of wine. It tasted sour to her and she pushed it away and pulled her water glass closer to her plate. Charlie and Paul were talking about what might happen if you rigged a sail to a canoe, and the grown-ups were talking gardening and types of compost.

Teagan started asking Lilly about school, but this made her feel like a boring auntie, so she switched subjects and asked Lilly instead, "What kind of riding do you want to do?"

"We're mostly going to do trail riding, right now."

"You're a pretty good rider, aren't you?" Teagan said.

"I took lessons," Lilly said.

"That's what I meant. You could do shows if you wanted to, along with trails," Teagan said. Teagan and Susanna had been to one of Lilly's horse shows. Teagan had seen how quietly Lilly rode. She wasn't aggressive in any way. She didn't place, but she was gentle, and Teagan thought that was more important. Ribbons didn't mean anything.

"You should get an older horse. Something you won't need to train," Teagan said, realizing that she was talking to Lilly about Ian, to see if she would be interested in him.

"That's kind of what my dad said. I think he's going to talk to your mom about it."

"That's a good idea," Teagan said. She pictured Ian and then she pictured Lilly riding him. Teagan sipped the wine again to taste the bitter thought, which ended sweetly.

With Charlie and Seth both at the table, the grown-ups had a clear shot and took advantage of it, asking what colleges Charlie had been accepted to and where Seth might apply. The two boys sat up straighter in their chairs and fielded questions. Teagan felt relieved to not be part of that conversation, until Joan turned to ask her about going back to Hunting Hill.

"I'm not going back," Teagan said, catching everyone's attention.

There was a slight silence, and Susanna said, "It will be good to have her home."

"I'm going back to Kerner High. I'll be in classes with Grace. I'm looking forward to it," Teagan said, employing the phrase Susanna had suggested she use. It sounded wooden to Teagan, but the grown-ups nodded happily. Since Robert had left, Teagan noticed that grown-ups talked to her differently. She sometimes felt that they were sorry for her, which confused her, because it wasn't as if her father had died, he was just somewhere else. She didn't know how to feel about it herself, but her mother seemed to expect her to be sad, or angry, or to do something to express sadness or anger.

Teagan felt like everyone's attention was still on her, so, without planning to, she made an announcement. "I think Ian would be a good horse for Lilly."

Joan and Susanna looked at each other, confirming something. Lilly looked at Teagan, smiling.

"He's perfect for you, don't you think?" Teagan asked Lilly.

"Sure," she said.

"Which one is Ian?" Seth asked.

"He's mine," Teagan said.

Seth opened his hands as if to say he needed more information and Charlie filled in the description of the horses at Blue View to help Seth figure out which one Teagan was talking about.

"You just won something on that horse, didn't you?" Seth asked.

Teagan smiled down at her plate.

"Teagan did very well at the combined training show," Susanna said.

"I didn't win it." Teagan laughed.

"She looked so cool on cross-country," Lilly said. "You take these jumps over a huge field."

"Cross-country is just kind of cool," Teagan said, and Lilly agreed.

"You could do that with Ian," Teagan said to her, feeling earnest at last. "If you worked with Hope, you could start with pre-novice level. It's easy and Ian already knows it all."

"That might be fun," Lilly said.

"It's really fun," Teagan said, and then she leaned closer to Lilly and tried to say just to her, "I'm just not riding that much anymore. I really think you and Ian would have a great time together."

Lilly smiled down at her plate.

Charlie was looking at Teagan, his hand resting lightly around his beer on the table, as if he had forgotten to let go of it. Teagan felt his eyes on her and glanced up. He smiled at her but looked a little bit sad. Teagan straightened up and gave him a big smile and then dug into her pile of potatoes with her fork. Everyone was still too quiet. Teagan took an enthusiastic bite of chicken and saw Joan and Jim and Susanna leaning in and talking quietly. She heard Joan say, "Okay, we'll discuss it."

Teagan felt her embarrassment begin to burn. They all thought that Ian was so important to her. She thought, hotly, that maybe she was not the girl they knew. She thought, I am a different girl now.

Paul had asked Charlie if he was playing any club sports at college, and Charlie was explaining how the different teams were organized. Teagan thought they were off the subject when she heard Jim ask her if Lilly could come over to ride Ian to try him out.

"Sure. She can come tomorrow," Teagan said, deliberately not looking at her mother.

The conversations rose in volume again and they all tucked in to their plates, eating every delicious bite all the way through to the lattice-top cherry pie.

"Girls clear plates, boys light fires," Paul called out, rising from his seat.

"I want to light fires, too," Teagan said.

"You didn't say it first." Paul grinned.

"Paul, you didn't ask if everyone was finished," Joan said.

Paul looked doubtfully at the people sitting in front of their emptied plates.

"Anyone want anything else?" he said. "There are some clean napkins and water left, I think," he said, looking as if to make sure.

Teagan and Lilly laughed. Everyone began to get up from the table and carry their own plates, but the boys went quickly outside.

"You girls go too," Joan said, ushering out Teagan and Lilly, while Susanna gathered plates.

The wooden benches around the fire pit were Jim's handiwork. Long, slender green sticks were leaning on a bench. Paul and Lilly had whittled them to points, perfect for spearing marshmallows. Jim and Seth rearranged the logs because Jim thought some of them were too green and would only smoke, but soon the fire was going and they all were sitting around it, as the sky blackened and the stars popped through. Teagan instructed Lilly on her personal favorite method of setting a marshmallow on fire on purpose, then blowing it out and pulling off the black, crisp outer skin, crunching it in her mouth, then sucking up the melted inside off the stick. Lilly tried it, but she didn't like the burned bits as much as Teagan did. Lilly had the patience to turn her marshmallow slowly and let it toast lightly and not burn.

Charlie and Paul talked, both patiently turning their marsh-mallows near an ember, browning them. Charlie perfectly roasted a couple and gave them to his mother. Susanna liked her marshmallows nicely browned, but when she was talking to Joan she kept distractedly catching fire to hers. Joan and Susanna gave up on marshmallows and sat back on their bench, discussing something about a trial.

"Who's having a trial?" Paul asked suddenly.

Teagan was watching Seth snap twigs and add them slowly to the fire.

Joan turned to Paul. "Honey, it's a sad story. I shouldn't tell it tonight."

"I'll hear it," Teagan said, sloughing off another marshmallow skin with her fingers.

But Joan didn't say any more. Teagan knew that she was a social worker and she sometimes had interesting stories about people's lives.

Seth tried to say quietly to Teagan, "Someone died."

"Someone died?" Teagan said too loudly and turned to him.

"In the hospital," Joan quickly filled in and gave Seth a disapproving look, but he shrugged. "You know, people try to do what they think is right," Joan said, as if that explained everything.

"But then some people end up dead," Paul said.

Charlie laughed and then swallowed his laughter.

Jim put a hand on Paul's shoulder. Paul busied himself with some sticks and pretended not to react to his dad's touch.

"Let's hear the story," Teagan said, thinking that was probably what everyone wanted.

Joan was quiet, but she must have felt pressured, so she said, "There was a man who was supposed to receive daily in-home care, but some of those services are not as well organized as they ought to be."

"Daily care? So, someone forgot to check on him one day?" Teagan suggested, and Seth caught her eye and nodded.

"Something fell through the cracks, you could say. Or someone wasn't doing a good job," Joan said. "He was not getting consistent care."

"I don't know why he didn't call someone," Lilly said.

"Or complain," Teagan said.

"Maybe he wasn't able to call," Joan said, thoughtfully. "Older people can become confused."

"He couldn't call if he was dead," Charlie muttered for Paul's benefit. Paul choked a laugh. Teagan looked at Paul and Charlie. She didn't like that they thought a confused dying man was funny. Charlie was funny, he had a sharp sense of humor, but he could be mean, Teagan thought.

"Was he dead when they found him?" she asked. She wanted to sound matter-of-fact, but she couldn't help but picture a gruesome scene. She wanted to know if it could really be true.

"He died in the hospital," Charlie said, reminding them of the fact.

"Right," Joan said. "He ended up"—she trailed off, then finished—"not in a good way."

"Did he starve to death?" Lilly asked, and Teagan frowned for her benefit.

Joan shook her head. "Honey, I don't know the cause of death. Some people have a lot of medications and they can easily mix them up or forget to take them, and some people have serious medical conditions that need constant monitoring."

"I thought you did say that he wasn't getting enough to eat," Paul said.

"I don't know if I said that," Joan said. "And, Paul, you can't repeat these things."

"We don't know who he is," Seth said.

"He was dehydrated," Joan supplied, in a succinct tone. "Certainly his health was compromised, and he declined, even in the hospital."

"Someone's getting sued," Charlie said.

"He can't sue," Teagan said.

Seth snorted. Teagan hadn't meant to make a joke, but she smiled as if she had.

"Somebody is in trouble, if there's going to be a trial," Charlie said.

Teagan shook her head at him. How did he know anything?

"The suit has to do with neglect," Jim said.

"It's a locally run company. It's very sad. I've worked with them for several years," Joan said.

"So why didn't this man's family take care of him in the first place?" Teagan asked.

"They didn't live close by," Joan said.

"They didn't want to take care of him. That's why they hired strangers." Charlie snapped a twig.

"At least they tried. Nobody wants a relative left alone," Susanna said.

"Except they had incompetent people who killed their relative," Charlie said.

Teagan gave him a look. She didn't know why he was talking like that.

"I don't think the family was aware of the problems," Joan said.

She seemed to be talking to Charlie, but Teagan thought Charlie just needed to shut up.

"They could have known if they wanted to." Charlie sounded scornful.

"Charlie, what's your deal?" Teagan said.

Joan said, "It's complicated. It always is. There's always more than one thing going on. It's unfortunate. Nobody wants to lose a family member that way."

Teagan stared at Charlie, trying to signal him to drop it, but he didn't look at her.

Jim stood up, brushing off his jeans. "Let's change the subject and have some fun. I say we go inside for a game of Spoons."

"Spoons?" Susanna said.

"It's Dad's favorite game ever," Lilly said.

"But he cheats," Seth said.

"It's part of the game." Jim smiled.

Inside, Lilly gathered a handful of clean everyday spoons.

Jim brought out two packs of playing cards. "You've never played this?" he asked Susanna.

"I still think you're kidding," Susanna said.

"No, no. Not kidding," Jim said, sitting down and beginning to shuffle the cards.

Lilly arranged the spoons, bowls in, handles out, in a circle in the middle of the table.

"Anyone want apple cider? It's not spiked," Joan said.

"Why not?" Seth asked.

"Is there any of that wine left?" Susanna asked.

Jim said he'd open a new bottle. Susanna protested but lost. Wine was poured, but Jim suggested that people keep their glasses off of the table because things could get ugly.

"Have you played this before?" Joan asked Teagan.

"No," she said.

They crammed around one end of the kitchen table.

"Pull in close. You need to be able to reach to the middle," Jim said. "Okay. Ready to learn? Let's see. We've got too many players, but that doesn't matter. Everyone starts with five cards and the rest go in a pile. I'll be dealer for this game, just to start us out."

"Here we go," Seth said, indicating that Jim would cheat.

"There are eight people, but there are seven spoons on the table," Charlie said.

"Yes. I'm glad you pointed that out, Charlie," Jim said.

"Good counting, Charlie," Lilly said.

"Thank you, Lilly," Charlie said, bowing slightly to her.

Jim continued. "The top card is turned over and starts the discard pile. So, the first card is a six of spades. Charlie, since you are sitting to my left, you start. You put down a six or a spade. Just for practice, tell us what cards you have."

"I have a two of spades."

"Okay, lay that card down. And when you lay down a card, you have to say what it is, just like Charlie just did."

"I have a two of spades," Charlie said again.

"Yes. Thank you," Jim said.

Lilly clapped lightly for Charlie's demonstration.

"Now. Charlie had two options. He could play his card, or he could hold it, but then he has to draw. Let's say he draws a card he can play; he can play that card right away. If he doesn't, then the person to his left goes. The goal is to play all of your cards, but you have to announce when you are down to one card. If you don't announce it and we catch you, then you have to draw another card. Everyone with me so far?"

Susanna shook her head, so Joan leaned in to help.

"A few more rules. If you lay down a queen, that reverses the direction of play. So if Charlie plays his two, and Lilly lays down a queen, then play goes back to Charlie, instead of on to Seth. The eight of any suit is a wild card. It changes the suit. If you lay down an eight, you can call out whatever you want, diamonds, hearts, clubs, spades, and that's what the discard pile becomes."

"When do we get a spoon?" Susanna asked.

"Ah. You get a spoon when you are out of cards. Whoever plays all his or her cards first grabs for a spoon, and when that happens, everyone else can grab, too. If Teagan plays all her cards and I see her reaching for a spoon, then I know that I'd better grab one. This is where it can get rough. Everyone should cut their fingernails before we play."

"Or sharpen them." Joan wiggled her fingers to show her nails. Susanna wiggled hers back.

"This could end badly." Teagan smiled at Lilly.

"And whoever doesn't get a spoon is out," Paul said.

"Oh no, I'm going to lose!" Susanna said.

"Don't get anxious yet," Joan said.

"Should we play?" Jim said. He shuffled the cards again and dealt five to each person, stacked the rest, and turned over the top card. Charlie started. He laid down a heart.

"Draw again," Teagan yelled.

"Why?"

"You didn't say your card," Lilly said.

Charlie drew again.

"Hearts," Lilly said, laying down and drawing.

"Hearts." Seth played his card and drew.

They went around the table. The laying down and picking up of cards began to happen faster. Names of suits were said by one person and the next.

"Eight. Diamonds," Lilly called out.

"Damn!" Susanna said. She had to draw.

Cards were laid down and picked up at a crazy pace.

"You skipped me," Teagan complained, but Lilly kept playing.

Around they went again. The pace increased. Cards slipped off the table. Then Joan lunged for a spoon. A yell went up as everyone else realized what had happened and tried to grab a spoon at the center of the table. Charlie threw a friendly elbow into Paul, and there was general scrabbling and clanking of metal on wood.

When the struggle subsided Jim called out happily, "Who has a spoon? Hold 'em up."

Everyone who had gotten hold of one held up the proof of a spoon.

"I didn't get one," Teagan said, pulling a sad face and slapping the table with her empty hands.

"Loser," Charlie said.

Joan leaned against Teagan in sympathy.

"Who took the first spoon?" Susanna asked.

Lilly quietly raised her spoon.

"That was so sneaky. I'm going to have to watch this girl," Susanna said.

The game started again, and even faster they slapped down the cards, so that when someone called out the name of a card it overlapped with the next, and the game verged on chaos. Teagan noticed that Seth had stopped looking at the cards that were passing in front of him, and was only watching the six remaining spoons. She laughed when he called out the name of a card that was different from what was in his hand. "Seth's cheating," Teagan happily informed the table.

Then Susanna screamed that she was out of cards and grabbed for a spoon, and a wrestling match between Seth and Paul took them off their seats.

"Foul," Jim called out, gleeful.

Teagan laughed and slopped cider on her shirt.

Everyone recovered and the next round started.

One spoon was on the table. Joan was out of cards first, but Susanna won the spoon.

Fairy Tale

Once upon a time, there was a girl who loved horses. More than anything she wanted a horse of her own. One day her father said to her, "I will build a barn."

It was a good barn.

"We must find a horse," the father said.

The daughter was happy.

On the other side of the village, there was a young woman who had a beautiful horse, but she no longer wanted it. She went to her good mother and said, "I want to give my beautiful horse away."

The mother said, "If it is your wish, I know of a girl who hopes for a horse."

The young woman said, "Let me take my horse to her."

Riding Lesson

Even though she could not tack a horse as quickly as Hope could, Teagan's best time was approximately fifteen minutes. She wasn't faster because she enjoyed grooming her horse. It was the only time that she moved seamlessly, the movements of her hands articulate. When she brushed his face with a soft-bristled brush, Ian would close his eye on the side Teagan was working on. She often captured his whole head in a hug and pressed her face to his white blaze. When Ian had had enough cuddling, he would nip at her side, and she'd have to move. Ian was tacked, and Teagan patted his neck and was thinking about walking him around when she heard the sliding lock move on the door in the run. Teagan turned Ian to the door and saw Lilly, who was looking relaxed and a little shy. She wore jeans and paddock boots, and carried a faded black-velvet-covered helmet.

"Hi."

"Hi," Lilly said.

"Here's your horse," Teagan said. She felt happy. She gathered Ian's reins.

Lilly walked to Ian and stroked his head, saying hello to him. Ian sniffed her shirt and flicked his ears forward. He nosed Lilly's arm and side, checking her out. Lilly stood quietly, letting him. Teagan brought his attention back by reaching the reins to his neck, putting pressure on the bit, and Ian followed the pressure and quieted his head. Then his ears flicked forward and his head went up and he tensed. Teagan looked at the sky; she saw black bodies disappearing into the trees and heard the cawing noise of crows. It was nothing, but she saw Lilly looking up at Ian's raised head.

"Tell you what," Teagan said, "why don't I put a halter on him, and I'll lead him, just to start."

"That sounds good," Lilly said.

Teagan handed the reins to Lilly and got a halter, then fed the reins through the halter so that Lilly could use them, and buckled the halter over Ian's bridle. She clipped a lead rope to the halter and flung the tail of the rope over his neck.

"You hop up," Teagan said.

Lilly fastened her helmet and led Ian to the mounting block. She stood on the wood step and placed her toe in the stirrup. Teagan stood at Ian's head, but she didn't have to do anything, because he stood quietly. Lilly settled onto the saddle. Teagan checked Lilly's stirrup lengths.

"Put them up a hole or two on both sides," Teagan said.

Lilly moved her leg back and flipped up the saddle flap. She slid up the buckle on each stirrup leather, which shortened the stirrup length. With the toes of her boots she found the stirrups, got her feet in them, and pushed her heels down.

"How's that feel?" Teagan asked.

"That feels better," Lilly said.

"Stand up and then sit down again, thinking about pushing your heels down," Teagan said.

Lilly did, and Teagan said that her leg position looked better. "Okay. I'll lead him down to the ring, but go ahead and hold the reins and keep your leg on him. Just get used to him a little bit."

Lilly gathered the reins and moved Ian into a walk. Teagan held the lead rope loosely in her hand and walked at Ian's shoulder. They walked toward the riding ring.

"How's he feel to you?" Teagan asked.

"He's the tallest horse I've ridden," Lilly said.

"He likes to stretch out. He's got a long stride, but he's also really even, which makes him comfortable to ride. At least I think so," Teagan said.

"Yeah, he's got a nice walk," Lilly said, after a moment.

Teagan glanced up at Lilly on Ian, taking in the picture. She was happy with the way Lilly sat, lightly and easily in the saddle. Ian's walk was relaxed. His head was down and he was taking his usual long ground-covering strides. He seemed to be accepting of Lilly as his rider, and he wasn't giving her any trouble, at least not yet. Teagan hoped he would continue to behave himself. He could be a wonderful horse, or a really tough one, and she wanted to give Lilly the best version of Ian that she could. Teagan felt that she and Ian had worked well together, despite how difficult he had been for her at first. She saw that her work, and his, was paying off. Ian was calm and paying attention to Lilly.

Teagan opened the wooden gate and they walked into the grass ring. Lilly turned Ian's head to the gate and Teagan, still holding his rope, closed it. "We'll walk around once on the lead," Teagan said, "so you can get a feel of him on the flat, and then I'll turn you loose."

Going to the right (Ian's right shoulder was toward the fence), Teagan walked on Ian's left. She held the lead loosely, so that Lilly could take the feel of his head. Teagan could tell that Ian was taking his cues from her, rather than from Lilly. He was matching his pace to Teagan's. When she began the turn around the end of the ring, Ian matched his turn with hers. She was pleased that he was so in tune with her, but she wanted to give

Lilly a chance to engage with him. Teagan stopped walking halfway around the ring, and Ian stopped when she stopped.

"He's following me," Teagan said.

Lilly smiled. "I know. I'm not doing anything."

"Let me take off the halter and see what you guys can do together."

Even with the halter and lead off, when Teagan walked toward the middle of the ring, Ian turned to follow her. Teagan did not look at him, and she heard Lilly speak to him as she turned him away and put him on track around the ring. Standing in the middle of the ring, with Lilly and Ian tracking along the rail, Teagan could look over Lilly's position. She watched what her legs and hands were doing. Teagan saw that Lilly was working hard to keep her leg in place, but she wasn't feeling Ian's movement. It looked as if her leg was hovering away from the horse's side rather than moving with it. That could be fixed. Teagan liked Lilly's hands, which were soft. She held the reins too loosely, but for now that was okay. Her hands were also relatively still, hovering above Ian's withers, which Teagan liked to see.

"Are you going to ride more?" Teagan asked.

"Yes. I'm probably going to take lessons with Hope. Your mom is going to get us in touch with her and help set things up," Lilly said.

"That's great," Teagan said, and then she switched into speaking like an instructor. She had a student to teach, and she wanted things to go well for Lilly.

"First things. This leg looks pretty good." Teagan placed a firm hand on Lilly's calf. "It's in position, but I want more contact." Teagan pushed Lilly's leg against Ian's side. Ian shifted a little but didn't take a step. "See? He should feel you. You want to be able to feel him. That way, you can always tell what he's doing, and he can listen to what you are doing, and more importantly, you can feel what he is about to do, in case you need to get more control."

"What do you mean, feel what he's about to do?" Lilly asked.

"Let's say you are on a trail ride, and your horse gets worried about something on the trail. A deer or a funny shadow or something catches his attention, and if you have your leg on, you will be able to feel him stiffen up, and then you know you have to make a decision. If he tries to turn, or run, or shy, you will be able to feel which way he is leaning, and then you have enough time to react. But don't worry, he's a good trail horse." Teagan smiled, trying to soften her comment.

Lilly smiled a small smile.

Teagan said, "Or let's say you are in the ring, heading to a jump, and you feel him bulging to the right or left. With a steady leg on you can feel that, and straighten him out in plenty of time."

"I'm not sure what you mean," Lilly said.

Teagan said, "So, you should be able to ask him to move sideways by just using your leg. With this horse, you don't even need to use the reins. It's like this." Teagan pushed on Lilly's leg, pushing it against Ian's side; she kept up the pressure until Ian's back hoof stepped underneath him and he shifted his hind end over. Teagan said, "Did you feel that? Did you feel him take a step?"

"Yeah. That's cool," Lilly said.

"Now you have to do it without me." Teagan gave Lilly's leg a pat and she moved toward the middle of the ring. She said, "You've got a good horse. He's sensitive. That means he responds to the signals you make with your legs and body position, as well as your hands. So, be really clear about giving those signals." Teagan knew that she was giving Lilly too much information, but she thought it was good to give it anyway.

Teagan said, "Try to ask him to go forward using only your leg. Don't touch the reins." She could see Lilly's seat shift in the saddle, and she was pressing her leg against Ian, but he stood.

"Keep going. You've asked him, so you have to keep asking for what you want. Don't let him get away with not listening," Teagan said, raising her voice. "More. Heels down. Put your leg on. Keep going." Teagan watched as Lilly tensed other parts of her body, her arms and back, but she wasn't getting a result, and Ian was being stubborn.

"Stop," Teagan said. "Take your feet out of the stirrups. Good. Now sit deep in the saddle, but don't round your back. That's it. Good. Let your leg hang loose. Good. Now, put your leg on again, and wrap as much of your leg as you can against his side." Teagan could see Lilly flex her leg. Her leg position looked better.

"C'mon. You can do it. Think, Walk, and think about pushing him in front of you," Teagan said.

Then, as if it was the first time Lilly had asked, Ian began to walk.

"There you go," Teagan cheered.

Lilly let out a breath. "I felt like I couldn't get my leg to do anything."

"He was also giving you a hard time," Teagan said. "The thing is, once you really start to feel that, you'll be able to do it all the time, and you won't have to do as much to get him to go forward." Teagan was turning slowly, following Lilly and Ian as they covered the ring. Lilly held the reins loosely.

Teagan said, "Come back to the middle and we'll talk a little bit about the reins. And then we'll do something other than walk. I promise. Actually, keep him on the rail and I'll come to you."

Lilly halted Ian along the rail, and Teagan walked over.

"So, you know you can use your leg without the reins. Now, add the reins back in, because you want to control his head. The way I want you to think about the reins is that you are simply allowing him, or not allowing him, to move forward."

Lilly nodded, although Teagan didn't know if she really understood.

"So, if you are at the walk, and you want a faster walk, you allow him to go forward by giving him more room to move forward. If you want a slower walk, you take away some of that room."

Lilly patted Ian's neck as if she already considered him hers. It hurt Teagan a little to see that, but it also made her proud that Lilly wanted to take him on and learn how to ride him.

"The other thing," Teagan continued, "is how to use the reins to assist in turning him, instead of using the reins to turn him."

"How?" Lilly smiled.

"Like this," Teagan said. She showed Lilly how to shorten one rein and loosen the other. "The idea is to prevent him from going in one direction, while giving him the ability go in the other. So, let's say you want him to move to the right. Hold the left rein against his neck. Open the right rein, and for now let's make it really obvious." Teagan moved Lilly's right hand almost a foot away from Ian's neck. "Now, use your legs as before, but think about using your left leg to push him over to the right, as if pushing him into the space you've created with your right hand."

Again, it took Lilly some minutes to coordinate her movements and to push strongly enough to get Ian to respond, but finally he shifted to the right. Lilly gave Ian a pat.

"You're patting him, but you did the work," Teagan said.

"You remind me of Hope," Lilly said.

"Yeah, well, she taught me, so really everything I'm telling you is from Hope," Teagan said.

Teagan sent Lilly back out to the rail, and Lilly put into practice the things she was learning. Teagan saw that Ian was responding better to Lilly, now that she was riding him more closely to the way he was used to being ridden. She moved on to the trot and then the canter. They worked in both directions, and then Ian halted beautifully when Lilly asked him.

"Nice work," Teagan said. She looked at the dark horse and the bright girl.

Last Ride
(Though She Did Not Know It Yet)

They decided to take a long route on a nearby farm. They came down from the mountain and the sun was low. The black fences were duplicated by their shadows. They walked their horses beside the large barn, past a row of stalls with the top doors open, from which the heads of curious horses stuck out, looking at them as they passed. Teagan wiggled her left rein and pushed Ian a little with her right leg to keep him straight and to tell him to ignore them. They were both tired from the hack, and Ian dipped his head down and walked on. He knew the direction of his own field.

Susanna turned Duchess down the run, a grass lane closed in on both sides by four fenced fields. In two big fields, one on either side of the lane, two pairs of yearlings picked up their heads and looked. Their big heads on their skinny bodies made them look even more delicate and young. They were green, green like the supple wood of new tree growth, and spindly, as if they would never fill out to become like the calm, muscled horses Teagan and her mother now sat. Even from a distance Teagan could sense the complete attention the yearlings focused on the lane. The lines of the yearlings' backs against the deepening sky looked as if they were a brushstroke each in Japanese ink.

Ian suddenly noticed them and stopped. His head turned left to look at one pair, and then right to look at the other pair. As if Ian's stop was a signal, each pair tossed their heads, and wasting a lot of energy kicking up their hooves and hopping, they fell into a gallop, a mirror image of young horses approaching from across a field, and Teagan and Ian were the midpoint.

Susanna and Duchess were far enough ahead to have almost reached the end of the lane. Teagan shortened her reins, making more contact with the bit in Ian's mouth. She locked her heels down in her stirrups and used all her weight to push Ian forward, but the horse did not respond. His body tense, his ears forward, she could feel his energy building as the young horses barreled toward him from both sides. The instant she felt Ian move, she let go of the reins and with one hand grabbed the pommel of her saddle; with the other she grabbed a fistful of his wiry mane; she gripped with her legs and she held on.

Ian spun like eddying water whirling, and she felt a moment of weightlessness as she was carried, and then her gravity returned and she stuck to the saddle as he galloped up the lane, back the way they'd come. She had no control of his head, but he slowed when the barn blocked the view of the fields. She relaxed, relieved that she hadn't fallen. Her horse was walking, and she gathered the reins, stroked his neck to say he was all right. She was all right, and she turned him again to go down the shoot. It was the way home. She saw Susanna on Duchess, halted at the other end. She let Ian stand and look. The yearlings were messing around at the fences, biting and lunging at one another.

The biggest excitement was over, and soon they were bucking and leaping and squealing, and running the other way. As if Ian understood, as he looked, that the young horses were not worth his attention, he walked forward at Teagan's leg, but she also kept her reins short and wiggled the bit in Ian's mouth a little by squeezing her fingers on the reins, just to remind him that she was there and that he should stay focused. Her heart was still beating fast. At times a horse was an animal under control, and at times a horse was his own creature, even wearing a saddle and a rider in that saddle.

She tried not to wonder too much why the horse ever let her tell him what to do, since in an instant he could let loose power that she couldn't overcome. In another moment he was attentive and obedient to the directions she gave him. Pretending that she was fully in control, and not at all concerned about the fact that seconds before she'd been run away with, she looked straight ahead at the figure of her mother at the end of the lane, and her horse continued to walk calmly.

When they were on the gravel road that was the last leg home,

Teagan slackened her grip on the reins and sat more easily. She looked at her mother and laughed. She slapped Ian's broad neck, patting him. "That was unexpected," she said.

Susanna let out a breath of relief. "You were a whirlwind. I didn't want Duchess to copy you, so I kept going. I could not have stayed on through that." Susanna smiled.

Teagan nodded and unconsciously played with Ian's mane. "I got lucky. There wasn't anything I could do. He spun on a dime. But he stopped at the barn."

"At least he stopped," Susanna said, with a laugh.

"Yep." Teagan laughed.

"All right. Should we go home?" Susanna said.

"Let's just walk," Teagan said and moved Ian beside Duchess. The horses knew the way toward home and walked on.

Lilly and Ian

"Be a good boy. Be a good boy," she caught herself whispering to Ian, and she stopped. Teagan pulled the stiff brush down Ian's neck, over his back, down each leg, both sides of the horse. She sprayed slippery stuff on his long black tail and worked out tangles with her fingers until the tail swished and slapped her on the leg. She combed his mane. She brushed his face with a soft brush. She picked out his feet and painted polish onto his hooves to make them shine. He would get dusty the moment he walked into the new field, but when she brought him off the trailer she wanted the horse to look impressive. She oiled the leather halter with the brass nameplate on it and ran the sponge over the leather lead with the brass chain. She would leave the leather halter with him; it had his name on it.

She hadn't ridden him in weeks, not since the ride with Susanna. She hadn't meant for that to be the last time she got on him, but it turned out that way, the way things turn out without planning them. He seemed to know something was up. She wasn't saddling him. It wasn't early morning, she wasn't taking him foxhunting. She was quieter. Susanna didn't even come in the barn. There was a solemn feeling to the event, and it made Teagan irritable. This wasn't an end. It was a shift, a slight step to the side, a little bit of a new look at things. The horse was still a horse. He would be ridden. He would live in a field and be fed in a barn and a little girl would groom him and care for him and ride him on long trails in the woods. Ian's life would not be so different. Teagan's would be different.

She walked Ian onto the trailer, and Susanna lifted the heavy ramp and locked it. Teagan unclipped the lead rope and stepped out. Ian ignored the hanging net of hay and looked out of the opened side door. Teagan pushed his nose back inside and closed and locked the door. Susanna started up the truck, and they drove the quick miles to the Garretts'.

"This will be good for Lilly," Teagan said.

"It's a generous thing you're doing," Susanna said.

Teagan didn't like the sound of that and looked out the window. *Won't you miss him?* It seemed the question no one was willing to ask out loud, but it was in Susanna's voice, in all their voices, and in Teagan's own head. *You will grieve the loss of him.* She tried to silence her own voice in her head. *I will not.*

The rolling hills and oak trees out the window did not slow her thoughts, and instead she saw herself rolling along the line of each hill on horseback, the down and up. Her eyes rode them.

Feed

I imagine Ian looked at everything. I can see that he looked for a long time until he knew something. I believe he listened, flicking his long feathery ears forward and back, judging what the sounds were, and how far away. I remember he used his mouth to pull on the cloth of my sleeve, to grab the skin of my arm. To be understood he needed to communicate. For the most part he had been able to communicate his needs, his desires, and his decisions, even those a horse decides. He did not want to stand still. He wanted to move. He was a horse, a creature who needed to move in order to live. To create motion is to live, to walk and run over the ground, every day, day after day. He did this.

He was a horse who was born surrounded by people, instead of other horses. He lived day after day with people. He lived surrounded by a fence, he slept in a barn, he was called for, he was cared for; he knew this. I was a girl who had her particular scent, a smell he knew well. I also sometimes smelled like apples, and he liked apples. He would stand still for me, accept the things I did, like brushing him, putting a heavy saddle on his back, sitting in the saddle, asking him to accept a cold metal bit in his mouth. He did what he was told. (Why did he?) When he accepted these things, he was then asked to move, to walk and run over ground, which was something he liked, I know. When he was inside his fenced field, I did not pull or push him, I did not speak in tones that went up and down, and he could rest, and eat, or roll in the dust if he wanted, and he was comfortable, I think, and maybe content.

But he was taken to a new place and it smelled different, I imagine (of course it did), and there was no mare to share the field with him. He walked the fence line, perhaps, smelling what was there, different trees, grass, new mineral dirt. It was not unfamiliar, but his old scents were missing. Everything he had memorized had been rearranged.

Of course he would have to work to get his bearings, to learn the sights from the new field, the way the ground felt different under hooves, the rises and dips in a different order. He had to pay attention. He had to learn all of it to know it. There was a pony in his field also. A gelding, not a mare, and he didn't care for the pony. He bared his teeth and flattened his ears and told the pony to get away if he came near. When the pony was grazing far away, it was better.

He had to learn quickly. What other choice did I give him? His old field had been familiar, but it was gone. I imagine his confusion when he couldn't smell any of the regular smells, the ones he had become used to, and also I wasn't there, and I was the person whose scent he knew, who probably sometimes smelled like apples. He stood waiting to hear me, to see me, but I wasn't there. Maybe he had not been able to rest since the moment I was there and then I was not there. I was the person he knew. I was the person he expected to arrive. I was there for him and then I was not.

Instead, there was a new person who spoke to him, who

smelled different, and she sounded different, and he was curious about her, but he couldn't love her, yet. And now he was in the new field, and it was dark, and he was hungry. The one who usually brought him grain in a bucket had not brought him grain in a bucket, and he was hungry. Somewhere he could smell grain, and maybe he could get to it.

The pony was in the field, but he didn't care. He did not tell the pony to follow him. He walked to the barn that he could reach from the field. The barn was in the field. There was no fence separating him from the barn. It was not his usual barn, the one he knew, but inside the new barn he could smell hay, and he could smell grain, and he could smell that this barn was a place where he would be brushed and saddled, and also where he could be fed. I know that Ian is an intelligent horse, as far as such judgments are made, and to him two of the doors smelled empty, but the third smelled full. Of course he knew that there was food behind the third door. He could easily smell, as I could have, a warm scent of hay and a sweet vegetable smell of grain that he liked to eat. He would get to it.

I picture that he knocked against the door with his hoof, something I have seen him do before. It was a sturdy door, and he must have knocked against it, and I imagine hearing it rattle the way a closed door sometimes will, but it did not open. The smells of food were stronger when it rattled, when there was a gap of air that carried a scent of hay, a scent of grain, to his wide nostrils. He breathed into the crack in the closed door. He smelled up and down, and while he did this his soft, sensitive nose bumped a cold thing. He'd tasted these things before. They tasted like the metal he wore in his mouth when I put the bridle over his head. He licked the metal and then he pulled on it with his lips, because he was determined. I bet that he tried chewing it and that he pushed at it with his nose. If he licked it and chewed it and grabbed the part of it that stuck out, and was able to shift the part of it that moved a little, and felt it wiggle when he pulled and pushed, and if he kept doing this, pushing or pulling and licking and biting and working on this problem, a puzzle that slowly began to be solved, if he did not give up, because there was food on the other side of the obstacle, then eventually, he opened the lock.

And then, I imagine, if he knocked his hoof against the door again, and then again, the door began to bounce in its frame. Each time it bounced a small gap was made, so he could smell the scent that was fresh and strong, hay and grain. He kept working, because why not, and then the gap was wider, bigger, and then, I can see that he stopped and he waited. The darkness was soft. The smell was there, but I did not arrive. I, the apple-scented person, was not there, and I would not come to give my hungry horse some food, so he put his nose into the gap that was big, and then he pushed and the space widened, and the darkness was there but he could tell that he could walk through it, and he could go inside the place. Of course he went inside the place, and from there it was not difficult to find the tall metal can that held fifty pounds of grain. At last, he had found the food, and all he would do then was eat. He could smell the grain and how easy to knock his sturdy hoof against it. I can hear, in my imagining, the can fall and make a clatter, and the *shush* of grain sliding out onto the barn floor, and Ian, my sweet horse, backed away, but the clatter would stop and the grain was accessible on the floor, and finally he had food, and so he stood still and he took big mouthfuls and he ate, and there was no end to what he would eat.

Notify

Later, when the details could be discussed, I was told that Ian ate so many pounds of grain that his body became disfigured from swelling. When Lilly discovered him in the feed room and tried to move him, Ian fell over, knocking her over and pinning her feet under him. She pulled herself free, but her feet swelled and she had to lie in bed with bags of ice on them for days. It was Lilly's mother, Joan, who made the phone call to my mother, Susanna, to say that Ian was dead and needed burying.

Build Your Own Horse

The Build Your Own Horse™ kit that I ordered online came today; it was carefully padded with air-filled recycled plastic bags. I sweep the concrete floor in the barn and lay out the pieces. I don't need the booklet of instructions; I know how this goes. I hold a long, pointed ear, covered in soft hairs and lined with softer, feathery hairs. In their pair, the ears attach on either side of the poll. The neck, broad and supple, is in two parts, which fit together over some vertebrae, including the atlas and the axis. The hair on the neck grows down, toward where the shoulders will be. The mane was braided for shipping, but I undo the plaits with my fingers and let it lie loose, on the right side, preferably.

The skull is in its skin, and I lift it with one hand on the mandible, which makes the cheek curve, and one under the divot behind the chin. Whiskers grow around the nose, which is (it is cliché) velvet soft, and the comma-shaped nostril will breathe hot exhales when this kit is finished, assembled into a horse. The head attaches to the neck, and I fluff the forelock into place on the face, between the ears. I brush a little dust from the eye. It is wide, but it tapers at the ends like an almond. Like pairs of shoes I pair the hooves. Two front, two back, two to a side, four in all. The back are labeled with cannon bone (named for its tubular shape. Tube bone would sound less categorical) and the front with splint bone. I scrape off the stickers with a fingernail. I'm distracted and pick at my hangnail. One of the hooves topples and reveals its frog. Lifting the horse foot, I trace the V ravine with a finger. The bottom of the V points forward, the opening points toward the heel. The grooves are not too deep or shallow, the raised flesh of the frog sufficiently springy. The leg I line up to the knee, which is located about halfway along the leg's length. Long hairs fall at the back of the leg, and the rest lie close and smooth. The back legs line up to the hocks, the joint about parallel in height to the front leg's knee. To a back leg I join its muscular upper part; it includes the stifle joint, and the big haunch of the horse encases his femur. Upper and lower legs affixed, I lift a front leg to the chest of the almost-horse. If I would point to my own chest and say *pectoral,* on him (I ordered a gelding) I would have to name *deltoid*. As if my human arm was the front leg of a horse, the horse has biceps and triceps there. Legs and head are made, and now I need some tools. Two pine sawhorses prop up the large pieces of my would-be horse. The torso is enormous. The long back, containing the muscle with the many *s*'s, the latissimus dorsi, I align at the top. The eighteen pairs of ribs are preassembled, and I'm careful not to damage one. This horse will be a Thoroughbred. The additional information booklet said an Arabian horse has seventeen pairs, and the American mustang is short one vertebra from the usual thirty-six. Legs attached to body, neck to chest, the head on, and now I fit the tail, unbraid it, and it hangs long and wiry. This horse is complete, but something's not quite right. He lacks a sort of glint to his eye, and he doesn't seem to love me. More of an it than a horse, somehow.

New

I want a completely different horse. One that is a different color. One that has a new name. (What would be the point of naming the new one the name of the dead one?) One that is chestnut or dappled; one that is eating an apple, happily dripping apple-scented slobber from its living, chomping, big flat teeth. This one reminds me of the past one, though. No, it isn't different. Here is the same horse, again, as if alive; he looks the same and moves the same and he smells like dark, like the black moonless heat his living body gave to the skin around my eyes.

Conversation

"You loved it?"

I thought that the artist was talking about Ian, but she meant riding, in general.

"I loved him."

The artist looked confused.

I said, "He was a horse I loved."

Artist

Anything in particular, the artist asked. The artist wore a brightly colored scarf and I wasn't too happy with her but liked her price. The artist was chewing gum. It wasn't bubble gum but she made a squelching sound when I tried to answer. Particular? About his appearance, she said. He had large, round eyes. Most horses do, she said. His personality, then. Every animal has a personality, she explained, as if I would deny it. Did he do anything unique? What was his posture? How did he greet you when you went to ride him? He didn't like to be caught, I said. He would dribble a line of sweet feed onto the lip of the stall wall along the iron barred window and after he'd finished what was in the bucket he'd nibble his leftovers. Really? the artist said. I nodded. The artist said, Well, I can't draw that.

Particular

Can you describe anything particular? That the horse was from my father.

ᵇ

Portrait

The artist's result was typical. The horse looked too delicate to be strong, and yet too bulky to be balanced. It also did not seem to love me.

Grief

Grief is a dead horse.

The body must be buried where it lies. Who can move the weight?

Memorial

And we are standing at the edge of red clay, freshly mounded, and I believe that a once beautiful horse is lying, bloated and disfigured, underneath. Joan begins a song about horses and hounds (and how does she know such a song), and I've never heard the tune, but I suppose I'm supposed to connect the march to the death of my animal, his kind eulogized in cavalry songs. The dirt is damp, and the clotted-dust smell familiar. The shining dirt is so fresh that the light seems to bake it, and before it hardens in the keening of voices, I think I might reach slowly down (no one will notice) and push the dirt away with one finger, dig down and touch the rim of his nostril, it must be just an inch or two away, and touch the soft skin, and prick of wire hairs that sprout from the water-soft side of the nose.

Offering

The shiny green apple was smooth against my mouth. I took a bite and chewed the tangy flesh, then placed the bitten fruit on the wet, orange dirt (an orange ocean, a green boat, one bite a passenger).

Jim told me, "The next morning the apple was gone." His expression asked, How could it? My expression replied, Ian ate the apple.

Letter

Dear Grace,
Death is no longer a secret.

It was a letter I let slide into the wire trash bin. I didn't finish it, and I didn't send it. My friend already understood me. She and I went for walks and didn't talk much, like we were horses, constantly in motion, because to stop moving means to begin to fail, spirit then body.

Me, Ian, Robert

I had a quiet day, and Grace called. By the time we hung up, the light outside the window was darkening. A pile of paper on the floor caught my eye. It was the stack of cards I'd saved. The card from my father lay on top. I flipped it open and read it, then stuck all the cards on the bookshelf between two books. I briefly thought of work and putting in laundry, but then pulled my father's card from the shelf and looked at it as if it were a photograph.

I imagined myself and Ian and my father. Ian was a horse who had to do what he was told. He accepted a saddle and cinch of girth, a rider and a metal bit, which rested in the back of his mouth, where he naturally had no teeth. It is as though a horse evolved to fit a bit. Robert was the father that he was.

Mammoth Cave

The surface of Mammoth Cave National Park encompasses about eighty square miles.

Kentucky. I always wanted to take a road trip with my dad. I hoped he'd suggest one. Let me pretend that Dad bought the groceries and I made some mix tapes. We packed spicy beef jerky, turkey sandwiches with mustard, and Frescas for the drive. He drove the interstate. We looked at the scenery. He took Cave City exit. Dad chose the Historic Tour.

We considered walking the River Styx Spring Trail. I looked around for something I could pretend were coins. (On the path I would have to explain the joke.) Under the earth, in the cave, the ranger who was the tour guide stopped in Booth's Amphitheater, where Edwin Booth, brother of assassin John Wilkes, had once recited Hamlet's famous soliloquy. (Edwin is such a better name.)

"What's the line about angels?" I asked Dad. He didn't know what I was talking about.

We saw an eyeless, colorless cave shrimp and a cave cricket. At the campground, Dad grilled hot dogs and I opened a bag of potato chips and put out the ketchup and mustard and the relish. We ate and talked about what it was like to be in the cave, and the history of what had happened there. I read a poem to my dad and he was interested. None of this actually happened, but the poem was "The Man-Moth," by Elizabeth Bishop. The original title was misprinted. It was supposed to be titled "Mammoth." Let me pretend that my dad saw the connection. Whatever it was supposed to be called, I said, I like the line "He cannot tell the rate at which he travels backwards."

Spirit

When I woke, I remembered that my dream had included my father. We were at the barn. My father had brought an apple for Ian, but he didn't understand that Ian had died. My father seemed embarrassed that he had brought an apple for a dead horse. Charlie, my mother, and I walked to the field. My father couldn't come with us.

"Everything looks old," Charlie said. He said this because all of the colors were sepia tone.

I pointed to a horse across the field.

"Look, there's Ian," I said.

He was a spirit. I understood that I couldn't ride him, but I was glad he was there.

Tree

My dream had been about a tree. In the dream, it was an old, tall, and sentient father, a beech with leaves that shone green in sunlight, making a watery yellow patterned canopy that looked good enough to swim in. All of the slim silver trunks near the old tree were its seedlings. I realized it was an intelligent tree and it could speak to me. I was walking toward it, and I was eager to hear the voice of the tree.

"You can speak?" I asked it, just to be sure.

It didn't say anything, but I felt it listened. Nothing else happened, so I kept walking.

Woods

I wanted to see the big old beech tree that had seeded the forest with little beech saplings. I walked up the trail my father had bush hogged. It was already growing in. The path was rockier than the others, which was why I liked it. Chunky pieces of white quartz seemed to bubble up through the red clay, as though foam from a receding ocean wave were pinned in place. I remembered that beyond the second bend in the trail the quartz pieces would be bigger. The largest rocks were near the roots of the big silver beech. I was always curious about digging them out, but I never tried.

I left Barker and Max at the house, which now felt like an unfair thing to do, but I'd wanted to walk by myself. A strong late afternoon sun shone, and I stopped to look around. Beech seedlings were everywhere, some only the thickness of a dowel but several feet tall, bearing their tenuous infancies in competition with one another. The effect of sunlight through so much new green was like being underwater in a swimming pool, I thought, like opening my eyes in clear water.

I reached the big tree and said aloud, "There you are." I didn't feel how I'd expected to feel. The tree was so familiar that seeing it again felt ordinary. It was dull silvered, tall and lovely. I spent a few moments looking up at the branches and the leaves, until I started to lose my sense of place and I had to look down at the ground. It was time to head back. I went down the trail I had just come up.

Them

The telephone rang. Susanna answered it. Teagan knew that something was wrong. Then Teagan knew that something bad had happened. Then she knew that her mother was having a hard time telling her. Susanna was standing in front of her. Teagan hesitated, then asked her mother, "What is it?"

Susanna reached out to her daughter.

"What is it?" Teagan said again.

Susanna simply held her arms out and started to cry.

Teagan took her mother's hands, closing her arms. "Tell me what's going on."

"Oh, honey. I'm so sorry. I am so sorry for you."

"What is it?" Teagan asked. She felt terrified, but she still didn't know why.

Susanna looked at Teagan, her face stricken, but she didn't say anything.

"Mom," Teagan insisted.

Susanna tried to hold her daughter. Teagan pushed against her. "Mom, please tell me what's happened?"

"Teagan, Ian has died."

After a moment Teagan said, "Ian?"

"Joan says he got into the feed room, and he got into the grain bin. He overate and it killed him."

"It killed him?" Teagan repeated.

"He ate so much that he had a heart attack or a stroke. He ate from a new fifty-pound bag. He didn't stop eating. Sometimes horses don't stop. They'll just keep eating."

Teagan turned away.

"Teagan. Honey."

Teagan stared out of the window. She could see the roof of the barn. She hadn't been back to see Ian. She had left him, and he had died. She felt that she wanted to scream, so she kept her mouth shut.

Both

The telephone rang.

"Hello?"

"Teagan."

"Charlie?"

There was a silence. Charlie didn't say anything.

"Charlie, what's up?"

There was more silence from the other end.

"Do you want to talk to Mom?"

"Not yet," he said.

"Is something wrong?"

"It's Dad," Charlie said.

"Dad. You said Dad?" Teagan said. She didn't want to talk about her father.

"Yes."

"What is it?"

"Dad's at the hospital," Charlie said.

Teagan studied a single square of glass in the window to see what it framed. "What happened?"

"He's dead. He died."

They were both silent, then Teagan yelled into the phone, "Our father?"

Charlie said, "Yes."

Teagan sat down. "Our father is dead?"

Charlie said, "Yes. He's dead."

"I want to go to him," Teagan said.

"He's at the hospital," Charlie said.

"Let's go, now. I want to go now," Teagan said.

"I'll come get you," Charlie said.

Teagan saw her mother standing in the doorway.

Epilogue One: Cowboy Party

I'm sitting on the porch, waiting for Grace to wake up. When I've had too much to drink, I wake after a few hours of fitful rest and that's it. It was the cowboys. The skinny, dusty men who smelled of leather and earth.

Before driving here, I didn't know anything about Arkansas. Not the flatness of it, the black soil, or the beauty. Where we are is a plain green valley between two canyon walls. A low stream cuts it in half. I had no idea Arkansas did this, that it canyoned and it valleyed. Grace told me about the canyon, but I was not prepared for how the rock would simply meet the ground, like someone plopped it there.

Grace mentioned cowboys. I did not picture real ones who herd horses and ride fences and wear the same pair of jeans every day and wear white embroidered roses on the chest of a black western shirt. I did not form in my mind worn cotton, oiled leather, dust from the coats of horses, dust from the grass of fields, and what I did not imagine caught me off guard.

We arrived late in the day and walked to the lodge to find the office and pick up keys to a cabin. Inside was a dining hall. Grace found the stairs. Downstairs was a game room. A door so plain it might have been to a closet opened. A cowboy walked out. He wore embroidered brown leather boots, and a western shirt with silver snaps; he nodded to us and went up the stairs.

Grace and I looked at each other. She reached for the door-knob. Behind the door was an office, as narrow as a hallway. Inside were the slim bodies of cowboys, seated in chairs lining the walls. They looked at us. They each seemed to wear a beautiful shirt, and their light-colored jeans were brown with dust along long thighs, and their boots, which I mostly examined because I was too overcome to look at faces, were lovely, stitched in patterns with white thread, or black and decorated with roses.

I wanted to visit each face, to look into eyes that looked over the Arkansas ground from horseback each day. I wanted to run my fingers over callused palms of hands. They practically encircled us. I tried to keep away from a knee that was nearly touching my leg, in case I caressed it. Grace was between my shoulder and the wall, as if she was using me as a shield. I also wanted to get out of the room, away from cowboys, before I told them all how beautiful they were.

Grace had said we needed to ask for Jim, but Jim was obvious. He wore a cotton polo with HORSESHOE CANYON embroidered over the pocket. He was obviously used to interacting with guests. He chatted with us and lifted keys off a board, but when I handed over my credit card, he couldn't get the machine to run, and then the receipt printed as a streak of pink. I started silently counting, a habit I have to overcome nervousness. I thought about what I was wearing, exercise tights and an old windbreaker. I felt as if I was wearing a space suit in front of some self-possessed race of decorated beings. Jim asked if we were going rock climbing. I said yes. Grace said yes.

Then, to a cowboy shirt, I suggested, "I think it's supposed to rain."

"It's gonna clear up," a voice said.

"I heard it was going to rain," I said again.

I don't know why I disagreed. The cowboys probably always knew the forecast from looking at the sky, or from the National Weather Service. Jim couldn't get the cartridge to fit, so I said, "Don't worry about it," and Grace and I left the office. The game room felt cool. I let out a breath.

As we were leaving the lodge, a cowboy held the door for us. Before he walked away, he turned and said, "There's a party tonight. Y'all should come."

Grace and I walked on the gravel path in the gray afternoon. I turned to Grace but then couldn't think of the thing to say.

"Cowboys," she said.

"Oh, yes," I said.

We climbed the pine porch steps of the cabin.

"So we got invited to a party?" I said.

"We don't have to go," she said.

I said, "Let's go."

Our first order of business was to make coffee, then to lie on the quilted bed, paging through magazines. After the sun set, I stretched and pulled on sneakers and jacket. We walked the gravel road. Through the windows of the lodge I could see families eating in the dining hall, and I caught the smell of beef stew. Grace pointed out lights in the woods. We walked and found an A-frame house fully lit up. From it drifted the garbled noise of conversations happening over rock music. A circle of jackets stood around a big fire pit in the yard.

One of the jackets turned and said, "Hi."

There was a folding table and a bloody paper plate piled with raw hamburger patties and another piled with hot dogs. An old-fashioned metal grill was set in one side of the fire pit.

"Hi. Somebody at the lodge invited us," I said.

"Sure. Glad you're here."

"Who was it, d'you know?" another jacket asked.

"I don't know. He had a blue shirt on," I said.

A cowboy stepped closer. "There's beers inside. Help yourself and come back out for a burger."

We said thanks and walked to the house. In the open living room there weren't just cowboys; there were cowgirls, too. Maybe they weren't cowgirls, but there were more jeans and boots, western shirts with pearl buttons. Grace and I looked like we had gotten lost on the way to the gym, in our sneakers. By a blue cooler we met Billy, and next to him was Doug. I drank a beer too quickly. Billy casually scooped up another for me. We talked with them. Soon Doug was talking only to Grace. At one point I saw him tug on the sleeve of her shirt. I watched them for a moment.

Billy saw me looking. "He's okay," he said.

"Okay," I said.

Doug seemed okay to me. I sipped my beer and over the heads of cowboys saw a long bleached skull on the wall. It wasn't a deer. I'd seen those. It was a horse. I gestured with my beer.

"That's a horse skull, right?"

Billy looked around. "It is a horse skull. Never seen one?"

"Not on a wall," I said.

"Why's that?" Billy asked.

"I think the riders I know would bury a horse." I thought of Ian, and I thought of myself.

"They ain't pets so much, here," Billy said.

"The riders I know spend so much time on one horse."

Billy laughed and walked over to the beer cooler, but I was

glad he came back. While he was gone I looked over at Grace. She and Doug had moved farther away, but she caught my eye and checked in. I smiled at her. I thought about saying we should go out to the fire and get some food, but I just never did, so the second beer hit me. I started liking Billy's looks. I checked out his boots.

"Like your boots," I said.

"Had these for five years," he said.

There was something wrong with our conversation. We weren't hitting it off, but I stayed and Billy stayed, too.

"Where do you live while you're here?" I assumed cowboying was a seasonal job.

"In a house on the other side of the creek."

I wished I hadn't asked, in case he thought I wanted to go there. "That makes it easy to get to work," I said.

"I'm up at five," he said.

I stopped myself from saying, *That's early.* I finished my second beer and without thinking, used both hands to crush the middle of it, for something to do.

"Want another?" Billy said.

"Sure," I said, wondering what I thought I was doing.

Billy got me the beer and I popped it open and took too big a swallow and coughed. Billy smiled and patted me on the back, then he dug into his pocket and pulled out a roll of breath mints. He offered one to me. I took it. While I was trying to pop out the mint with my thumb, I saw him look across the room. I popped the mint in my mouth and handed the roll back to him. He shoved the roll in his pocket, smiled at me, and walked away.

I didn't know what to do. Grace didn't seem to be in the room anymore, so I used that as a reason to walk outside. The cold air hit me and I felt more awake but felt the beers in my system, too. I was drinking the third way too fast. I thought I should go see if there was food by the fire when I heard my name called. I wasn't sure where Grace was. She stepped onto the porch and Doug appeared with her. He fit his arm around her waist.

"Where are you going?" Grace said.

I meant to say that I was going to get some food, but instead I said, "Back to the cabin."

"Already?" Doug said.

"I want an early night. We're climbing tomorrow," I said, looking at Grace.

She looked right back at me and nodded. "I'm going to go, too," she said to Doug.

Doug glanced at me. To him I thought, Yes, I am taking your girl, and so I stepped away so they could say goodbye or whatever it was they needed to do.

I walked off the porch into the dark between the light from the house and the light from the fire, and waited there.

Morning sun lights the stream. Two horses graze. From here there are no fences I can see. Past the barn, two young boys walk. They wear plaid coats, and I think how nice it must be for them that they can walk out on this land and be kids alone. They approach the horses. The bay ignores them, but the Appaloosa lifts her head and one boy strokes her face. I want to remember this. The boys over there, early blue sunlight, and the horses, easy, standing close by, and the interest the boy has in the horse, and the horse in the boy, in the early canyon morning. Grace comes onto the porch, coffee cup in her hand. She leans on the railing, her back to the stream, and sips from her mug. Since there is coffee, I get up to get some. As I walk outside again, I have a clear sense that I am plainly earth and muck, a body at work in habitual rhythm, a heart that beats. In the furrow of our hours, all things cede to love.

Epilogue Two: Horseshoe Canyon

Grace led the way up the trail to the cliffs. She carried a map. Teagan knew it was a map of climbing routes, but she hadn't looked closely at it. She watched Grace hold up the page of squiggly black vertical lines and compare it to a rock face that rose far above their heads. Grace looked from the lines to the rock and said, "I think we want the next one."

Teagan smiled. She looked at the valley they had walked through. "Look, those can't be sheep." She saw a group of animals moving slowly toward the trail she and Grace had come up.

"Those are goats," Grace said.

"It looks like they're following us," Teagan said.

"There's this beautiful herding dog that stays with them."

"What's beautiful about him?" Teagan asked.

"He's got a look of patience."

Teagan looked at the goats again. She couldn't make out a dog among them.

Grace started along the narrow path below the cliffs. Teagan followed. When they were at the climb Grace had chosen, they started unpacking the gear. Teagan could be helpful in organizing, but she didn't ever want to be responsible for the equipment herself. The climbing ropes, harnesses, belay device, and metal pieces of protection to place into crags to create a system for holding the rope, these were a new vocabulary for her.

From her backpack Grace pulled the tight-fitting rubbery climbing shoes. She tossed Teagan her pair. Teagan looked around for a good rock. She moved off the trail to sit down on one. Grace sat down on a different rock, closer to the path.

Teagan pulled off her sneakers, then looked the way they had come. She said in a quiet voice, "Grace, there's your dog. He's huge."

They watched the enormous figure of the dog coming closer, his head down, moving through his familiar territory. It wasn't like seeing a dog; it was like observing an animal in the wild. He would pass right in front of them if he kept his direction. He approached and they stayed still. When he reached Grace, he paused for the smallest moment and laid his chin on her bent knee, and then trotted on, as if they were already forgotten.

Acknowledgments

With heartfelt thanks to everyone who read a version of *Horse,* for your time and care, and for encouraging me to press onward. Writing requires community, and I thank my community for much support, especially Madison, Beth, Diana, Ayesha, and four more. Thanks, Maple, for scribbling on some pages, and Bel, for being wonderful. Thanks to Trina for sharing her bravery and curiosity. Thanks to some horses and other animals.

A NOTE ABOUT THE AUTHOR

Talley English received the Academy of American Poets' Gertrude Claytor Poetry Prize. She lives in Charlottesville, Virginia, with her family.

A NOTE ON THE TYPE

This book was set in Adobe Garamond. Designed for the Adobe Corporation by Robert Slimbach, the fonts are based on types first cut by Claude Garamond (ca. 1480–1561). Garamond was a pupil of Geoffroy Tory and is believed to have followed the Venetian models. He gave to his letters a certain elegance and feeling of movement that won their creator an immediate reputation and the patronage of Francis I of France.

Composed by North Market Street Graphics, Lancaster, Pennsylvania

Printed and bound by Berryville Graphics, Berryville, Virginia